The American Food Scandal

THE AMERICAN FOOD SCANDAL

*Why You Can't Eat Well
on What You Earn*

by **WILLIAM ROBBINS**

William Morrow & Company, Inc., New York, 1974

Design by Helen Roberts

Printed in the United States of America.

1 2 3 4 5 78 77 76 75 74

Library of Congress Cataloging in Publication Data

Robbins, William (date)
  The American food scandal.

  Bibliography: p.
  1. Food industry and trade—United States. 2. Food prices—
United States. 3. Cost and standard of living—United States.
4. Consumers—United States. I. Title.
HD9006.R6   338.1   73-19841
ISBN 0-688-00251-X

For Winnie

Contents

I
The Hoax Is on Us

One of the oldest propaganda tricks is the technique of the big lie. The theory is that, if people are told the big lie often and emphatically, enough of them will believe to make the trick successful. The theory is obviously true.

For it has helped to perpetrate a hoax of mammoth proportions on the American people. It is a hoax that is a composite of many deceptions, and it robs American families daily of millions of dollars of the money that they spend, knowingly and unknowingly, for their food.

Abetted by government agencies, the businesses that form the nation's food-supply chain are the authors and beneficiaries of the deceptions. They are a vast complex, of infinite variety, including corporations that produce and corporations that process and sell, as well as conglomerates that have a hand on each link of the chain that runs from field to supermarket. They include also the industries that serve and supply the others. They are an amorphous mass, grouped under the mongrel name of agribusiness but unified by the common goal of taking all that

1

they can from consumers. They have been outrageously successful.

The food industry, or agribusiness—the terms are almost interchangeable—has succeeded partly because it has been one of the world's most skillful practitioners of the technique of the big lie. Americans, we are told, are blessed with better food at lower costs than anyone in any other country. So we are told by the industry, which is the world's largest concentration of financial power. We are told so by the industry's lobbyists, who compose the most potent political force in Washington. And their message is chorused by Congressmen and bureaucrats in the national capital who guard the industry's interests and do its bidding.

We have been told the big lie so often that few skeptics are left among us, and even fewer raise the pertinent questions.

Better than what? Our food is grown, processed and impregnated with chemicals, with hardly a passing thought from the industry about their effect on the consumer's health and little show of concern when an ingredient, after long use, turns out to be carcinogenic. We have been robbed of variety by stores and distributors and of taste by nearly every hand that touches our food.

"Let them eat the Delicious," say the buying officials of the supermarkets if we want apples. And where are the Rome Beauties, the Northern Spies, the Grimes Goldens, the Baldwins and Yellow Newtons of yesteryear? Their delightful flavors, like the tart sweetness of a fresh blackberry or the exotic tang of a ripe persimmon, have been sacrificed to a mythical god of efficiency, and our children may never know the riches of which they have been robbed.

Our tomatoes have become hard, grainy and tasteless because government researchers, serving agribusiness rather than the consumer, breed them for toughness rather than quality. And, as our supply system has been corrupted, those hard tomatoes, developed primarily to withstand the steel fingers of mechanical harvesters, are picked green and reddened with a gas spray while being shipped over vast distances. In the stores we get the same dry, pulpy, boxed-and-shipped vegetables whatever the season and whatever juicy and tasty varieties might be offered by small local farmers.

And how can we believe that our costs are lower when we are bled by hidden costs, both financial and social? We have paid billions in subsidies to wealthy farmers and giant agribusiness corporations and billions more because their prices were artificially supported by the Government. And we pay additional billions to be bombarded by advertising messages designed to persuade us that worse is really better.

Our food costs also include the billions spent for unnecessary processing that diminishes both quality and taste, for extravagant packaging and for preparation of "convenience" foods that offer us the flavor of cardboard, often with less time saved than we could achieve with a pan and a can opener.

The hidden costs include, in addition, hundreds of millions of dollars in extra taxes. Consumers must pay more because of tax dodges that let farming corporations pay less, while wealthy absentee investors in farming schemes often pay no tax at all. We pay, as another hidden part of our food bills, the billions in welfare costs brought on as small farmers and farm workers are driven from their fields. And still higher and more devastating are the social costs of our desolated rural villages and country lanes, left behind by the dispossessed people who crowd our slums.

Oh no, we are told, what is meant is that Americans pay at the food counters a smaller percentage of their income—

less than 16 percent—for food than other nations do. That, too, is deception. Again the pertinent questions: Which Americans? The poor? A family of four at the poverty level —among the most tragic victims and the easiest marks for advertising frauds—spends nearly half its earnings for a meager subsistence. The average wage-earner? That family of four, if it moved up to the median tax bracket, would pay nearly a third of its income for food, and if it should advance to the relatively higher income average of suburbanites, it would still pay over 25 percent. Only among families with relatively high incomes do we reach a level where less than a fifth of spendable earnings goes for food.

The government and industry claims rang more hollow than ever in 1972 and 1973 when soaring costs virtually eliminated meats from the diets of low-income families. The resulting loss of food value came at a time when, according to a report by a Senate committee on "Hunger— 1973," twelve million Americans were still malnourished.

Poorer families in 1973 were forced to seek substitutes for such old standbys as hamburger and hot dogs, and red meat was cut from the federal surplus-food programs long depended upon by the needy, the schools and other institutions.

In the twelve-month period ended at midyear the cost of the roast in a roast beef dinner rose nearly 22 percent. Buying by families seeking a cheaper alternative drove the cost of the chicken in chicken dinners up nearly 29 percent, and eggs, cheese, fish and other main dishes were climbing at similar rates.

These were high prices for the consumer to pay for a combination of industry practices and governmental actions that included politically motivated restraints on production and poorly managed export programs.

But the industry, and its hucksters, should never be allowed to dodge the issue of real costs with its specious equation of cash-register prices and some mythical average of total personal income, which lumps the wealthy in with the poor. The relatively little that a wealthy man must pay does not ease the strain on families of moderate income. And any accurate assessment must include the hidden costs. All of us long ago could have got tax relief—ranging from a few hard-earned dollars for the poor to thousands upon thousands for the well-to-do—had it not been for the subsidies and tax advantages that have become a form of welfare for the wealthy farmers and farming corporations, and if not for their jobless victims and the costs of helping them survive in their newfound urban squalor.

A new farm program passed in 1973 may reduce the subsidies and it has some other advantages over previous legislation, but it also insures that the cost of food will never again fall below the high levels that were reached in 1972, whether those costs are paid through prices or taxes.

The principal advantage is that price guarantees to farmers, provided in the program, help to restrain scarcity-induced inflation because they encourage growers to produce as much as they can.

But the problems in our food-supply system amount to more than the situation as it exists today, shot through though it is with waste and inequities and laced though it is with deception and outright fraud. Bigger problems threaten our not-so-distant future. Until recently, despite the needless costs, food has been a better buy than, for example, our automobiles or the gasoline that speeds them relentlessly toward the junkyards.

For those are products of industries in which trends toward shared monopolies—oligopolies, as the economists call them—have run their course. They are products, like many others, of industries in which prices for an entire segment of the economy are "administered," that is, dictated by the executives of the strongest company rather than by the forces of competition. Because a few companies control the market in follow-the-leader fashion, our cars can be sold for style rather than durability, to be changed when the makers decide that the buyers of one fashion must be tempted with another.

Forces in the food industry have already quietly accumulated the power of similar shared monopolies, and they are displaying their strength. Two companies share the production of soup, for example; four control the cereal shelves; one company is dominant in cheese. Trends point toward a similar leverage in other phases of processing, as well as in production, marketing and retailing. And in food the forces of control grasp more than a luxury. They seize on our most vital necessity. In the taste, purity and variety of food, they capture an essential element in the quality of life. The iron hand of control reaches for our throats.

And that is not strange, for the prize is great. The American food industry is the largest in the world. It is a $150-billion-a-year industry, bigger than automobiles, steel, oil or even the defense establishment.

The National Commission on Food Marketing, in an excellent but largely unnoticed study in 1966, analyzed the gathering forces and reported to Congress and the President on present and potential effects on the consuming public. Control of the food supply, from processing to the retail counter, the Commission found, was passing into the hands of ever fewer and larger companies. Competition was declining, and a live-and-let-live attitude prevailed among the surviving corporations and conglomerates as they pursued their common goal of carving up the consumer's dollar. The less competition, the higher the price. And monopolistic positions in product lines were protected by heavy advertising that both increased consumers' costs and barred competing brands from the grocery shelves.

The National Commission on Food Marketing was created by Congress, and its members were appointed by the President of the United States, the President pro tempore of the Senate and the Speaker of the House. Its final report, "Food from Farmer to Consumer," was a summary of ten book-length technical studies. Staffs for the work were drawn from several government agencies, but none contributed so extensively as the Federal Trade Commission, which wrote a key study, "The Structure of Food Manufacturing."

Yet after the temporary National Commission's landmark report, the effort to systematically assess the trends was dismantled. Since then no broad-based, concerted attempt has been made to curb or reverse the movement toward shared monopoly that was found.

Against a background of much foot-dragging on the part of politically appointed commissioners of the F.T.C., what progress has been made has been largely the result of initiatives from dedicated staff directors and economists within the agency. Guidelines have been drawn to curb mergers of retailers with annual sales of more than $100-million, but no effort has been made to roll back concentration of power that already exists or even to slow its expansion through the proliferation of a chain's supermarkets in areas where the company already has a big share of monopolistic power.

Attacks on overwhelming market power have been largely piecemeal, taking the form of individual suits by the F.T.C. or the Justice Department against prominent mergers or flagrant violations of antitrust law.

Lacking an adequate budget and often the freedom to carry the attack, many staff economists of the F.T.C. have grown discouraged, the more so because they also are barred by government-protected corporate secrecy from vital information on the state of competition in the economy.

Many people, including economists who should know better, have felt that the consumer was offered some protection by the simple nature of food production. Farming, the first link in the food-supply chain, was the freest form of competition in the American society. Productive resources were fragmented among millions of free and independent farmers.

But what farmers had was a freedom to commit economic suicide, and they have been doing that in large numbers. Processors long ago gained a foothold by growing on their own lands much of the produce needed to fill their cans. Now other national corporations and conglomerates are moving massively into food production and the so-called independent farmers are falling like wheatstraws before a scythe. Trends now in motion, unless checked, will finally give agribusiness control of that last bastion of free competition.

Statistics understate the forces that are at work. By 1969, when the Department of Agriculture made its most recent study, corporations were said to have gained control of only 1 percent of the nation's farms. But that 1 percent represented an amalgamation of what were once many other farms, the end result of the merging of small farms into ever larger production units. Those corporate farms, although only 1 percent of the total number, owned 7 percent of all farmland and produced more than 8 percent of all cash income from farming, the Agriculture Department says. Still, according to the department, many of those corporate enterprises are only family farms organized as corporations. A subsequent review of census figures confirmed the basic conclusions, the department has said.

But some caution is necessary when dealing with Department of Agriculture statements. Top officials at the agency have long been apologists for agribusiness, from where most of them came and to which they hope to return, at far higher salaries. Agriculture officials tend to regard the fading of the family farm as an inevitable trend and to disregard their own mandate to protect it. And these men seem even to regard the trend as a phenomenon eminently to be desired, despite proof that the family-size farm can be more efficient than vast operations structured in layer upon layer of administrators and supervisors.

Even the department's statistics have been thrown into question by a follow-up study led by a rural economist, Professor Richard Rodefeld of Michigan State University. In heavily documented testimony before a Senate monopoly subcommittee, he said that he and a group of other researchers had found glaring inaccuracies in the department's basic data for Wisconsin, with understatement of corporate holdings ranging up to 216 percent.

But even if Agriculture Department figures were accepted as accurate, they are misleading. What they do not make clear is that the corporate invasion of farming has focused largely on the most strategic sections of the country, where control can pay off in the highest cash earnings. What is clear is that the number of farms is rapidly declining and that the independent farmer is a threatened species.

Since World War II, the number of farms has dropped by half, from over six million to fewer than three million. Until 1972, when abnormal influences temporarily slowed the trend, more than two thousand independent farmers a week were leaving their farms and the land was usually swallowed up by larger and wealthier farmers and farming corporations. The pattern of the future is one often seen now: Once a large but independent farmer assembles neighboring acreage enough to be attractive to a corporation, he in turn is swallowed up. If the trends continue, within a decade large national corporations can control the output of the nation's farms and dictate prices along the food chain, from the land to the grocery counter.

They will be able to accomplish that not only by the acreage they own but also by other production which they control. For the corporations that enter farming today often rent more land than they own. Further, they often control through contracts with once-independent farmers far more land than they farm with their own hired managers. About 75 percent of vegetables sold for processing are now grown under contracts with food-manufacturing corporations.

More and more farmers are surrendering their independence in return for the semblance of security to be found in a contract with a corporation. It is only a semblance, for farmer after farmer has found himself in debt to his corporate client and headed toward bankruptcy. In such cases, the corporation is often only too glad to relieve him of the problems of landownership.

What all this means for the consumer of tomorrow is indicated by what it already has brought him today. He may, on Thanksgiving Day, as a witness at a Senate hearing testified, bow his head to his deity, but the immediate source of his fare is more worldly. Describing a Thanksgiving dinner of 1971, the witness said: "The Smithfield ham comes from ITT, the turkey is a product of Greyhound Corporation, the lettuce comes from Dow Chemical Company, the potatoes are provided by the Boeing Company and Tenneco brought the fresh fruits and vegetables. The applesauce is made available by American Brands, while both Coca-Cola and Royal Crown Cola have provided the fruit juices."

The thanksgiver cannot, however, find the cost of his dinner a matter for rejoicing.

II
Beachhead in the Sun

In late summer of 1972 two men walked out to a small plane and, under a blistering sun, took off over the San Joaquin Valley of California. This fertile midsection, lying between the Sierra on the east and the Coastal Range on the west, is a segment of the vast Central Valley. The valley, which runs from north to south, spans a distance almost as great as the Eastern Seaboard and embraces a variety of climate and agriculture that is almost infinite in its richness.

The takeoff was from Mendota, a town bearing the blight that is often associated with surrounding corporate farms. Its main street with its grimy storefronts sleeps idly in the sun and its dusty backstreets are lined with the hovels of often idle farmworkers. From there the plane soared into the grandeur of a sky so clear that its two occupants could see the land below stretching away for fifty miles in all directions. When the pilot leveled off at 3,000 feet, wheeling northward, the land unrolled in broad swatches of crop-green, plowed-brown and the dry yellow of semi-desert crust.

In a few minutes, the San Luis Reservoir was a small silver coin gleaming in the distance but growing larger until it dominated the horizon, the sheer face of the new dam that hemmed it into the Coastal Range looming like another mountain above the valley. New concrete-lined canals stretched away to north and south.

The sighting of the San Luis complex on the first leg of the flight seemed symbolic, for it was soon to become clear to the plane's passenger that this was a part of a vast scheme of agribusiness and government to provide the water that supports land power in California.

Over the reservoir the plane banked again and turned south to fly toward Tulare Lake, which is not a lake anymore but a broad dry basin, its waters drained away long ago to slake for a time the unending thirst of the valley's fields. And now the lakebed itself has been plowed and another vast underground basin has been mined to water the crops.

There the fliers looked down on one of the principal strongholds of agribusiness. Lands of the J. G. Boswell Company, Salyer Land Company and South Lake Farms reach outward for hundreds of square miles from the old lakebed. More than 140 square miles of cotton and grain belong to J. G. Boswell and these crops support a processing complex of mills, gins and seed crushers and a large feedlot for cattle. Boswell is a corporation that has been supported by one of the biggest multimillion-dollar federal subsidies. Through varied interests Boswell is interlocked with the rest of agribusiness in California and thus with corporations that reach across the continent.

Salyer's somewhat less extensive spread, which also has collected millions in federal subsidies, supports a similar processing establishment. And the lands of Boswell and Salyer are indistinguishable from the broad miles of South Lake Farms, which has had its own millions in subsidies.

South Lake is operated by the old Producers Cotton Oil Company. But "Producers" is a misnomer, for the company is now a subsidiary of Bangor Punta, the big conglomerate that also owns, among other holdings, the Piper Aircraft Corporation.

At the edge of the Tulare basin squats the town of Corcoran, another like Mendota that has been blighted by the corporate presence and infected chronically with one of the state's worst epidemics of unemployment.

At a point south of the Tulare basin, the pilot pointed ahead beyond the whirling propeller and indicated land that stretched away to the distant horizon.

"There," he said, "as far as you can see, almost all of that is new money. That's Southdown land just ahead, and beyond that there's Getty Oil and then Belridge Oil land. And off to the right there, beyond those low hills, that's Lazard Frères land. They call it the Blackwell Corporation, but that's just a front for Lazard Frères." The Lazard Frères he mentioned is the Wall Street investment house with multinational operations.

The pilot was a tall, taciturn businessman who knew the valley well. Its sun and wind were burned into his face and its landholdings into his brain from long hours often spent plowing through files in the valley's halls of records. He was not a man who was given to easy displays of emotion, but there was a sense of smothered rage in his voice when he spoke of the land and big money's easy conquest of California.

From the air it was almost impossible to distinguish where the land of one corporation ended and another began. There were few hedgerows or windbreaks. Only by changes in pattern and texture could the lands of almonds, peaches, nectarines and oranges be distinguished from the strife-torn grape country around Delano where sheriff's deputies had manhandled striking pickets. Except for irrigation ditches and canals and the rich burden of crops, signs of a human presence lay miles apart. In between there was only a sense of vast desolation.

Farther south were spread hundreds of miles of fields that until recently were part of the empire of the Kern County Land Company. The old corporation, the creation of nineteenth-century land sharks, has been taken over by Tenneco, the oil, shipbuilding and manufacturing conglomerate, in one of the largest outpourings of the new money that is flowing through corporations into agriculture. Tenneco, with its treasury gorged with the tax benefits of oil-depletion allowances, is the king of the newcomers. In taking over the Kern County Land holdings, it acquired properties twice the size of the state of Rhode Island.

With the plane's gas tanks running low, the pilot turned back before reaching Bakersfield, which is the core city of agribusiness control in California and where, from a sprawling, eight-acre plant, one company—a subsidiary of Tenneco—exercises its control over many of California's crops and significant portions of the nation's produce.

The flight was instructive in many respects. It helped this observer to register the broad reach of increasing corporate control over the vastness of California's productive resources. It also enabled this reporter more easily to grasp the relationships as they were soon to emerge between old frauds and present deceptions and between old policies of disregard and present evasion and misinterpretation of the law.

California, of course, is not alone. A design for takeover and control by conglomerates and giant corporations is being carved across the land. It can be seen in Florida, where corporations have seized control of the major crop to produce most of the nation's orange juice and where they own broad fields of fresh vegetables, old canefields and new cattle lands. It is evident in Maine where twelve corporations now control 52 percent of the land. Again, in Arizona the corporations, including those operating in California, are taking over lettuce, fruit and cotton production. In Colorado, Oregon, Texas and Washington—call the roll of the states that are rich in cash crops and nearly everywhere the takeover is under way.

It follows a pattern that appeared long ago and is still growing in Hawaii, where, beyond the facade of the island paradise of the travel commercials, corporations are in the saddle and they ride the consumer. Eight corporations collect 73 percent of all farm receipts in the islands. They include names like Del Monte and Libby as well as others such as Castle & Cooke, whose activities are rarely discussed beyond the tall monuments to financial power on Wall Street, but whose interests reach halfway around the globe and into a dozen industries.

The same corporations that control production in Hawaii are often dominant in California, where Castle & Cooke has its retail division, among other holdings. And it is in California where the pattern of takeover can best be examined, in part because it is the richest prize.

California leads the nation with a cash farm income of $4.5-billion a year from crops with a market value of over $17-billion. More important, its production is concentrated in crops with the highest cash value.

For many of these crops California is nearly the sole source of supply. It produces 40 percent of the country's fruits and vegetables and over one-third of the canned and frozen versions of those crops.

A look at the high-profit cash crops and some of the major varieties of produce brings the picture into sharper focus. California grows, for example, nearly 70 percent of the country's lettuce and is nearly the sole source of supply in some seasons. It also produces 65 percent of the tomatoes and 50 percent of the winter and 67 percent of the late spring potatoes. In addition, California supplies 92 percent of the table grapes consumed in the United States.

California's share of the nation's other high-value crops is equally staggering. This includes 44.7 percent of the carrots, 50 percent of the spinach, 55 percent of strawberries, 60.9 percent of celery, 76.3 percent of cauliflower, 80 percent of lemons, 94.6 percent of brussels sprouts, 96.3 percent of apricots, 98 percent of honeydew melons, 98.4 percent of walnuts, 99 percent of figs, 99.3 percent of dates, 99.6 percent of artichokes, and 99.9 percent of almonds and olives.

Obviously, if agribusiness could dominate a sizable share of production in a state where so many food crops are concentrated, it would be well on the way toward seizing control of the nation's food supply. The corporations have not been slow to respond to California's lure of riches in the land.

Old-line food companies have long had a hand in agriculture, but it was principally in the last half of the nineteen-sixties that outsiders, including the conglomerates, became fully aware of the wealth contained in the nation's limited land resources and the riches that might be reaped from control of the means of production. And California lay there, richly beckoning.

Conditions peculiar to California made it both attractive to the conglomerates and a logical place to seize a commanding position for the conquest of agriculture. One was the concentration of fruit and vegetable production in the state. Another was the consolidation of lands that had already occurred.

In California, schemes and deceptions of the present are rooted in frauds of the past, some of which helped to create the largest of the state's landholdings. They were plotted by men like Henry Miller, James Ben Ali Haggin and Lloyd Tevis.

Miller, a German immigrant arriving in San Francisco in 1850, started out in the New World as a butcher. But while thousands around him went mad over the lure of gold dust, this wily settler turned his attention to the land itself and he saw the water that flowed through its streams as liquid gold. Although he had stepped off a ship with only six dollars in his pockets, he was soon buying up property along the rivers. And before long back-country homesteaders, cut off from water, were selling out to Miller at distress prices. He acquired other vast stretches from land speculators who had obtained their rights by one means or another while working as surveyors to open up the new country for the United States Government.

But Miller's most grandiose move was the bold fraud by which he obtained title to thousands of acres of grasslands under terms of the Swamp Lands Act of 1850. The law provided that a settler could claim swamp land if it was underwater and could gain title free of charge if he would agree to drain it. Miller, learning of the law, saw it as a chance to greatly expand his holdings. So, loading a row-boat on a wagon and hitching a team of horses to it, he climbed aboard and, sitting high and dry in the little vessel but without even a paddle in his hand, had himself pulled across a vast dry expanse. Then, when he filed a map of the sections along with a sworn statement that he had traversed the area in a rowboat, he became the owner of the coveted land.

By the time Miller died he had amassed fourteen million acres. And although quarrels among his heirs split his empire, several large corporate holdings today are his legacy.

The brashness of Miller's scheme was almost equaled by another plot in the same era, this one by Haggin and

Tevis. The two had already acquired hundreds of thousands of acres by buying up the often dubious claims of old Spanish grantees. But their boldest land grab came under the provisions of another act of Congress, the Desert Land Act of 1877. The law was ushered through Congress by men obligated to Haggin and Tevis, and under its provisions land that was said to be worthless desert could be sold in 640-acre sections at twenty-five cents an acre to settlers who would agree to irrigate.

Haggin and Tevis, of course, had their eyes on land that was far more valuable than dry desert. In fact, some of the land they sought lay along the Kern River and some was already occupied by homesteaders who had not yet perfected their claims. The San Francisco *Chronicle* in 1877 told the story this way:

"The President's [Grant's] signature was not dry on the cunningly devised enactment before Boss Carr [Haggin and Tevis's agent in the San Joaquin Valley] and his confederates were advised from Washington that the breach was open. It was Saturday, the 31st of March [1877]. The applications were in readiness, sworn and subscribed by proxies. . . . All that Saturday night and the following Sunday the clerks in the Land Office were busy recording and filing the bundles of applications dumped upon them by Boss Carr, although it was not until several days after that that the office was formally notified of the approval of the Desert Land Act."

Peter Barnes, writing in the *New Republic* of June 5, 1971, added this to the *Chronicle* account: "Thus by hiring scores of vagabonds to enter phony claims for 640 acres and then by transferring those claims to themselves, Haggin and Tevis were able to acquire title to approximately 150 square miles of valley land before anybody else in California had even heard of the Desert Land Act. In the process they dislodged settlers who had not yet perfected their titles under old laws and who were caught unawares by the new one. The *Chronicle* called the whole maneuver an 'atrocious villainy' and demanded return of the stolen lands. A federal investigation followed, but Haggin and Tevis, as usual, emerged triumphant."

Haggin and Tevis's holdings later became known as the Kern County Land Company, which was taken over in 1967 by Tenneco.

There are other large holdings that are based on vaguely defined legacies of the Spanish crown, some with more valid claims than others. According to Barnes:

"Almost immediately they [the grants] fell prey to wily speculators and defrauders, who either bought out the heirs of the grantees or forged phony title papers and bluffed their way through the courts. Several of the original Spanish grants are embodied in giant holdings today: the Irvine Ranch (68,000 acres in Orange County), the Tejon Ranch (268,000 acres in the hills and valleys northeast of Los Angeles, 40 percent owned by the Chandler family, which publishes the Los Angeles *Times*), Rancho California (97,000 acres to the northeast of San Diego, jointly owned by Kaiser and Aetna Life), and the Newhall Ranch (43,000 acres north of Los Angeles, owned by the Newhall Land and Farming Company)."

Thus, control of millions of acres by corporations in California is rooted in claims that reach into a shadowy past, though there is probably no legal basis for questioning rights of the present holders.

But other holdings survive today under circumstances that appear difficult to defend. Those are the vast lands originally turned over to the railroads by Congress as a device to speed the opening of the West. During the third quarter of the nineteenth century 130 million acres of land were turned over to them to help pay for laying rails across the trackless expanse of plains and mountains. That was a total land area equal to the size of California and Florida combined.

In general, although the details varied in different concessions, these were the conditions laid down by Congress: The lines were to receive the land in alternate square miles, checkerboard fashion, in a band extending outward for twenty miles on each side of their rights of way—that is, half the land in a forty-mile-wide ribbon stretching along their thousands of miles of new track.

The purpose of the plan was twofold. Besides helping to defray costs, it was a device intended to assure settling of the West by small, independent farmers. To promote that objective, Congress usually wrapped its gift in certain restrictions. The railroads were to sell the land to settlers in homestead-size plots—that is, generally in divisions of 160 acres—at prices of no more than $2.50 an acre. In some cases the top price allowed was $1.25 an acre. In addition, the railroads were barred from using the land, the timber on it and the minerals under it for any other purposes.

There was usually another, highly significant condition. If for any reason the tracks were not laid, the grants were to be canceled and the land returned to the public domain. And if the land was not sold it was to become subject to claim by homesteaders. The Government has recovered millions of acres of those lands either because of failure of the railroads to keep their part of the bargain or because of outright fraud, but the railroads have fought the retrieval bitterly, and litigation and subsequent legislation have been required.

Today, 12 million acres of those original public lands are still in the hands of railroads that received them only in the role of conduits for conveyance to settlers. One of the biggest shares, 3.8 million acres, is held by the Southern Pacific, and about 3 million acres of that is in California, much of it rich in crops, timber and minerals. And although the original conveyance provided that the railroads were neither to farm, mine or to cut timber from the land except for the prescribed purpose of rail construction, the Southern Pacific gets a gross income of over $24-million a year from the land. The income is from the prohibited uses—from oil and gas leases, from timber sales and from farm rents.

A team of researchers sponsored by Ralph Nader, the consumer advocate, has charged that the railroads have no remaining legal right to hold or use the land. Meanwhile, a public-interest group called the National Coalition for Land Reform has filed a petition with the Department of the Interior demanding that the landholdings be investigated. The petition suggested that the investigation would show the need for some or all of several remedies: Sale of the land under the original stipulation of a price no higher than $2.50 an acre, forfeiture of the land to the Government, and reimbursement to the Treasury for any illegal income taken by the railroads over the years from illegally held lands.

The petition was obviously a first step toward a public-interest lawsuit, and the legal questions will eventually be settled in court. Meanwhile, one thing is clear. The lands retained by the Southern Pacific have abetted the exercise of corporate power in agriculture in California.

The Southern Pacific, like other landed corporations, generally deals with others of its kind. Its agricultural lands are leased to interests like Giffen, Inc., one of the biggest landholders in California and, as the recipient of millions of dollars in agricultural subsidies, one of the largest beneficiaries of the federal dole. But whether a breakup of Southern Pacific holdings into family-size farms would materially slow the movement toward corporations' control of agriculture is open to question. The history of such holdings has been marked by a process of merger into larger and larger farms.

The process operates in case after case like that of John Garabedian, a Californian who now runs a fruit-packing and shipping business in Fresno, not far from the Giffen holdings. Born of Armenian parents who were unable to send him to college, Garabedian began farming during the Depression on land leased from neighbors. Through sweat and brains Garabedian built up a fruit farm of 2,000 acres, expanding gradually when older or less industrious or fortunate neighbors went out of business. Along the way he opened the packing and shipping business to handle his own produce and that of nearby farmers. But in early 1972 Garabedian's farm fell into the hands of the Superior Oil Company.

Today Garabedian derides the fears of farmers and farm groups who tremble as they hear the rumble of corporations closing in around them. Garabedian maintains that he and others like him could always farm more efficiently than any large corporation. But like others before him and others around him today, in an accelerating process, he found himself unable to resist the lure of big money. Despite Garabedian's claims of greater efficiency, Superior Oil had pockets deep enough to dig down and pull out a cash offer that he could not refuse.

More important, probably, corporations have found a way to limit competition from efficiently operating farmers like Garabedian. Following a practice that has spread widely, Superior engaged him as a consultant with a contract that is likely to prevent him from reentering agriculture as a rival, at least for a period of years. Such contracts have been mentioned in proceedings of the Federal Trade Commission charging violations of antitrust policy but thus far without effect. The F.T.C. was particularly interested in contracts signed by former let-

tuce growers who have been bought out by a conglomerate. The terms specifically barred them from reentry as
competitors for a specified period of years.

Instances of the corporate takeover are legion in the
area around Garabedian. There is the case of the Pacific
Lighting Company, the big utility that also owns Southern
California Gas. Pacific Lighting bought the farming operation of W. D. Fowler & Sons in 1970—4,000 acres
planted in pistachios and citrus and a $2.4-million packing
house. In 1971 the utility bought Blue Goose Growers, an
operation with twenty-eight farms totaling 5,000 acres of
fruit and with control over 20,000 acres more. The deal
included packing houses and marketing operations.

Federal law restricts subsidiary activities of public utili-
ties, but the impotence of federal agencies in dealing with
the phenomenon of mushrooming agribusiness control of
production was strikingly illustrated in a Pacific Lighting
case. After a look into the utility's farming operations, a
deadlocked vote in the Security & Exchange Commission
prevented regulatory action.

Besides Superior, four other oil companies were entering or expanding farming operations in the nearby Fresno,
Tulare and Kern County area. Between them, Superior,
Belridge and Getty Oil farm over 89,000 acres in Kern
and Fresno Counties, and Belridge has bought a majority
interest in the Lost Hill Produce Company. Buttes Gas &
Oil bought 5,000 acres of wine grapes, a move that gave it
a 20 percent interest in the Guild Winery Cooperative,
one of the state's larger wine producers. Southdown, Inc.,
a Texas firm that has its headquarters in the Tenneco
Building in Houston, has bought a major interest in
32,000 acres of orchards in the valley.

The Lazard Frères holdings in Kern County total 18,000
acres.

But the San Joaquin Valley is not the only California

area where expansion of corporate power is notable. It goes on apace in other areas, such as the Salinas and Imperial Valleys, where conglomerates have seized command of lettuce production, farther north in the low, rich delta area of vegetable production around Stockton and in other strategic areas of high-value crop concentration throughout the state.

Alarm over their own future spreads as farmers call the roll of big names never associated with agriculture until recent years, names such as Xerox and Kaiser. Val Tabarini, for example, a farmer in Madera County, testified at U. S. Senate hearings conducted in 1972 by Senator Adlai Stevenson 3d, Democrat of Illinois, on the corporate takeovers. He told of large holdings assembled by L. D. Properties, a front for the Hershey Company, and others by John Hancock Ranches, a subsidiary of John Hancock Insurance, and by Kaiser Steel and Standard Oil of California. Responding to questioning, the Madera County farmer said:

"Since L. D. Properties, or Hershey Company, has bought the almonds we have had quite an exchange of land in our county. We have Newhall Land and Cattle, which is connected with Standard Oil; we have Kaiser Steel that has come in and bought large amounts of land. . . . Now, one of the latest sales that has been made is John Hancock Ranches. . . . They came in and they put in elaborate sprinkler systems and planted grapes."

Statewide figures give only a hint of the scope of corporate concentration in California agriculture, for the corporate interests are centered in the areas of highest crop values. For example, the census figures show that corporations owned 16 percent of the state's 35.7 million acres of farmland in 1969. But that figure belies the degree of control that it makes possible. Much of the state total is poor land that makes little contribution to the concentration of food production in California. Only 8.6 million acres of the state's land is actually planted in crops. And the corporate farms, totaling nearly 4 million acres, tend to be the richest of the land, intensely cultivated and productive from boundary to boundary.

Some crops statistics from the 1969 census of agriculture give a clearer picture. For example, corporations controlled 89 percent of the state's cotton acreage, 62 percent of the lettuce land, 35.6 percent of the corn, 30 percent of the citrus and 32.5 percent of the potatoes.

Still, ownership and production figures give only a partial picture of corporate power in agriculture. Much of the land that the food-producing corporations do not own they control through contracts with smaller farmers. About one-third of California's food production goes to the processing industry, and most of what companies like Del Monte and Libby do not grow themselves is raised under contract with the growers. Californians, for example, grow over 70 percent of the nation's processing tomatoes, and it is almost impossible for a grower to find a market unless he signs a contract that gives a processor exclusive rights to his crop.

And if anyone doubts the degree of control exercised through such contracts, he need only talk to farmers around Stockton. One big producer there, who asked not to be named for fear of retaliation, explained how the processors exert their power. At the beginning of each crop year the companies present a united front although they deny collusion. Somehow each company offers tomato farmers the same price as its "competitors" for the farmers' crops. The growers plant and cultivate under instructions from the processors, and if any farmer attempts to retain any degree of independence, or if he complains about his treatment, he faces severe economic retribution. He finds himself the next year without a contract or a market and with a substantial loss of income.

A Stockton farmer who cannot be identified for fear of further retribution learned the consequences when he dared to show independence in his dealings with one of the nation's biggest processors. As a result the company ignored his contract and rejected his crop at harvest time. Angered and severely hurt financially, he sued and won a substantial out-of-court settlement. It would seem that he should have been pleased with his victory, but he told a neighbor:

"I won the battle, but I lost the war. I cannot find any processors or distributors who will do business with me. I am dead."

III
Land Syndicates:
And The Rich Get Richer

Money, or what antitrust lawyers call the "deep pocket," is the principal tool of the corporate takeover. For the independent farmer finds it impossible to compete with the corporations in the bidding for the most desirable land. Though he might be more efficient as a grower, he finds it futile to bid against corporations like Tenneco and the other oil companies or against United Brands, which has acquired much of the best land in the areas of California where most of the nation's lettuce is grown as well as in the secondary areas, in Arizona.

And now an ingenious device is being used to bring still more money into the takeover of farmland. It is one that clearly results now in increased corporate control, with side effects that are likely to cause severe dislocations and higher consumer costs in the years ahead.

The trick is a tax gimmick that is used by promoters who buy, or contract to buy, large assemblages of acreage from independent farmers. The promoters form syndicates and print prospectuses that they then mail to professional

men, such as high-income doctors and dentists. The litera-
ture offers limited partnerships in the syndicates. Oddly,
the chief attractions offered are the losses that the prospective investors can be promised.

Odd?

The explanation is simple. Federal tax law allows most
of the capital investment that is put into developing an
orchard, a poultry flock or a livestock herd to be written
off as ordinary expenses. Obviously, for a man in a 50
percent tax bracket, the write-off means that half of what
he would spend to develop an orchard is money he would
otherwise pay in taxes. Or, put another way, a $100 outlay
for development costs him only $50 in real income.

Under the scheme, the payoff comes when the investor,
after a few years, sells the developed orchard. He will then
pay his taxes at the capital-gains rate, or half the rate of his
ordinary income tax. Thus, if he only gets back the money
he invested, he will still show a profit. If the payment he
receives equals the money he has spent, he will have a
gain of $25 for each $100 that he put into the venture,
which is a pretty good rate of return for a bad way of
farming. In fact, by farming the public till, well-to-do investors can even show a book loss on the sale and still
make an actual gain, so long as the loss does not exceed
the $25 windfall per $100 allowed by the tax law.

As a simple example, the wealthy investor may put
$10,000 of his income into a syndicate as his share of the
costs of developing an orchard. Since he is in the 50 percent tax bracket, he would normally pay $5,000 in taxes on
that part of his income. But since the development costs
of the orchard are an ordinary deduction, rather than a
capital investment, he pays no taxes on the $10,000. And
since, after taxes, his $10,000 would really have amounted
to only $5,000, the actual cost of his investment is only
that $5,000.

After about five years, when the trees are ready to bear fruit, the orchard will be put on the market. Suppose that it is sold at a bad time, when the fruit is in surplus supply, and the venture shows no profit. The investor finally recovers only the $10,000 that he spent for development.

At that point he has regained his own $5,000 plus the $5,000 that, except for his investment, would have been due the Government in taxes. Now the Government must be paid. But the capital-gains rate, which is half that of ordinary income taxes, now applies. Thus, his tax now is 25 percent rather than 50 percent of that $10,000. The tax due the Government is $2,500 instead of $5,000 and what the investor can keep is $7,500 rather than $5,000. His gain is $2,500 on an actual risk of $5,000—a whopping 50 percent return on his real investment.

Some legal experts see still more of a windfall in such tax "shelters." The investor is allowed to use tax money—funds due to the Treasury—for his own private investment and to keep it invested interest-free. In five years, if he had borrowed the money at an interest rate of 6 percent for his venture, the cost would be $1,500. And that is the approximate cost to the Treasury of borrowing $5,000 to meet the taxpayer's deficit. Thus the actual tax windfall on his real risk of $5,000 is increased by $1,500, and his interest saving plus the reduction of his tax is an actual cost to the Treasury of $4,000.

As if all this were not enough, there are still other advantages to many wealthy investors. Those seeking to build up estates for their heirs can finally escape not only ordinary income taxes but the capital-gains tax as well. Under federal tax law, if such an investor keeps his orchard holdings until his death, his heirs will escape the income-tax collector entirely. Only the inheritance tax that would be due on an estate whether or not it had been subject to income taxation could be exacted. This quirk of tax law has led Charles Davenport, an expert at the University of California at Davis, to coin the macabre saying:

"Death clinches the prize in the tax shelter game."

Syndicates are sprouting all over California, many of them formed by big corporate interests such as Buttes Oil, Pacific Lighting and the Tejon Ranch, the corporation that is partly owned by the Chandler family of the Los Angeles *Times*. The prospectuses are all carefully drawn to avert any liability on the part of the promoters, and they are reviewed and approved by the California Corporation Commission.

Some wealthy investors have benefited from syndicates in other states as well. Governor Ronald Reagan, for example, in one widely publicized case, was able to escape all income taxes in 1970 partly through investments in Kansas City cattle syndicates.

But the terms and conditions of the sales as clearly printed in the prospectuses often raise a question as to whether even the interests of the investors are protected. Most include exorbitant charges for start-up and administration of the syndicate and for management of the farms involved.

Not unusual was a prospectus of a syndicate called "1971 Treecrop Company," organized by Treegrove 1971 Management Corporation, a subsidiary of Buttes Gas & Oil. The large and clear print contained many warning flags that appear to have done little to deter investors. A previous syndicate, "1969 Treecrop," had realized a tax loss of $3,447 per $5,000 in its first year of operation and $2,345 in the second, the prospectus noted, or "115.8 percent of the purchase price paid for each $5,000 unit." Two pages later it gave this breakdown of uses to which the investors' money would be put:

Of the total, $500,000 would go to Buttes as a down payment on the land involved, and $505,672 more to Buttes as prepaid interest. Buttes would get still another $316,045 for the financing fee, and $713,903 would be prepaid to a farm management company under a contract that appeared highly beneficial to the managers. The contract provided for a fixed fee ranging up to $312.50 an acre with increments for inflation, plus reimbursement for its planting, cultivation, harvesting and marketing costs plus an additional fee of 3 percent of those costs. In other words, it appeared from the contract, the more the managers spent, the more they would earn. In the event that the venture should ever show any earnings, the managers could also share in part of the profits. In addition to the other prepaid expenses, $47,000 of the investors' money would go to prepay property taxes and $11,000 for miscellaneous expenses.

Of $2,100,000 to be put up by the investors, the total, after expenses, to be "held as capital," according to the prospectus, was exactly $6,380.

It seemed entirely superfluous for the prospectus to warn: "There can be no assurance that the groves and vineyards will be commercially profitable."

As if to underscore other pitfalls lurking for the investor, the offering went on to add: "It is possible that certain existing and anticipated activities of Buttes or Treegrove may create conflicts of interest between Buttes or Treegrove and the Company or that such activities may place Buttes or Treegrove in direct competition with the Company."

No responsible agency of the Government makes any attempt to keep an accounting of the number of such syndicates or the acreages involved. But it is known that hundreds of thousands of acres are being planted under the syndicate schemes, and they throw a new distortion into Agriculture Department estimates and census accounts of the scope of corporate control in agriculture. In most cases, the new acreages are under the direct or indirect control of large corporations, some through management arrangements and some through marketing agreements.

Whether or not the glitter of tax windfalls at the end of the investment trail turns out to be fool's gold, as it well might, the epidemic of syndications promises increased control for the corporations and new troubles for the independent farmer and thus for the consumer. The thousands upon thousands of acres of baby trees and vines now thrusting toward maturity are the agricultural equivalent of the population bomb. Agricultural experts at centers of learning like the University of California at Davis and the University of California at Berkeley shudder when they think of the reverberations that will occur when fruit from those new plantings hits the market.

Not only will the new crops increase the concentration of agribusiness power but growers inundated by waves of surpluses are likely to become easy prey. Big corporations, with "deep pockets" of profits from diversified operations that enable them to weather any bad times in agriculture, are likely to be the top bidders in distress land sales. Prospective surpluses and resulting low prices, of course, promise some temporary benefits for the consumer. But the ensuing increase in concentration of agribusiness market power can only be bad news for the future, when shoppers at the supermarket can expect little mercy.

IV
California's Water Fraud

One of the biggest boons to agribusiness corporations in California has been the public handouts that they get in the form of subsidized irrigation water. It is the public that pays for projects like the San Luis Reservoir, and the corporations that are the chief beneficiaries pay not even their fair share of costs of operations that move the water to their fields. The circumstances of this additional windfall outline a gigantic fraud.

This too is rooted in old frauds, going back to a reclamation law of 1902 that has been most notable for its history of circumvention and violations by public officials as well as large landholders. The law, lobbied through Congress by representatives of powerful interests in the West, authorized the Bureau of Reclamation to build reservoirs and related canal systems to provide water in areas of scarcity.

One of its purposes has been well served—too well served, according to many experts. At a public cost put at about $10-billion by the Bureau of Reclamation—and far more than that by others who are knowledgeable—the projects have opened more than ten million acres in the West to cultivation. They have, indeed, made the deserts bloom with crops. But, in a curious conflict of goals, in the years when the Government was spending most of those billions to open new lands, it was spending other billions to take already productive lands out of cultivation.

On the one hand the Government was paying $10-billion to open land that would augment surpluses of acreage and crops; on the other it was paying out tens of billions to try to solve farmers' problems created by the surpluses. The total of direct costs of subsidy payments to farmers has now passed $50-billion, and there are untold additional billions in related costs. Besides the money paid to farmers to keep land idle, additional sums have gone to buy surplus production and keep it off the market. And the government funds spent for those surpluses have resulted in an additional cost to consumers, who finally have had to pay increased prices. The indirect cost of farm programs, the inflated prices that have resulted from government actions, has been estimated at more than $4-billion a year.

The fundamental effect of reclamation projects and farm programs has been, in each case, to transfer income from one sector of the public to another. Reclamation has transferred income from east to west and both programs have transferred income from consumer to farmer.

On a national scale, reclamation projects have caused severe hardships in many areas, particularly the Southeast. Farmers there have seen production in crops that were once their own migrate to the West where public subsidies, which their own taxes have helped to pay, create conditions with which they cannot compete. More important for the future, the subsidies for irrigation have accelerated the concentration of production in California and the West. Still more important, they have promoted the concentration of market power in the hands of agribusiness corporations.

Obviously, the Reclamation Act has been a boon to the owners of land in dry sections of the West, as it was intended to be. But the high cost of opening arid lands with subsidized water raises questions as to whether the program has served the national interest. In fact, several study commissions have found the projects and the national interest in conflict, but congressional logrolling goes on and new funds for the reclamation boondoggle are voted each year.

Another clear intent of the Reclamation Law has been ignored, circumvented or blatantly violated by public officials and powerful agricultural interests alike. The public has been abused and defrauded, and its interests have been trampled into dust turned to mud by illegal water. The unequivocal wording of the act of 1902 as well as congressional debate that preceded its passage made it plain that the law was intended to aid family-size farms and not to produce windfalls for speculators and big landed interests. It said:

"No right to the use of the water for land in private ownership shall be sold for a tract exceeding 160 acres to any one landowner, and no such sales shall be made to any landowner unless he be an actual bona fide resident upon such land or occupant thereof residing in the neighborhood."

And President Theodore Roosevelt, in signing the law, underscored the intent when he said that it was "designed to secure that use for the people as a whole and to prevent it from being absorbed by a small monopoly."

Thus it seemed obvious that the irrigation projects were to serve directly only those families who had moderate-sized holdings and who lived on the land they farmed. But a series of commissioners of the Bureau of Reclamation have seemed unable to understand the simple language of the law. They have allowed the bulk of the project water to serve corporations and wealthy individuals with great landholdings and much of the water to go to absentee investors. Some have simply ignored the law, others have called it a bad law and blatantly violated its terms, and still others have circumvented it by strange interpretations of its strictures.

From the beginning, the law was interpreted as limiting water service to users with no more than 160 acres for each member of a family, so that a strict limit of 160 acres per farm was never applied. That construction was probably in keeping with the spirit of the law. But the water was also allowed to go to the big landholders, and under an interpretation that strained both the letter and the spirit of the law. All the owners needed to do was to promise to dispose of excess land to buyers who could meet the legal requirements. Few expected to be required to keep the promises and, indeed, few have been kept.

In some cases, papers were drawn up including enough names of relatives to create a dummy organization big enough to prevent a breakup of extensive holdings. But the most blatant excuse used for ignoring the acreage limitation was a letter, written in the last days of the Hoover Administration by Secretary of the Interior Ray Lyman Wilbur. The letter simply asserted that the law did not apply to the Imperial Valley.

The letter has been used by reclamation commissioners over the years as a legal basis for decisions. And as recently as January, 1971, a federal district judge in San Diego, Howard Turrentine, held that the letter, not the reclamation law, applied to federal water projects in the valley. Strangely, although the Justice Department had supported the law in the case, it declined to appeal the decision.

No effort has ever been made by public officials to enforce the residence requirement, although it was upheld in November, 1971, by another federal district judge in San Diego, William Murray. The requirement is likely to remain paralyzed through a long series of appeals to higher courts.

Today, hundreds of thousands of acres continue to be served by water from federal projects in violation of the law. As Paul Taylor, professor emeritus of the University of California at Berkeley, an acknowledged expert on land and water resources, testified at a Senate hearing in 1972:

"On the west side of the Central Valley, federal construction proceeds to serve with water 500,000 acres or more, around two-thirds of which are ineligible to receive it; a single owner holds over 100,000 acres within the project.

"In the Imperial Valley, 233,000 acres exceed the legal limit."

Overall, Professor Taylor testified, there are 900,000 acres of land in California that are being served with water in violation of the Reclamation Law, including 120,000 acres of the land held by the Southern Pacific Railroad.

In Congress, Senator Fred Harris shortly before retiring expressed surprise at "the Federal Government's acquiescence in what amounts to a giant land steal and raid on the public treasury." He noted that the subsidies to western landowners for water cost the public $600 to $2,000 an acre.

Senator Harris added that in the Imperial Valley, where a network of canals and dams has been built at a public cost of $200-million, water service was being provided illegally for vast blocks of land owned by such agribusiness giants as Purex, United Brands and the Irvine Land Company. He charged other big corporations receiving water illegally through federal subsidies included Tenneco, Getty Oil, Standard Oil of California and, again, the Southern Pacific.

"The record elsewhere is no better," the Senator said. "In the Pacific Northwest water from the Columbia River will soon flow to the vast land held by Boeing Aircraft, Burlington Northern, Utah and Idaho Sugar and Amfac of Hawaii."

Nevertheless, recent years have at least brought more pretense of enforcement although interpretations of the law continue to be extremely liberal. Under pressure from some Congressmen and public-interest groups, large landowners are being required to sign contracts agreeing to dispose of excess lands. It remains to be seen how vigorously sympathetic public officials will press them to keep their agreements.

In the past, any enforcement has been far from even-handed. While some, for example an elderly landowner in the San Joaquin Valley, have been forced to sell, others, such as a subsidiary of Tenneco that bought his land, have been allowed to escape the limitation. The device used by the Tenneco subsidiary was to put the land, undivided, in the names of company officials and minor members of their families.

Even where sales may be required, the illegal water service provides a windfall. During the period before the sale —ten years' leeway is being allowed—the landholders get the benefits of the subsidized water. And although the regulations require the sales to be made at pre-water prices, the provision is liberally interpreted, and the actual prices allowed bear little relationship to what the land would be worth if there were no federal water in prospect.

But in California the most grandiose scheme to fleece the public was a plan hatched in the late nineteen-fifties when big landholders began to fear that the Reclamation Law might indeed be enforced as a result of growing outrage. The idea was to take a series of water projects in the state away from the Bureau of Reclamation and build them under the auspices of California agencies. It was a transparent device to undermine the acreage limitation of federal law, although the system would be linked with federal projects, with federal costs.

California would, indeed, assume most of the construction costs, but under the plan those would be foisted onto the general public rather than being paid by the water users. Representatives of the landed interests pressed the plan in both Washington and Sacramento and finally, in 1960, won its adoption.

The result has been one of the most monstrous pieces of thievery from the public. A gigantic extension of dams and canals has been built to bring water from northern California to the big farms of the south at a cost to Californians that will exceed $12-billion before it is paid for. The cost will be about $500 for every man, woman and child in the state; the result will be the coup sought by the landed interests, who are the principal beneficiaries. There will also be service to cities and towns, but facts that have emerged since the selling of the plan indicate that their modest needs could have been met more cheaply.

Although the California plan is linked to federal facilities, and although Congress in approving the plan specifically refused to exempt the area served from the acreage limitation, that restriction has been circumvented. The big corporations with their thousands and hundreds of thousands of acres have been served with project water at a public cost of more than $1,000 an acre. And not only do their water charges fail to reflect construction costs; they do not even reflect the operating costs of the system. In fact, the Nader team found, the rates charged amount to less than half of operating costs. And operating subsidies were found to amount to hundreds of thousands of dollars a year for some of the biggest water users.

V
Conditions for Conspiracy

The concentration of corporate power is increasing on many fronts—in the processing and selling as well as in the production of food. It happens almost as if the corporations were working in concert and, as economists at the F.T.C. and elsewhere have noticed, where the interests of large corporations collide in the marketplace, there is a mutual backing away from serious forms of competition.

In fact, the explanation stops short of conspiracy, for no actual collusion is necessary. The leading corporations are a closed society whose members work almost as one to promote mutually beneficial legal and business policies. All are kept aware of their common goals, as agribusiness executives and directors meet each other in private clubs and on the interlocked boards of the companies and their banks. The way the two largest supermarket chains seem to have divided the country into mutually exclusive territories to avoid head-on collisions may be one result.

What is more to the point is that the conditions for conspiracy exist in the interlocked directorates. Interlocks between companies in the same industry are forbidden under antitrust law, but here again enforcement has been notably lacking.

For agribusiness companies with California interests, the interlocks create an intricate network. The ties in the net may change from time to time, but the pattern continues essentially unaltered. The following are some of the interlocks found during one brief period by researchers for the Agribusiness Accountability Project, a Washington-based public-interest group. One link with one other company was all that was necessary to tie a corporation into the network.

The Bangor Punta Corporation, owner of South Lake Farms and its vast cotton and grain acreage in the San Joaquin Valley, had a director who also served on the board of United Brands, which dominates lettuce through the farms operated by its Interharvest division. More important, at United Brands he was in contact with directors from Welch's Grape Juice, John Hancock Life (owner of John Hancock Ranches and its vineyards) and a number of banks and investment companies, who, in turn, were in contact on those boards with other agribusiness directors. And so it goes in spreading veins of contact and interchange of influence and information.

Among other findings, Anderson, Clayton & Co., the conglomerate with interests in food, cotton and byproducts and the owner of Vista del Llano Farms and 52,000 acres in the San Joaquin Valley, had a common board member with Riviana Foods, Inc., a processor. Castle & Cooke, the landowning conglomerate that has expanded into retailing, was also interlocked with Safeway Stores, Newhall Land & Farming, Sunkist Growers, Inc., and Las Pasas Orchards. Consolidated Foods, whose subsidiary Union Sugar Company owns 11,000 acres in California, was interlocked with other corporations with large land and agribusiness investments such as Di Giorgio, Kaiser Industries and Standard Oil of California.

Del Monte, the world's largest producer of canned fruits and vegetables, with sprawling international land interests, has directors who meet others from a wide range of agribusiness on the boards of Broadway Hale Stores, Western Bancorporation, Southern California Edison, Pacific Lighting, Pacific Mutual Life, Pacific Gas and Electric, Pacific Gas Transmission and others.

Then there is Dow Chemical, among whose interlocks was one with Bud Antle, Inc., a giant farming enterprise from which Dow bought 17,000 acres of land in California and Arizona. Getty Oil, owner of 90,000 acres of California land, was interlocked with, among others, the Great Atlantic and Pacific Tea Company, and through that company with many others in agribusiness. Green Giant Company, the food-processing colossus, which owns or leases 285,000 acres in nineteen states and two Canadian provinces, was interlocked with, among others, Super Value Stores, Inc., a food chain. And the J. G. Boswell Company, owner of 108,814 acres in California and other land in Arizona and Australia, was interlocked with Safeway Stores and the Southern Pacific, which claims title to over three million acres of California land.

Safeway, in turn, was also interlocked with Southern Pacific as well as with Amfac, Inc., and Castle & Cooke, the two Hawaii giants, and Southern Pacific was further interlocked with Newhall Land and Farming and Del Monte Properties, among numerous other corporations and banks with agribusiness ties.

The linkages spread on and on. Newhall Land and Farming, in turn, besides its interlocks with Castle & Cooke and the Southern Pacific, has similar contacts with Las Pasas Orchards and Di Giorgio. Then the Ogden Corporation, a conglomerate whose food divisions include

Flavor Pict, Inc., a Florida-based grower and marketer of fresh tomatoes, had ties with Allied Supermarkets. And Pacific Lighting, one of the Del Monte contacts and the owner of Blue Goose Growers and thousands of acres of land, was also interlocked with Foremost-McKesson, the big dairy-products combine.

In a seemingly endless procession on go the names with agribusiness interests and broad agribusiness linkages: Standard Oil of California; Stokely-Van Camp; Sunkist Growers (a giant cooperative with many agribusiness corporations among its members); Tejon Ranch; Tenneco, Inc.; the Times-Mirror Company and Westgate-California.

It is not only that the director of one company serves on the board of another in the same or a related industry; the larger significance is that the directors he meets on each board often serve on several others where fellow members, in turn, have broad and intertwined agribusiness ties. It is a succession of interlocks that becomes finally like some monstrous tangle of jungle vines, almost impossible for regulators to hack through and impenetrable for the consumer.

More than anywhere else, all those interests come together on the boards of the big banks, whose doors are always open to the corporations but often closed to the grower with more modest needs. The Bank of America, for example, the biggest source of agribusiness financing, meshes with the network through interlocks with a list that reads like a roll call of the food industry: Producers Cotton; Di Giorgio, the processing conglomerate; Getty Oil and Kaiser Industries, owners of widely diverse lands; Consolidated Foods; Von's Grocery Company; American Potato Company; Standard Oil of California with its varied landholdings; Lucky Stores; Foremost-McKesson, the dairy conglomerate, and Newhall Land and Farming, producer of cattle and more than thirty crops.

As antitrust laws have been interpreted, they do not forbid directors of related or even competitive companies to serve on bank boards. But the bank boards are, at the very least, exceedingly convenient meeting places. And it should not seem strange that at banks where such big interests congregate, smaller farmers pay highly discriminatory rates in comparison with those charged the corporations.

California is no exception to a general condition of injustice in that respect. The corporations gain an unfair advantage over the small but efficient farmer in the cost of borrowed money, which is a critical need of agriculture everywhere. In times of tight money that small farmer often cannot obtain bank financing at all. He must turn then to the agribusiness firms themselves—to suppliers from whom he obtains his equipment and seeds and chemicals, to brokers who handle his produce and to processors who buy his crops. Agribusiness will usually supply whatever credit he needs, but only at high rates and on terms that make him a captive customer and supplier, subject to further discrimination in both the prices he pays and the prices he will receive for his crops. Thus he lives on borrowed time as well as borrowed money.

Preferential interest rates is only one of many advantages of corporations that are driving families off their farms and increasing concentration of agribusiness' power. But American consumers in an urban society are rarely stirred by injustices that mottle the agricultural scene. They are as unmoved by the plight of the small farmer as they are by the troubles of migrants and other farm workers. These workers have been denied, through the effectiveness of the agribusiness and big-farm lobbies, the benefits of the many laws passed to protect workers in other industries. They lack protection enjoyed by other workers in case of accident, against unfair conditions of wages and hours and against ill treatment when they attempt to bargain to improve their lot. Meanwhile, their children suffer malnutrition in the midst of plenty, they often lack a basic education in a nation that spends billions on its agricultural colleges, and they frequently are unable to find medical care they can afford.

What is surprising, however, is that Americans overlook their own losses as consumers when corporations are allowed unfair advantages and farmers like Ygish Bulbulian are lost from agriculture.

Bulbulian was born in Armenia and came to this country as a young man during World War I. He was penniless, but he worked in the fields for California farmers until he had scraped together $500 to make a down payment on twenty acres of land. The twenty-acre farm was not big enough to support Bulbulian and his wife and son, but it was a start. He continued to hire himself out as a laborer and his wife and son helped with the work while husbanding their money and adding bit by bit to their land. Today Ygish Bulbulian and his son, Berge, have 150 acres planted in grapes and currants.

But Ygish Bulbulian, now more than eighty years old, is a rarity on today's agricultural scene. In the future, Americans will see few like him. The nearly impossible dream of following in the Armenian's path was expressed in eloquent Spanish by Manuel Leon, a farm worker, to Senator Stevenson's subcommittee. Translated, his statement said:

"You will please forgive my simple nature because I am not an educated man. We are not jealous of the millions of dollars that are granted to rich farmers to hold back production. There is so very little that we ask for.

"It is a matter of record that many of us have all but managed the ranches at which we have been employed.

"And late at night, while we were struggling to keep a secondhand tractor, a dull disc harrow or a dilapidated plow in workable condition in some windswept barn under a dim light, we have felt despair and frustration because we were so aware that the farmer inside the house enjoying the warmth of his living room could have been us.

"Gentleman, this is a very difficult thing for me to say because I am not accustomed to making demands. My trust has always been in God and I have always left all things to Him. But now, deep within my heart, I feel that He is pressing me to ask for one thing. Please, gentlemen, make it possible for my people to be able to buy their own land and to care for it with the hands that are full of love for the soil. As a simple man I do not know how this can be done. But if it is, we will be able to build a life for ourselves that will make this country more fruitful."

The impossibility of Manuel Leon's dream became clear to the subcommittee through testimony of Berge, Ygish Bulbulian's son, who also indicated how agriculture and the economy suffer when such men are unable to farm their own land. He told Senator Stevenson's panel:

"Probably the biggest obstacle we face in our struggle to save the family farm is the attitude of many Americans, including some farm people, that the family farm is obsolete, it is inefficient, and therefore unable to compete with the efficient and well financed conglomerates.

"Well financed they are. Efficient they are not. I challenge any giant agribusiness corporation to match my efficiency. There is no way a large concern with various levels of bureaucracy and managed by absentee owners can compete in terms of true efficiency with a small, owner-operated concern. I cannot hire anyone to perform with the level of competence and efficiency that I perform. I seldom do one job at a time, but often two and three jobs simultaneously. While driving the tractor I watch for other things that need to be done. I watch for pests, for nutrient or water deficiency and generally consider management problems while doing a purely physical job. I work long hours each day and seldom have a Sunday completely without work.

"I am the manager, personnel director, equipment operator, maintenance man, bookkeeper, laborer, welder and so on. When I do hire labor, I usually work with them.

"With 150 acres of vineyard, I believe that we are at or near the optimum level of operation for our type of farming. No, I can't sell for a loss and make it up in taxes, nor can I lose on the farming end of the business and make it up at another level as a vertically integrated operation can. I have no political clout, and lobbying to me means writing a letter to my Congressman or Senator. But that is not what efficiency is all about.

"Efficiency has to do with the relation between input and output. No, the big agribusiness firms are not efficient except in farming the Government and, even if they were, do you think that that efficiency would be translated into lower prices to consumers when and if a small handful of agribusiness giants control agriculture?"

Berge Bulbulian's views of the relative efficiency of his farming and that of the corporations is supported by economists of the University of California at Davis. What their studies have found is that after a certain size—normally as much land as one family and occasional hired help can manage with modern equipment—no additional economies accrue through expansion of operations. There are no savings in further increases in size. That and other evidence indicates that, with their "various levels of bureaucracy," the big agribusiness concerns can compete with the smaller farmer only because of advantages that are due to their power—advantages such as lower interest rates the concerns obtain and lower prices they pay for their equipment and supplies. Subsequent studies by the Agriculture Department have confirmed those findings, but they have been little publicized.

Why then cannot a Manuel Leon or another Ygish Bulbulian hope to go into farming in competition with the conglomerates? Berge Bulbulian's testimony put the answer in simple terms. After explaining how his father, with only the equivalent of a fourth-grade education, had built up a farm and sent young Berge to college, Bulbulian said:

"Obviously, no semi-literate farm worker would, in his wildest dreams, dream of owning a major landholding. This is not surprising, nor is it particularly a problem. What is a problem is that he cannot even dream of owning a small piece of land. A forty-acre vineyard sells for approximately $80,000 in my area, with about $24,000 needed for a down payment plus the cash or credit to farm and live through one crop year, at least. On such a farm one can expect to earn a meager living at best if he has to pay interest and principal but can survive if he owns the farm outright. It would take at least eighty acres of grapes to farm with some degree of efficiency, to earn a satisfactory living. In short, the ambitions of people like my father were often realized in the nineteen-twenties and thirties, but today no young man who is not a part of a farm family dreams of owning a piece of land big or small.

"It is simply an unrealistic dream."

What has made it an unrealistic dream, in large part, is the unlimited capital that corporations have poured into their acquisitions. They have created land scarcities by their buying, and have thus driven the cost of land beyond the reach of the ordinary farmer. Meanwhile, in part through the risks created by their unfair competition, they have driven up interest rates that must be paid by smaller farmers.

In terms of the consumer's interest, what they have achieved is an enormous increase in the costs of farming that translates into extra billions of dollars that Americans must pay for their food.

What is more, as landholdings slide into fewer and fewer and bigger and bigger hands, the bidding will grow stiffer, the holdings larger and harder to manage efficiently. Finally, the costs to the consumer will climb still higher.

VI
Giants of the Earth, Shadows on the Land

Hollis B. Roberts sat behind his desk, his eyes closed, a cigar protruding from heavy lips, folds of flesh drooping over an open collar. The desk, a great, cluttered horseshoe, enclosed his girth. The plush furnishings in his office were arranged in awkward groupings as if movers had not quite finished their job.

"Look out for Roberts when he closes his eyes," a former associate had warned. "That means he's thinking."

Roberts, a 300-pound giant, opened his eyes and stared at the interviewer. "What kind of slander you gonna write about me?" he asked in a high-pitched Texas drawl.

He had been a hard man to reach. Only by camping in the outer office had this interviewer been able to get himself admitted to the big man's presence. Seeing him would hardly have been worth the persistence except that Roberts is a linchpin between several of the giant corporations involved in California food production. His peculiar dealings with a big banker also help to illustrate the link between financial institutions and agribusiness control in

California. Through land deals, quid-pro-quo agreements, management contracts and labyrinthine relationships, he is tied in with the vast landholdings of such corporations as Tenneco, Westgate-California, Buttes Oil, Getty, Texaco and Prudential Life. In addition, Roberts himself is of considerable importance to consumers and the future of the nation's food supply because he produces more than one-hundredth of his state's massive fruit and nut output on the 130,000 San Joaquin Valley acres that he controls. It would not take many like him to dominate production.

Roberts's office, near the town of McFarland, was in a low, sprawling, Spanish-style building that houses the multiple Roberts enterprises and was hard by his private chapel where he can pray and, at the push of a button, listen to hymns accompanied by the amplified tones of organ music. There are those who say that Roberts has much to pray over.

He looked troubled as he glared at the interviewer, and that was unusual. For the first time in his life, reporters were beginning to say unpleasant things about him. In the past, newsmen had often enjoyed the Hollis Roberts style of lavish but homespun hospitality and known the weight of the man's heavy arm draped across their shoulders. And the reporters had written glowing accounts of a rags-to-riches saga.

It was not that the stories had proved untrue. They told how Roberts, a poor dirt farmer, had fled the Texas dust bowl in 1936, his wife, two children and all the belongings he could carry loaded into a battered 1929 Chevrolet. He headed for California and once there began scraping together money to buy some more land of his own. Now, after years of farming and land dealing, he could have been musing behind his closed eyelids about how his life had changed. Instead of a shack in the dust bowl and his old Chevy, he owned Cadillacs, an eighteen-passenger airplane and an estate in a private mountain preserve near San Diego. But most important of all was his 130,000-acre empire. The stories were true—as far as they went.

"I believe in the land," Roberts said. "It's worth more today than it was yesterday, and it'll be worth more tomorrow."

Well he should believe, for it is that faith that has built his pyramid of wealth—though it may not do as well for the hopeful doctors, lawyers and dentists that he has gathered together as converts to his land-investing religion.

But now a worrisome federal agency was beginning to ask questions about his relations with a San Diego banker; a partner who had been driven to the verge of bankruptcy in one enterprise was suing, blaming Roberts, and reporters were beginning to ask questions about his ties with the biggest corporations in agribusiness. Some wondered why he had submitted so easily to the unionizing of his farm workers, and one had even suggested that his pyramid of wealth could sink in the loose sands of heavy debts and that he was keeping afloat only through new loans and by churning more and more investors' money into his land schemes.

But what seemed to trouble Roberts most was the blow to his pride when one writer suggested that he was only a tool in the hands of the San Diego banker. The inference was that the banker was likely to keep him in operation only so long as he remained useful to the banker's agribusiness and land schemes and some other, questionable interests.

But the full magnitude of the Roberts role and his usefulness to agribusiness in California has never been widely told. For example, he obtained a large chunk of his land empire by relieving a giant agribusiness corporation of part of its problem when it ran into trouble with the

F.T.C., and he has been accused of holding the country's largest commuter airline for the San Diego banker, who ran into trouble with the Civil Aeronautics Board. Other links tie him to the land operations of other agribusiness giants.

Roberts was already a fair-sized farmer, though he had some serious problems, when some years ago he formed a friendship with a southern Californian who was chairman and chief stockholder of the United States National Bank of San Diego. As it turned out, for a farmer with big ideas and credit problems, it was better to have a friend at U. S. National Bank than at the Chase Manhattan.

The banker was C. Arnholt Smith, a friend and financial angel of President Richard Nixon. Smith would later run into trouble with the Securities and Exchange Commission and the Internal Revenue Service over his methods of operation as chairman of Westgate-California, a big agribusiness and transportation conglomerate. On May 31, 1973, the S.E.C. charged him with converting assets of Westgate-California, which owned airline, taxicab, tuna-canning and land and farming corporations, to his own enrichment and that of several friends, who were named codefendants. The S.E.C. said he used his bank to further the schemes. The I.R.S. said he owed $22.8-million in back taxes.

As investigators probed more deeply into Smith's affairs, his troubles multiplied. Late in 1973 the Controller of the Currency and a platoon of examiners moved in, declared U.S. National insolvent and overnight transferred its $1-billion in assets to the big Crocker Bank of San Francisco. Among massive loans of doubtful collectibility cited by investigators as contributing to the bank's insolvency were debts totaling $67.1-million owed by a "Hollis Roberts group."

Shortly afterward Smith was able to settle the S.E.C.'s fraud charges by agreeing to give up control of Westgate-California.

Before that, however, Smith's principal problems were with his own auditors. For such difficulties, it was useful for the banker to have a friend in farming like Hollis Roberts.

The Smith-Roberts relationship is a tangled skein of multiple multimillion-dollar deals with, on occasion, the same piece of land passing through several transactions, all in the names of mysterious companies with addresses that looked curiously like Smith's own or those of members of his family or close associates. Several strands also lead to another millionaire, Michael J. Coen, who was a codefendant with Smith in conversion of Westgate-California assets.

In Smith, Roberts was dealing with a man who had used the bank he heads to finance the land schemes of his corporations and in one case in an attempt to show on his corporate books what appeared to be an inflated corporate profit for an unusual deal. He was also a man who, finding one appraisal inadequate to support a land deal, would simply hire a different appraiser, and who has been known to fire an auditor because of a frank statement on his company's condition. One of the things an auditor did not like was Westgate-California's payment of $1.8-million to a design firm owned by Smith's wife for decoration of Westgate Plaza, a plush hotel built by the conglomerate.

The deal in which Smith had to go to several firms before he could find a cooperative appraiser was one in which Roberts repaid past favors by helping Smith enter a much-needed $8.5-million profit in Westgate-California's books. It was in 1970 that the agribusiness conglomerate sold a 12,000-acre cattle ranch to Coen and some other Smith associates. The deal was financed through three Westgate subsidiaries with loans from Smith's U. S.

National Bank totaling $12-million. The auditing firm employed by Westgate boggled at his attempt to put an $8.5-million profit on the deal into the corporate books. When an appraisal that the auditors ordered showed the land worth only $8-million, they said the $12-million in notes on an $8-million piece of land was a liability that could revert to Westgate and injure its stockholders. C. Arnholt Smith contacted other appraisers and finally found one who would put a value of $15-million and still another appraiser who provided a valuation of $20-million on the land. But Haskins & Sells, the highly reputable auditing firm, still refused to change its original decision.

The firm's determination was not hard to understand, since the land was said to be alkaline. It would have cost additional millions to develop it for fruit crops, the only agricultural use that could justify the price being paid. Haskins & Sells, which also questioned the Westgate deal with Smith's wife, did not last long with the company.

Before the auditors were discharged they finally approved the land deal because Smith was able to find a benefactor—Roberts. Ownership of the three Westgate subsidiaries and the $12-million liability for the U. S. National Bank notes were transferred to Hollis Roberts, but the three subsidiaries went on operating as before from offices in the U. S. National Bank Building, which was also Smith's headquarters—and mainly with Westgate-affiliated officers. There was only one visible change. Roberts began to be listed as the president of one of the companies. Later the land was recorded in the names of three newly organized companies, but the brand on their cattle continued to be listed as Westgate's. Any purchasers of cattle would have had to make their checks payable to Westgate-California, the brand owner. Also, unlike other Roberts enterprises, the ranch was said to be paying its bills with reasonable promptness.

The deal went into Westgate-California books as a clean, profitable sale. The S.E.C., in its 1973 charges, alleged inflated profits from questionable transactions were often keys to Smith's schemes. It said Smith often turned out to be "on both sides"—that is, both buyer and seller.

Another land deal, this one also involving the trio of Roberts, Smith and Coen, was blocked by the California Department of Corporations. California securities laws require that sales of land syndications must reflect "fair, equitable and just" prices, although the department has often allowed pyramiding of fees, financing charges and management contracts to mount higher than the cost of the land.

In this deal, a Kansas City group headed by Coen bought 2,814 acres from Smith's Westgate-California Realty Company for $7,740,506 and formed a syndicate to sell it to investors for $10.1-million. The department balked because it considered the land overpriced and it said that, besides, there was not exactly an "arm's-length" relationship between Smith, Coen and Roberts, who was to have been the farm manager. Roberts's was to have been a highly lucrative contract much like that provided in the Buttes Oil-Treecrop syndication. The farm management in that deal was also contracted to a Roberts company.

With the Coen syndication blocked, the land was transferred through seven corporations, each with the same Los Angeles address as a brother of C. Arnholt Smith or that of Arnholt's daughter, in a series of twelve transactions financed by the U. S. National Bank at prices that climbed to $10.5-million, considerably above the level previously rejected by the Department of Corporations.

The association with Smith has been profitable for Roberts, the one-time refugee from the dust bowl, who began his California career slopping pigs with scraps scavenged from restaurant garbage cans while plowing a few acres of cotton and working as a roustabout on oil rigs.

Roberts had built his holdings to about 9,000 acres before he tied in with C. Arnholt Smith, but the land was heavily mortgaged and, according to Dun & Bradstreet, his net worth was only $40,000. Also, his working capital was a minus figure, he was badly in need of financing, and his credit at the banks was far from the best. A friend at a bank that was not inclined to be overly cautious was exactly what Roberts needed, and that was what he found.

It was in 1968, after cattle breeders had already shown the way, when Smith began what is said to have been the first of the big treecrop syndications described in Chapter III. Smith, the banker, brought Roberts, the farmer, into the deal, a 5,880-acre promotion called Jasmine Groves, and it started Roberts on the way to the big time. He reaped a quick $8-million profit from the sale of the land, most of which was Roberts's, and he was given a ten-year, $25-million management contract with an assured $3-million in profits. In the same year, after he was turned down for short-term loans at both the Bank of America and United California Bank, Smith, his friend at U. S. National, came up with money that he needed. U. S. National Bank has continued to carry him, sometimes when others wouldn't. In early 1972 a report showed Roberts owing U. S. National nearly $3-million in short-term notes. Several bankers in the San Joaquin area told a reporter from a business magazine that Roberts still found it hard to get unsecured loans anywhere else, partly because of his heavy indebtedness and partly because of haphazard bookkeeping.

But, although the Jasmine Groves deal sent Roberts on his way to the big money, the investors in it did not fare so well. The land was planted in citrus, and most citrus syndications have turned out badly for their investors. But that has not prevented Roberts from selling the dream of quick riches in other syndications, promoted as paths to big profits and low taxes.

Although Smith was one of the first big friends to open doors for Roberts, he has not been the only one. Besides Roberts's relationship with Buttes Oil as a farm manager he has been named to contracts for similar services with such landowning giants as Getty, Texaco and Prudential.

But the most important of all his liaisons, and the occasion of his biggest indebtedness, came after Tenneco, Inc., the conglomerate that bought Kern County Land Company, found itself under investigation on antitrust grounds. Its officers decided that Roberts could be useful to them, too. Apparently in response to the antitrust charges, Tenneco sold Roberts 70,000 acres for $65-million, a fancy price for the land, much of which was undeveloped.

Neighbors in the area wondered how long the land would remain sold, for Tenneco held a sizable mortgage on it. But best of all for Tenneco, the corporation retained control of the crops and, through a ten-year marketing agreement, tied up much of the fruit from Roberts's farms. The increase in volume provided by the contract was significant even for a company that already controlled 10 percent of the nation's table grapes and still larger shares of other crops.

VII
Corporate Hands on the Plow

"Lady, you just pinched your last peach," says the large print on a leaflet that Tenneco has sometimes packed into containers of produce. The words have a snarling, just-before-the-arrest sound, as if in the next instant the peach-pinching shopper were going to feel handcuffs clamped around her wrists.

Of course, the words were not meant to sound threatening, although Tenneco has developed the market power to give ominous overtones to the leaflet. As its small print explained, Tenneco was enunciating a relatively new concept in the marketing of fresh fruits and vegetables. The message the shopper was intended to get was this: Though your mother might have taught you to paw and pick over the produce, Mother did not know best. But Tenneco's experts do and they select it for you. You can't check the quality because the produce is packaged in plastic and paper, but you can trust Tenneco.

The leaflet was part of a costly advertising campaign designed to convince shoppers that experts had scientifically studied every orange or peach, every plum or bunch of grapes and made sure that its quality was the finest before it could go into a package under Tenneco's label.

The idea had seemed to officials at Tenneco well worth the try. After all, one of the basic findings of marketing economists has been that phony differentiation of products by brand-name promotions is one of the most successful devices for achieving market control. It holds down competition and at the same time it helps the advertiser to get a little more for his product. And it elevates company-versus-company rivalry to the more profitable plane of competition through claims rather than through pricing and value.

In its few short years in the farming and marketing business Tenneco has gained the power to make the plan work.

Like many other acquisition-minded conglomerates, Tenneco entered the farming business in the late nineteen-sixties. It was another big jump for a company that had taken a running start in 1943 and, many long leaps afterward, had become one of the biggest companies in the United States. Before it moved into food, Tenneco had become a major factor in oil production, pipelines, chemicals, packaging and shipbuilding. It had assets approaching $4-billion and net income of more than $139-million a year, and those figures were climbing with each annual report.

Tenneco had its scouts looking for land when they spotted one of the biggest holdings of all. It was the old Kern County Land Company, the empire put together in the land-grabbing days of Haggin and Tevis. An article, "The Company Twice as Big as Rhode Island," that appeared in the March, 1961, issue of *Fortune* magazine described Kern County Land as "2,800 square miles of land, with cattle, crops and oil royalties." A map of Kern County illustrating the article showed how aptly the company was named. Its land dominated the countryside around Bakersfield, spreading far and wide from both banks of the Kern River, whose excess water, incidentally, it was selling to other farmers and ranchers the way a utility sells gas and oil. Besides its 400,000 acres, but not shown on the map, were the million acres the Kern County Land Company owned in Arizona, New Mexico and Oregon.

It is sometimes difficult to grasp the dimensions of such vast landholdings under the control of one financial interest. To try to get the point across, one witness at U. S. Senator Adlai Stevenson's hearings in 1972 presented graphically the scope of the company's Kern County holdings: "That is roughly equal to a one-mile strip of land extending from San Francisco to Los Angeles." The distance between those two cities is more than 400 miles. "If you have trouble getting all of that," he added, "it is six miles wide from San Francisco to Sacramento"—a distance of 85 miles.

By the time Tenneco became interested, an old, conservative management of the land company had given way to more aggressive, expansionist policies. Kern County Land had gone into industrial products by acquiring Walker Manufacturing, a producer of automotive equipment, and the J. I. Case Company, an old and respected producer of farm tractors and machinery. Other divisions were also in land development and wildcatting for oil rather than merely collecting royalties as the company had in the past.

It seemed an ideal combination to go with the assets that Tenneco already had. At a glance it appeared easily possible to achieve near-perfection in the kind of integration that conglomerates worship, independent farmers fear and the general public gawks at. Tenneco could use chemicals from its own plants for fertilizers and pesticides;

it could till the land with tractors from its own J. I. Case Company, fueled with gas and oil from its own refineries; it could package the products in containers from its own Packaging Corporation of America and it could even market its products through the retail stores that it runs in conjunction with its service stations.

Tenneco, once the F.T.C. began looking over its shoulder, scoffed at the idea that it had ever considered any such thing. Its refineries were too far away for economical integration into the land operation, Tenneco pointed out, and it did not even use its own chemicals or packaging materials. But it would be naive to believe that an acquisition-bent company like Tenneco had no such idea for the future. Witness its own statement in its 1970 annual report:

"Our goal in agriculture is integration from the seedling to the supermarket."

That grand view has haunted Tenneco since the annual report first expressed it. The words created concern throughout the food chain, for the message enunciated a system that economists have noted as the worst threat to true competition. In such a system, even if the company uses costly predator practices to gain control or if it operates uneconomically at one step of the ladder, it can make up the losses at another. Meanwhile, when a company is widely diversified, rivals with an advantage in one market hesitate to compete as vigorously as they might for fear of retaliation in another market. The frank statement of Tenneco's goal may be one of the factors that attracted the attention of the F.T.C.

Another, though the federal agency has never even acknowledged its interest, may have been that Tenneco's agribusiness acquisitiveness did not stop with its acquisition of the Kern County Land Company in 1967. In 1968 Tenneco expanded its almond groves and began negotiations for acquisition of California Almond Orchards, Inc., an operation with plants that were processing nearly 17 percent of all United States almond production.

"Forward-looking steps were taken in 1969," the company said in its annual report, "notably the expansion of acreage under cultivation and advances toward integrated agricultural operations." It was still buying more citrus and almond orchards and grape vineyards; it locked up its deal for California Almond Orchards, Inc., and most "notably" it was negotiating for the biggest produce marketing firm in the world, the Heggblade-Marguleas Company, which had big landholdings of its own. In 1970, a year when Tenneco acknowledged "giant strides toward the development of an integrated agriculture," the conglomerate announced that "with a growing population to house, clothe and feed, Tenneco is well prepared to help meet this fundamental demand."

It was indeed. In fact, Tenneco was well on the way toward a shared monopoly in the feeding of that population. Early in 1970 it closed the deal to absorb the Heggblade-Marguleas Company, and it took over the facilities and marketing of the California Date-Growers Association in a deal that gave Tenneco control of 70 percent of the nation's date production. It also, continuing its land acquisitiveness, added on 4,500 acres of grape vineyards, including land acquired with the Heggblade-Marguleas merger.

The grape land was an important step toward its present control of 11 percent of California's and 10 percent of the nation's table-grape production, but perhaps just as significantly it also began promotion of its Sun Giant brand name for produce. Through its market control and brand-name promotion, it soon set the pattern for the future in its other produce. It was able to increase its price to consumers of its Sun Giant dates, and it even spun off some of its profits to the independent date-growers whose products moved under the Tenneco umbrella. There were other growers who were less happy, for Tenneco had begun to spread fear across its empire by evicting tenants who had been longtime farmers on the Kern County land. Some of them had put enough investments in their leased-land operations to qualify as agribusinessmen themselves.

By 1972 the company had put into operation the eight-acre plant at Bakersfield through which streamed fruits and vegetables for the nation's markets and supermarkets.

It was there that a visitor found the truth behind the Sun Giant claims of expert and scientific selection for the benefit of the shopper. Boxes of grapes moved into the cavernous buildings by the truckload, having been packed in the fields as fast as harvesters could pick them. Machines graded oranges and plums for size and uniformity. Some women watched a conveyor belt of oranges and occasionally tossed out one that was discolored or misshapen. Others bent over a receiving bin at the end of the line, packing boxes as fast as their arms could fly. The oranges that the machines dropped out for lack of uniformity and those with discolorations rolled into discard bins, destined to be squeezed and concentrated for orange juice. The plum discards rolled into boxes, destined only for hog feed.

What the shoppers' mothers could have told them, but Tenneco and other mass marketers never do, is what is general but never publicized knowledge among the experts at the Department of Agriculture: Fruit that grows in odd shapes and sizes or with off-color skin has as much taste and food value and as many vitamins as the large round fruits that are chosen purely for cosmetic reasons. Except for the money, time and labor wasted in the grading and culling process, economically troubled families across the

country could buy nutritious fruits and vegetables for
much less than they must pay now.

By 1972, Tenneco had stopped talking about "integration from seedling to supermarket." (At this point the
conglomerate was under F.T.C. scrutiny.) Its new slogan
was: "We put the pro in produce." The "pro" in its produce was Heggblade-Marguleas, where the top pro was
Howard Marguleas, a handsome, hardworking son of one
of the company's founders—a sophisticated marketing millionaire in a hand-tailored suit.

In a paneled office, hung with original paintings at the
end of a richly carpeted corridor, Marguleas talked frankly
and proudly about the operations of his company, now
the Heggblade-Marguleas-Tenneco division of the parent
company. He openly acknowledged that his company now
controls 72 percent of the nation's date production, and
10 to 15 percent of the California market in such fruits
as strawberries, peaches, plums, cherries and nectarines
and that it has become the primary factor in grapes—
F.T.C. investigators have found that Tenneco controls
10 percent of the national market in table grapes. Says one
economist at the F.T.C.: "Remember you don't have to
have all the production to control a market in agriculture.
All you need is a sizable share."

Although he did not elaborate, experts know that in
some seasons each big producer has a much larger share of
the market than he shows on the basis of an annual average. A minor change in supply—often as little as 1 or 2
percent—can have a major impact on prices, and a company able to effect such changes has the power to exercise
price leadership.

"Some people talk about us as if it were a crime to be
big, but I think bigness is great," Marguleas said, noting
how the company's financial power and its market control

and brand-name promotion were helping to get higher prices for date-growers. He added that the company's size also helped to get higher prices for the products of about two thousand other growers whose output is now under the company's control.

Apparently, eight Congressmen, members of the House Agriculture Committee, feel the same way about Tenneco's bigness. In April, 1972, when the company was already under investigation by the F.T.C., they accepted free rides in the company's plane on a tour of California. George Baker, a writer for the Fresno *Bee*, noted at the time that it would have cost them $1,000 to charter the flight. It is likely that ethical considerations never crossed their minds, because free rides in agribusiness planes have become commonplace for many Congressmen.

Peter J. Divizich, like Hollis Roberts, would have agreed that bigness was great if he had been asked during the years when he was building a sizable agribusiness operation of his own—before his ambitions collided with those of Heggblade-Marguleas and ran into some bumbling management help from the Bank of America.

Divizich, an elderly Yugoslav-American, has some bitter memories that he recounts in the halting accents of his native land. According to his testimony and the records of two court cases, he had spent a lifetime building up his expanse of more than 5,000 acres of orchards and grape vineyards when he first encountered Heggblade-Marguleas, the "pro" that Tenneco put in its produce. A brief filed in one of the cases tells the story of how Divizich, once the king of a sprawling domain of vineyards and orchards, ended up a broken man, and Tenneco wound up as the owner of his former kingdom.

There is no record of how many dreams of smaller farmers were shattered as their lands were absorbed into the

Divizich holdings during his rise. This is merely the story of his fall, as presented in a brief to the United States Court for the Eastern District of California, following a jury trial in the Fresno County Superior Court that ended in December, 1971.

Beginning about 1940, the Bank of America financed the farming operations and expansion of Peter Divizich until, by 1957, he had built his orchards and vineyards to the imposing size of 2,300 acres. At that point, he was told by Bureau of Reclamation officials that they were going to enforce the law limiting irrigation service to holdings of 160 acres a person. Since his 2,300 acres were being served by the Federal Central Valley Project, it appeared that he would have to sell most of his holdings.

Divizich obviously enjoyed his role as owner of vast landholdings. Perhaps that was his motivation as he embarked on expansion into new lands, which he would not be required to sell, but there was also a more practical reason. He had substantial investments in packing and cold-storage buildings.

Year after year, as he expanded, the Bank of America financed his operations and acquisitions on the basis of short-term notes, callable on demand, although each year the profits from his fruit fell short of clearing the debt. The money that he owed mounted steadily, increasing by $1,052,753 in 1963 and $714,058 in 1964.

Ostensibly, those short-term loans were merely to be used to finance current operations, but he was using much of the money to develop new orchards on newly acquired lands. In his brief, Divizich charged that the Bank of America, which monitored his business closely, knew very well what he was doing with the money. He pictured an arrangement with a tacit understanding that would keep the credit revolving because, he said, the bankers knew "at all times that the newly planted vineyards were not scheduled to come into meaningful production for a period of five years."

It was in 1965 that Divizich first encountered Heggblade-Marguleas, which was later to become Heggblade-Marguleas-Tenneco, and his deepening debt problem began a disastrous plunge.

As Divizich and his lawyers told the story in their federal court complaint, he was first approached by a vice president of Heggblade-Marguleas, a John A. Thomas, who suggested what appeared to be a mutually advantageous arrangement. The company proposed to take over the marketing of Divizich's fruit and, Divizich said, Thomas "represented" to him that Heggblade-Marguleas and some of its officials were interested in buying some of the land that the Bureau of Reclamation was forcing him to sell. Apparently this looked like a good deal to Divizich, and he signed a contract giving the Heggblade-Marguleas Company exclusive right to sell his 1965 crop, at a 9 percent brokerage fee.

Then began, according to the complaint and other reports, a curious record of selling by the brokerage company. Heggblade-Marguleas, despite its long experience and broad contacts in the fresh fruit business, sold the Divizich crops at prices "substantially" below what other growers were getting for comparable fruit, the complaint charged.

Divizich's lawyers later explained in interviews the basis of that complaint. Fruit was shipped from California on the basis of one contract price and often sold on arrival to large wholesale buyers for sharply reduced rates, with no adequate explanation for the reductions, they said. They reported examining ticket after ticket that showed final sales at prices that were sharply below the market. Yet, they said, no federal inspectors were asked to confirm damage or deterioration of the fruit and thus explain the price-cutting that slashed Divizich's income. There were few claims for damage to the fruit filed with the railroads that had carried it. Both recourses are available to a broker who is forced to accept below-contract prices because of the condition of his client's commodity and who wants to show good faith.

The complaint charged that Heggblade-Marguleas, because of its size, was able to victimize its client and carve out a still bigger share of market control for itself by underselling the market to favor big buyers in return for promises of expanded future purchases of other fruit or in return for favors on previous purchases. Such practices are reportedly widespread in the manslaughtering world of fruit and vegetable brokering.

Whatever the reason, in his year with Heggblade-Marguleas, the misfortunes of Peter Divizich grew and his debt at the bank mounted. His budget deficit for 1965, while his affairs at the market were in the hands of Heggblade-Marguleas, amounted to $1,470,731—nearly twice that suffered the year before.

One year with Heggblade-Marguleas was enough for Divizich. He dismissed the company from its role as his broker both for its sales performance and because he was beginning to suspect, according to the complaint, that neither the company nor its officials had really intended to buy from him the reclamation lands that he was being forced to sell.

According to Divizich's complaint, next came an assault on his standing at the bank. It charged that Thomas, the vice president of Heggblade-Marguleas, and its president, Howard P. Marguleas, began to "convey" to the bank that the old man was failing, because of his age, to market his fruit properly and to keep pace with modern farming practices. Those "untrue and malicious" representations, made with a "wanton recklessness," had an ulterior motive, Divizich asserted.

What happened in 1966, the year after Divizich discharged Heggblade-Marguleas for its sales performance, was one of the most curious parts of the whole story. Under threat of foreclosure, the bank forced Divizich once again to hire as his broker the company that he charged with responsibility for the worst of his problems the year before and to hire as a farm manager a man chosen by the bank and the top officials of Heggblade-Marguleas.

Although the contracts involved made it appear that Divizich was acting of his own volition, a separate paper that the bank required him to sign specifically took away any right of control over his lands and farming. The complaint charged that this was all part of a scheme by Thomas, Marguleas and their company to take control of his land and operations.

If his problems were serious in 1965, the first year of his relationship with Heggblade-Marguleas, the next two years were disastrous. The new managers lavishly spent money that he didn't have for long-term improvements to his property, the complaint said, and drove him "further into debt." His losses for the two years soared to $3-million.

From February, 1966, to January, 1968, Divizich noted, his debt to the bank doubled, from $4.5-million to $9-million. He charged that the bank, by its own management decisions, had created half the debt that became the basis for forcing him into bankruptcy and into a foreclosure sale that allowed the bank to take over his property on January 9, 1968.

It should come as no surprise that it was Heggblade-Marguleas and Tenneco that wound up with the Divizich land. Curiously, the bank turned down a higher bid by

an officer of Buttes Oil than the $5.75-million paid by
Tenneco shortly after the merger with Heggblade-Marguleas. The Buttes offer included a provision that would
have left Divizich with eight hundred acres of his land,
free and clear.

Another curiosity was the difference between the treatment that the Bureau of Reclamation gave to Divizich
and that accorded to Tenneco and its officers. Although
Divizich was ordered to sell his reclamation land, Tenneco was allowed to keep control of it by simply placing
it, undivided, in the names of Marguleas, Thomas and
various members of their families, with enough names
listed to bring their average interests technically into conformance with the 160-acre limitation. As usual, there was
not even an allusion to the residence requirement of reclamation law.

The Superior Court jury apparently believed the Divizich charges. They awarded the elderly victim in the case
$400,000 in damages—$200,000 each from the bank and
from Heggblade-Marguleas-Tenneco.

The federal case involved charges of antitrust violations,
with the complaint building toward the allegation that the
corporate takeover of Divizich's lands "may substantially
lessen effective competition through the control of price
and supply and tend to create a monopoly in the California
table grape market." Competitors were threatened, one by
one, with elimination, it said.

The antitrust case never reached a decision. Divizich
was induced to drop his charges and accept an out-of-court
settlement that gave him an additional $200,000.

Divizich's holdings were quite large, and it is at least
comprehensible that they might attract the attention of a
large corporation, but apparently no holding is too small
to attract the interest of agribusiness. It was the misfor-
tune of William W. Wiest, owner of only fifty acres and

a packing business operated out of a converted dairy barn, to come to the attention of a subsidiary of C. Arnholt Smith's Westgate-California Corporation.

In many ways, Wiest's story is similar to that of Divizich. Wiest, a farmer-businessman who once had visions of grandeur, told his story in timid, apprehensive tones after a bankruptcy hearing that reflected his dealings with a brokerage firm named Hooker-Corrin, which was a subsidiary of Westgate-California. The record of the hearing showed him winding up with a debt of $270,000 after a few years of experience with the firm—during which he was charged allegedly illegal fees, money due him was said to have been withheld, and interest charges were piled on interest charges at the high rate of 10 percent a year.

The record of the hearing included testimony of a former supervising auditor of the Bureau of Market Enforcement of the California Department of Agriculture, who had been asked to audit the accounts of Hooker-Corrin's dealings with Wiest. The auditor testified that in one instance he found $15,751 in illegal charges for cooling Wiest's fruit, fees that were also being paid by the buyers. He also reported finding that the average market price on the days when Wiest delivered his fruit to the brokerage house would have given $38,558 more than Wiest received. The auditor testified also that there were illegal brokerage fees, charged to both buyer and seller, while the interest charges deepened Wiest's debts.

Despite the testimony, Wiest was forced to accept bankruptcy and lose his orchards to the giant Westgate-California Corporation.

see p. 264

VIII
A Banana Named Chiquita

While Tenneco was swallowing up the orchards and vineyards, another big corporation—United Brands—was taking in the lettuce, which is an even bigger prize. It is one of the highest-volume products sold in the supermarkets—a $667-million-a-year commodity. The market looked like an easy conquest to United Brands in 1968, when the company decided to launch its invasion. First, the industry was "atomistic," as the economists say. That is, ownership of lands and shipping and handling facilities was fragmented among many interests, and there was no big, established leader. And, second, United Brands was fresh from a victory in a campaign similar to the one it planned for its takeover bid, one that appeared to have tested and proved the strategy of conquest.

Also, most of the nation's lettuce production was in concentrated sections of California and Arizona, with the Salinas and Imperial Valleys of California dominant. The year round, the two states produce 85 percent of the country's lettuce, and for six months of the year they have 90 to 98 percent of production.

The story of United Brands and lettuce has to start with bananas back in the days when the company was known as United Fruit. It is revealed in an internal company report obtained by the Federal Trade Commission when it began looking into the company's operations.

The year was 1960. United Fruit was in trouble. United States consumption of bananas, its principal product, had been declining for nearly ten years. Worse, United Fruit's share of the market had dropped from 66 percent in 1953 to 55.7 percent in 1959, though it edged back up to 57.1 percent in 1960. At the same time, the company's profits had been dropping steadily and at alarming rates. From $44.1-million in 1953 they fell to $2.2-million in 1960.

The heart of the problem was that prices were declining as consumption fell.

More significantly, the company had discovered something that has finally been brought home to most Americans only recently through problems such as those encountered by the giant Lockheed Aircraft and Penn Central Railroad companies: Size does not always—nor even usually—equate with efficiency. The greater the size of a company the greater its financial and market power—elements that permit it to swallow up small and middle-sized but vigorous and dynamic companies. Often, however, the economists find, those smaller companies lose their vigor in the process of being absorbed into the bigger mass.

United Fruit was the giant of its field, but its smaller competitors had learned to produce bananas of at least equal quality at a cost that permitted them to sell profitably at cheaper prices than United Fruit.

The company had to find a way to pass its higher costs on to consumers, and it turned to the big advertising firm of Batten, Barton, Durstine and Osborn to help find the solution. BBDO was not without an answer and, as might be expected, it found the key in advertising.

It noted that manufacturers of branded products were able to pass along rising costs because, through their advertising, they had built a "consumer franchise" for their products. "The retailer knows this, so he is willing to pay more for a well-known brand," says the company report, which covers the years 1960–67, when United Fruit was building such a "consumer franchise." The report was apparently prepared for the company by BBDO. It said:

"The consumer does not know United Fruit bananas from any other kind of bananas and, therefore, doesn't care whose bananas she buys. Assuming that the quality of the bananas is comparable, the lowest priced bananas get the sale."

United Fruit set out to change that, the report said, observing:

"In order to raise the price of its bananas, United Fruit must first build consumer preference for its own brand of bananas." It added: "The objective of the brand program was to sell United Fruit bananas for a higher price than they would normally get."

Realizing that "our bananas would probably not look any better than the competition's at retail," it decided: "We could not use any product claims that were checkable at retail."

The company, with BBDO's help, fixed on the brand name "Chiquita" because it was one that it had already been using in the wholesale trade, and hit on the claim, "keeps days longer." Market testing of brand-name promotion and advertising was set to begin.

It lasted only a short time in one of the test markets, Salt Lake City, for several reasons including one that was very simple: It found "very high quality competitive fruit at non-premium prices." But the company did not allow such a problem to interfere with its testing in other markets.

It had two principal goals: First, it wanted to "build a competitive edge based on a product advantage invisible at the point of sale." And then, by that device, it sought to get 20 cents more a box for its Chiquita bananas than others were selling for. The test seemed successful for, in the test markets, retailers were able to get average prices for Chiquitas of 19.2 cents a pound, against an average of 18.6 cents a pound for others.

Now the company was ready to go ahead full speed. It set an advertising budget for 1964 of $6-million and again it set a goal of a price premium of 20 cents a box over what unbranded first-class fruit would bring.

The first seven months of that year bore out the company's hopes. Its Chiquita bananas were selling for 14 to 23 cents a box higher at wholesale than other first-class bananas and 62 cents a box more than all other, unbranded United Fruit bananas. At retail, for the full year, Chiquita bananas were getting about 30 percent of the market at prices about 10 percent higher than other bananas.

For 1965 the company set a still higher goal: increased volume and 50 cents a box extra for the branded bananas while "maintaining a strong consumer franchise position capable of supporting a premium price structure and withstanding competitive countermeasures."

The results were even better than United Fruit had dared hope. It was getting 84 cents a box more for Chiquitas that year than for its other bananas, compared with 63 cents for the full year of 1964. The reason, of course, was the effectiveness of the device of brand-name promotion, as a consumer survey showed. Of women interviewed, 49 percent said they looked for Chiquitas when shopping for bananas; 27 percent said they would ask for Chiquitas

by name, and 25 percent said they would even go to another store looking for Chiquitas if the store in which they
were shopping did not have them in stock. Meanwhile,
more households were buying bananas and paying more
for them.

Some of the results were disquieting. Consumers who
were most receptive to the advertising claims were among
those who could least afford to pay a premium price for a
product that had no essential advantage of quality. Among
the most ill-used victims, those who tended most often to
buy the Chiquita brand when they bought bananas, were
low-income blacks of the inner cities.

In the beginning, the advertising message had some
slight basis in fact. The Gros Michel breed being promoted
does indeed "keep longer" than most other breeds, but
United Fruit's Gros Michels did not keep any longer than
anyone else's Gros Michels. But then, of course, United
Fruit did not say what keeps longer than what.

For production reasons, United had to shift to the
Valery breed and to shift from the "keeps longer" claim
because it was demonstrably false. The company switched
to the contention that Chiquitas were better packaged and
therefore less subject to bruising, but it had to drop that
claim because of complaints about bruising.

"Emphasis would be shifted to a less specific, less checkable claim," the company report said, "it being the company's desire to retain the good cooperation and sales
support of the trade." Its new claims were to be based on
wholesomeness and nutrition, but that did not last long
either because, the report said: "Parameters established
for campaign development were that copy emphasis be
more competitive than the existing campaign, yet less specific and checkable than the boxing/bruising story." The
new idea was to spread a message that the company was

"fussy about what we put our label on" and "to convince the consumer that Chiquita brand bananas achieve a quality level consistently higher than the competition."

It seemed to make little difference what the claim was. Each message persuaded more consumers to pay higher prices for bananas. By 1967 another consumer survey showed that 53 percent of shoppers looked specifically for Chiquitas, and the wholesale price spread had risen to 97 cents for the branded over the unbranded bananas. And most important of all to United Fruit, its profits were up $23-million a year since those depressed days before the Chiquita brand was hatched.

For the company, the stage was set for an ascent to the high echelons of conglomerates. A series of mergers, most importantly one with AMK, the former American Seal-Kap Corporation, a conglomerate that grew out of the container-cap business, lifted the combined corporation to Number 70 on the *Fortune* list of the top 500 companies. And now, fresh from its banana victory, it was ready to test a vision of big money in fresh produce.

Calling its Chiquita story "the most outstanding branding success in produce history," it began planning its strategy for invasion of lettuce, celery and cauliflower. A serise of highly sophisticated studies led first to lettuce.

There were many reasons for that selection in addition to the high volume and the fragmented ownership of lands and marketing facilities, which suggested that a dominant corporation such as United Fruit could easily establish leadership in pricing. Among the most important of the other reasons were the limited land areas where lettuce could be competitively and profitably planted. Those areas, in the Salinas and Imperial Valleys of California primarily and, secondarily, in the Salt River Valley and Yuma areas of Arizona, were already in cultivation.

What this meant was that, once the company achieved

its projected share of the market, it could easily protect its dominance. Competitors could not profitably plant new lands with lettuce and increase overall production so that it would threaten United Fruit's dominance. Allied with that consideration was another—the "inelasticity" of the demand for lettuce. That is, consumers who want lettuce usually buy lettuce, whatever its price. There is virtually nothing that can be easily substituted for it. Thus, if United succeeded in its design for elevating lettuce prices, as it had with bananas, people would continue to buy. Families that like tossed salad were unlikely to switch to cole slaw because of a change in costs.

At a meeting in July, 1968, the company's board of directors reviewed and adopted a proposal for invasion of the lettuce fields. Its goals and strategy were clearly stated.

"Our goal is to grow, pack, ship and distribute branded iceberg lettuce using the same methods that are being used for marketing Chiquita brand bananas," the proposal said, explaining the aim further: "Lettuce is now considered a commodity—there is no consumer-recognized brand. By applying Chiquita marketing techniques to lettuce, we expect to induce the consumer to pay a premium price for an established brand."

The invasion should encounter little resistance, it said, noting: "There is now a leadership vacuum in the lettuce industry. The largest grower only accounts for about 6½ percent of the industry and the second largest only about 4 percent."

Also, it indicated, consumers were expected to be just as gullible to lettuce branding and promotions as they had been in the Chiquita banana campaign: "Our marketing efforts will induce the consumer to purchase our branded lettuce at a price differential over unbranded lettuce. The price differential for Chiquita brand bananas during 1967 averaged about 35 to 40 cents per box over the seaboard price of competitive fruit. Our differential for a 24-head carton of lettuce is expected to be at least 60 cents; however, the cost of packaging is estimated at 40 cents per carton, in effect reducing the differential to 20 cents per carton."

The planners envisioned the substantial profit of 17.5 percent on money that would be invested in the operation. Part of that profit would come, under the plan, because of the company's size and financial power. First, it would establish its own manufacturing plant in the area to produce its boxes and packaging materials. It reasoned also that, because of its size, it should be able to get preferential rates on chemicals, fertilizers and materials. Not the least of its considerations was the advertising savings possible because of the advertising industry's rate structure. Volume discounts to big companies are enormous in comparison with those charged smaller, lower-volume advertisers. The savings would extend even to the company's bananas, because the plan was to "piggyback" a national advertising program for lettuce onto its banana-ad contracts.

To reach its goal of price leadership through industry dominance, the proposal said, it needed an annual volume of 20 million boxes of lettuce, or about 20 percent of the national market, and preferably 25 million, or one-fourth of the market. But it was afraid to move on such a scale too swiftly. To escape possible notice of trustbusters, it decided to start with a plan for 10 to 12 million cartons a year and gradually expand that to 25 million. As the proposal cautiously phrased the design: "An annual volume of 25 million cartons is needed in order to support an adequate national advertising program. . . . We have considerably reduced this volume, however, because of antitrust considerations and are now considering a volume of 10 to 12 million cartons annually. . . . We hope to expand the operation internally to the point where we

can plan a more efficient national advertising program."
That is, by stages that the company hoped would be imperceptible to antitrusters, it would build its market share
to the 25 percent that it coveted.

United moved swiftly to put its plan into operation.
Before the year was out it acquired Nunes Bros., which
included Toro Farms and control of vast acreages producing 1.8 million cartons of lettuce a year from fields in the
Salinas and Imperial Valleys as well as in Arizona. The
varied locations bracketed all seasons of the year. Then,
in quick succession, it acquired the Earl Myers Company
and its Demco Farms; Peter A. Stolich Co., Inc., a grower
and shipper; Monterey County Ice and Development
Company, a service firm with vacuum-cooling facilities in
Salinas and El Centro; Jerome Kantro Enterprises, another
grower-shipper; Salinas Valley Vegetable Exchange, also
a grower-shipper; Consolidated Growers, Inc., and the
Reliable Trucking Company, which would move the produce.

Generally, the officers and principals of the acquired
companies signed agreements not to compete with United
for a period of several years.

The company's aims, it became clear, were bigger than
lettuce. It called on BBDO to develop a promotion plan
that could be applied to a whole line of fresh vegetables.
Already, in its acquisitions, it was gaining a sizable share
in the celery and cauliflower markets, because several of
the acquired companies were also growers and shippers of
those vegetables.

It also became apparent very quickly that United was
going to be a tough competitor. It did not hesitate to
adopt practices generally frowned on in the lettuce industry. One was the shipping of cars known as "rollers." These
are cars that are moved east despite the fact that they
could not be sold on contract at the shipping point, on

the long chance that they can be sold en route for more than enough to cover costs of harvesting, packing and shipping. Usually they do not. In addition, they tend to depress prices with sometimes disastrous results for the entire industry.

With its "deep pockets," as an F.T.C. complaint said later, United did not need to fear the temporary losses it would incur with the rollers while gradually expanding its market. It shipped them, the complaint said, "in its anxiety to get more lettuce to market," even when the market was below harvesting, packing and shipping costs. Most shippers in such a market exercise restraint, the complaint noted. They pick only their highest quality and ship only when they can presell. What United was doing, the complaint said, "did not make sense, was not good practice economically and it caused other grower-shippers to wonder."

"Survival in the industry was no longer dependent on ability but in the case of United Brands [the name the company assumed in 1970] on a deep pocket," the F.T.C. complaint said.

In their wonderment, many of the company's rivals began to pull out of the lettuce business. In Monterey County, in the Salinas Valley, for example, the number of lettuce sellers declined from forty to thirty-two between 1968 and 1971, a drop of 20 percent. In the Imperial Valley, the decline was from sixty-three to forty-five shippers, a drop of 28 percent, and the same thing was happening in the major producing areas of Arizona.

Meanwhile, the operating costs of competitors were rising, partly because credit became dearer and harder to get. Because of increased risks of competing with a company that operated like United, banks were loath to put out vital financing.

At the same time, some of United's own costs could be

held down. Even though United was buying its fertilizer in smaller shipments than a few other growers, the company was able to demand and get substantially greater discounts, the F.T.C. complaint said.

Also, United was using to its advantage the easy access that officials of giant corporations have to each other. United executives were visiting the top officials of major supermarket chains. And soon United became, as it had wished, the price leader. Instead of waiting to see the market data and supplies that had governed prices in the past, chain stores began using United as a guide, waiting to hear its morning offering price before making any bids.

All this, of course, fitted perfectly with United's predetermined plan, and its takeover was running right on schedule. By 1971, in terms of the national market it was shipping over 10 percent of the nation's lettuce. More important, in some seasons its market share was up to its secret goal of 25 percent.

Meanwhile, it had become the leading shipper, also, of celery and had moved up to the second rank in cauliflower shipments.

But United did not, as it had hoped, escape the attention of the antitrusters at the Federal Trade Commission. On February 11, 1971, the agency filed a formal complaint. And in the proposed facts and findings of its investigators, the agency staff said:

"In February, 1970, United Brands had . . . plans on a long-range basis to diversify into a wide variety of agricultural and fruit-related products and services. These would be distributed through mass outlets, and would utilize the consolidated company skills in handling perishable products from their source to their ultimate consumers. . . .

"United Brands planned to package and brand lettuce, celery, celery hearts, cauliflower and develop a package for broccoli. Its objective was to market a line of branded produce, modify or alter existing distribution channels to most closely fit this requirement and to convey to the consumer a plausible justification of this action. The rationale of branding, or at least one of them, is that branding provides manufacturers or distributors more 'freedom in price determination' than would otherwise be possible. Without brands or other distinguishing marks on products, the market determines the price, as is true for many unprocessed foods. There is little or no opportunity for one firm to sell at higher prices than other firms."

The agency also noted the company's promotion plan, about which United had said in an internal paper: "Support objectives for our branded line will first convince the consumer that our products are of superior value and then motivate her to actively seek out and influence her store to stock. Our brand support strategy will be one of influence and we will aim the greatest part of our support at the consumer to influence the trade to stock our branded line. Similarly, we shall influence the trade to stock by convincing it that the consumer prefers our products and that it can make additional profit by supporting our vegetable crop marketing program."

The F.T.C. said that the company's test marketing had proved its estimates and predictions to be close to the mark, although the company later denied the accuracy of the agency's observation. Test marketing had shown that the United wrapped lettuce had brought higher prices "well in excess of the cost of wrapping." It went on: "Chiquita lettuce sold for $0.50 more per carton than other wrapped lettuce and $1.03 more per carton than unwrapped lettuce."

"One aspect," F.T.C. investigators said in one of the charges, "is uniquely a function of its position among the nation's large companies and the web of mutual interests and interrelationships between these companies. That is the ability to obtain access to the highest corporate officials of the major retail food chains, such as Kroger. United Brands did in fact establish an organized effort to meet directly with the officials in charge of fresh produce for these various large retail chains and endeavor to swing them over to Chiquita lettuce. No other grower-shipper had that capacity."

As the F.T.C. staff saw the company's scheme, it was a classic case of attempting to establish, in the jargon of economists, a "dominant firm model." They said:

"United Brands' activities as price leader of the lettuce, cauliflower and the celery industries is known as an oligopolistic situation denominated 'dominant firm model.' This model assumes that one firm in the industry is so large relative to the others that it sets the price. In the short run, such a firm will use its price leadership capabilities to establish its dominant position, usually by low pricing until marginal producers are driven out.

"Thereafter, it will use its price leadership capabilities to obtain the price that it administratively selects, permitting the other firms in the industry to sell whatever they can at that price and selling the remainder itself."

If the industry follows the usual trend for such "models," the investigating staffers saw a disturbing outlook indeed for consumers as well as for other growers and shippers now in business. It would be a future dominated by a few firms, able to "administer" prices and virtually bar the door to anyone else wanting to get into the field.

An administrative law judge of the F.T.C., formerly known as a hearing examiner, found the complaint justified and in 1973 ordered United Brands to get out of the vegetable business. The company promptly appealed to the full commission, in an action that apparently is the preface of a long run of litigation.

United Brands filed extensive briefs in answer to the F.T.C. complaint. Essentially, the company denied any plan that would be a violation of law. And besides, the brief said, the plan hadn't worked very well.

On appeal, the company offered a strange argument, one that would undercut claims of many other agribusiness corporations—that they can operate more efficiently than smaller farmers. United Brands said it enjoyed no advantage from "economies of scale"—that is, operational savings because of its large size. In fact, the company argued, its costs were often higher than those of smaller competitors. Such claims made it seem odd that United Brands would want to continue in the vegetable business.

Indeed, the company made many serious misjudgments; it operated inefficiently and it poured millions of dollars into the takeover scheme before starting to get very much out of it. But the F.T.C. investigators were not taken in. They knew that United Brands was still prepared to try, and it had the "deep pocket"—with millions more in it— to complete the takeover if it should win its argument with the Government.

IX
Giantism in Food Processing

The tendency toward giantism that is spreading in agriculture has already reached an advanced stage in the food-processing industry. Its manifestations are unlimited expansion to awkward proportions, voracious appetite for more companies to swallow and lethargy coupled with muscle-bound power. A highly contagious, often semi-paralytic affliction, it is continuing to thin the ranks of the food industry and sap the vigor of the survivors. People and society are bruised on contact.

The lethargy created by giantism in industry and the social and economic costs are well known to economists in and out of government. But even the most knowledgeable and articulate of them have not been able to change a widespread and ingrained public attitude. And something akin to hero worship comes through in the regard of public officials for chieftains of industry who say with Tenneco's Howard Marguleas that "bigness is great."

The Nixon Administration clearly agreed and it sent out signals to that effect early in the President's first term.

The signals had not far to go to reach the International Telephone and Telegraph Corporation, a giant centipede of a conglomerate with a foothold in many industries, including food through ITT Continental Baking and other subsidiaries. ITT's executives were able to get their message from the highest officials of government, relayed to them from President Nixon himself through the office of Vice President Agnew and John N. Mitchell, then the Attorney General.

The word was that Nixon had no intention of letting his antitrust agents pursue the giants because of their size. In fact, ITT and others were led to believe the Nixon Administration thought bigness was wonderful, a belief confirmed when campaign aides in 1971 and 1972 sought secret contributions from corporations that were having trouble with regulatory agencies.

The message was a great relief to ITT masterminds, of course, for they were locked in a struggle with the Justice Department to keep the financial power they had gained through a series of massive mergers. Richard W. McLaren, the department's antitrust chief, who seemed unable to understand the President's signal, was soon eased into a comfortable federal judgeship.

There are few better illustrations of the power of big corporate management, which is, in the words of the economist Carl Kaysen, "irresponsible power, answerable only to itself."

It is significant that, without even a reference to ITT stockholders, the company's chiefs could pledge its abortive gift of $400,000 to President Nixon's party and even promise $1-million to help the C.I.A. interfere with free elections in Chile, then a friendly neighbor.

ITT, of course, is a member of the fraternity of giants that dominates much of manufacturing—including the food industry—and more than half of the food industry, like the rest of manufacturing, is subject to monopolistic pricing because of that domination. The food industry, in fact, is one of the segments of that manufacturing fraternity where financial power, and the power for monopolistic pricing, is most concentrated. And the social and economic costs that have been identified with concentration of financial power in manufacturing overall apply more specifically to the highly concentrated food industry than to most of the others, authoritative studies have found.

One of the greatest costs of giantism and the accompanying monopolistic pricing is what economists call a "deadweight loss"—a loss to the economy resulting from restrictions on production caused by monopolistic practices. The respected scholar F. M. Scherer, in his recent "Industrial Market Structure and Economic Performance," put a dollar figure on the "deadweight loss." It costs the national economy about $10-billion a year, or about 1 percent of the gross national product, he said.

In the highly concentrated food industry, which accounts for more than 10 percent of the gross national product, it would be fair—conservative, in fact—to say that the "deadweight loss" is more than $2-billion a year. Such an estimate is buttressed by the fact that studies by the National Commission on Productivity have found the food industry to have one of the lowest rates of increase in efficiency.

But the deadweight loss is only a part of the drain on the economy caused by monopolistic pricing. There are several others, as many economists have noted. One drain is simply waste. Big companies in monopolistic industries, free from the pressures of competition, lack incentives for cost-cutting. Similarly, when high prices reduce demand and leave producers with unused capacity, operators in monopolistic industries tend to cover the expense of excess capacity by raising prices still higher, with the inevitable consequences of still further decline in demand. Consumers pay more for less—without even generating the benefit of an increase in industry profits.

Oddly, even the selling costs are increased when a few firms dominate an industry. Those with a deadlock on sales jockey for position and market share by expensive promotions and by the advertising of inflated claims rather than vying to offer the most value for the least cost. Few companies, for example, spend more than Campbell Soup does to promote a product, although Campbell has no one but Heinz to worry about in its industry.

Shared monopoly has paid off handsomely for Campbell Soup. Its profit rate of 1 percent on investment in 1972 was above the 9 percent that Federal Trade Commission investigators regard as grounds for suspicion that excessive economic concentration may be involved.

The champions of the promotional money-wasters, however, are the cereal companies. They spend thirteen cents out of every dollar of revenue on advertising, although four companies dominate the cereal market.

Perhaps more basic than any of the other effects of monopolistic pricing is the resulting high cost of production machinery and the high prices of commodities and supplies needed for production, for the results multiply along the entire line, from raw material to consumer. More important, the high costs of the most desirable machinery force producers to take the route of lower efficiency.

Farm machinery, for example, produced in an industry that economists call "oligopolistic"—or subject to monopolistic pricing—has been one of the fastest rising types of production equipment anywhere. Tractors that cost $10,000 ten years ago often sell for $20,000 today, and farmers who need a small step-up in production capacity must pay thousands of dollars for the smallest increase in horsepower

—often only an engine with slightly larger cylinders coupled to virtually the same gears and wheels as the less expensive model. As a result there are farmers across the country like John Lyman, a dairy farmer in Pennsylvania, who told this reporter:

"The machinery salesmen tell you you can't afford to be without it. But there comes a time when you just can't take the chance on more expensive machinery. You have to settle for lower efficiency. It's too easy to go broke down that road."

One man's loss of efficiency resulting from higher costs of machinery or commodities—a rise in feed costs had forced Lyman to choose a lower-quality mixture for his cows—can be multiplied throughout the economy, as H. Michael Mann, former director of the F.T.C.'s Bureau of Economics, explained in a recent speech.

"This," he said, "will necessitate a higher product price, forcing changes in production processes further up the line. The result is a widespread influence on efficiency throughout the economy."

F. M. Scherer in his study of market structure added up all the costs due to monopolistic pricing in the United States economy and came up with a waste of 6 percent of the gross national product, or about $60-billion a year. No estimate has ever been made of the food industry's share of that waste, but a conservative figure, considering the food processors' position in the monopolistic half of manufacturing, would be more than $12-billion a year. Citing Scherer's figures, Mann said:

"And these costs do not include the income loss to consumers which results from the holders of market power earning profits in excess of those needed to reward stockholders adequately for their investment."

The F.T.C. in a 1972 study found that overcharges to

produce monopolistic profits in only thirteen food lines were costing consumers over $2-billion a year.

Mann's chief complaint was that the antitrust law, at least as it has been interpreted in the past, does not provide the F.T.C. and the Justice Department with adequate tools to deal with the problem of monopolistic pricing. Observing that half of manufacturing fell into the category of "oligopolies"—and that it was thus able to engage in monopolistic pricing—he acknowledged the failure of antitrust policy to deal with abuses of corporate power. As he explained:

"Industries which are highly concentrated have been persistently able to engage in noncompetitive behavior with little risk of skirmish with the antitrust agencies. This anomaly exists because oligopolistic firms do not, as a general rule, need to resort to the familiar litany of antitrust violations to suppress competition: trade boycotts, price conspiracies, allocation of markets, exclusive dealing arrangements and the like. Rather, tacit understandings are sufficient to coordinate behavior so as to preserve a stable, comfortable arrangement with respect to the permissible bounds of competitive behavior."

The abuses of corporate power are an old story in the food industry, but perhaps nowhere else has that story been so widely ignored. Even when the effects of the abuses in the food industry were incisively identified and thoroughly documented in the landmark study by the National Commission on Food Marketing, Congress and government officials continued looking the other way. Professor George Brandow, who directed a commission staff drawn from many government agencies, remarked in early 1973:

"It was perhaps the best investigation that has ever been ignored."

The study traced the increasing concentration of power, identified the devices used by big companies to gather power unto themselves and hang on to it and suggested the costly effects on consumers.

While there were over 32,000 food-processing companies according to the 1967 Census of Manufacturing, their numbers were declining at the rate of 13 percent a year.

More important, the F.T.C. found, only fifty of those companies were earning 61 percent of the profits. All evidence indicates that the concentration of power and profits is still increasing.

One of several task forces assigned to the study found that the monopolistic companies in the industry have grown to their bloated sizes mainly through an almost cannibalistic process of swallowing up others of their kind. In fact, it showed, the biggest companies are able to keep ahead of the smaller firms only by merger; if they did not continue to feed on others through the process of acquisition they would eventually be overtaken. For the real growth of the largest companies, as opposed to growth by acquisition, has tended to lag behind industry averages.

What seems to happen is that both the acquiring company and the small but active company that it coveted tend to lose vigor in the larger mass. Meanwhile, other small companies with youthful trim and vitality manage to flourish and grow until they attract the attention of an overshadowing giant, whereupon they too are swallowed up and share in the problems of obesity. The whole picture outlined by the task force is proof enough of the relative inefficiency of the overweight giants.

The merger trend started early in this century, and it was the meat-packing industry that showed the way. The five biggest meat packers—Swift, Armour, Wilson, Morris and Cudahy—had gained a stranglehold on the industry by 1920. They owned railroad yards, stockyards, market-reporting papers, large wholesaling businesses that handled unrelated products as well as meat, and public cold-storage warehouses. They were moving massively toward a takeover of meat retailing operations in grocery stores when they ran into a setback.

The year 1920 was historic in the food industry, for it marked the successful end of a long and unusually vigorous fight by the Justice Department. The result was a consent decree—that sort of anomalous settlement of a legal action under which a corporation denies that it ever did any of the bad things charged and promises never to do them again.

In the case of the meat packers, the settlement involved more than the usually mild penalties. The decree required them to dispose of most of their unrelated activities and henceforth to restrain their appetites for acquisition.

But it was as if that decree were a signal to the other segments of the food industry. They rushed into the vacuum left by the meat packers' withdrawal from the struggle for acquisitions, and a wave of mergers began that did not slow down until the Depression that preceded World War II. Though, of course, it was not evident at the time, those prewar agglomerations formed merely a launching pad for postwar mergers of a nature that is more disturbing to economists.

The prewar mergers were mainly consolidations bringing together companies that were operating in the same general fields. A total of 2,191, for example, occurred within the dairy industry. The wave that has followed World War II has been marked more by mergers of the conglomerate type—with companies entering new fields through the acquisition route, gaining new products and broadening their territories.

It has been a logical if alarming process. As small companies acquired others and grew to middle size, they in turn have been swallowed up by still bigger companies—a phenomenon now being repeated in the more basic field of agricultural production. The biggest companies, with insatiable appetites and the financial power to swing deals, have been the most active acquirers. The most powerful most rapidly increase their power, and where power corrupts, the most corruptible are the biggest corporations.

In the four-year period between 1958 and 1962 the 200 largest companies in the food industry added assets through acquisition equaling 8.8 percent of their total size. The most acquisitive, naturally, moved upward in rank, while the least acquisitive moved downward, many of them finally being swallowed up by the others.

There were dramatic ascents for some into the upper echelons of wealth and power. Through mergers, Hunt Foods & Industries climbed from 47th to 9th in rank among food processors; Consolidated Foods from 43d to 16th; Foremost Dairies from a small regional company to a national rank of 26th; Beatrice Foods from 41st to 21st and Corn Products from 9th to 4th place.

The total effect, of course, was a rapid increase in concentration of financial power. The fifty largest companies in the food-processing industry grew 53 percent faster than the rest, and their total assets more than doubled. Meanwhile, their share of industry assets rose from 37.9 percent to more than half.

Significantly, however, their rate of real growth was slower than that of the whole industry. Had it not been for acquisitions the growth rate of those same fifty companies would have lagged 3.9 percent behind the overall pace, and their share of total industry assets would have declined. Here was proof that giantism saps vitality.

The effect on consumers shows up when the housewife goes shopping and brings home not necessarily what her family wants or needs for a balanced diet but what she found that she could afford. A task force of experts from

the F.T.C., which made the technical study, "The Structure of Food Manufacturing," for the Commission on
Food Marketing, found that while the big companies were
preying on other companies they were also gaining control over more and more of the items on the housewife's
shopping list.

What happened was a result of the nature of the food-
processing business—or any other industry where power is
concentrated among a few dominant firms. Officials of the
big companies know that it costs money to develop and
introduce a new product. It is easier and less expensive to
take over a company that is already in the business and
has a market, and that is precisely what the big companies
were doing. Consolidated Foods, for example, entered
eleven new product fields and Beatrice Foods entered
eight—but always by taking over the companies that developed them. Neither Consolidated nor Beatrice origi-
nated a single food product.

This is also a symptom of the fact that the big food companies, big spenders though they are for advertising and
promotion, are real penny pinchers when it comes to research. What research they do conduct, the investigation
demonstrated, is most often devoted to variations in combinations of foods and in blending, packaging and presen-
tation—that is, new ways to disguise the same old products.

The consumer, as a result of the big companies' choice
of takeovers in preference to innovation, loses not only the
benefits of price competition but also the prospect of
rivalry in diversity and quality and other dividends of
progress.

The investigators also found ways to gauge the effect of
the conglomerate trend, in which companies dominant in
one industry grasp for control in another industry and
then another and another. On average, the 200 biggest
companies in the food industry either controlled or were

controlled by companies that were major producers in more than six lines of business besides food.

Within the food industry itself, control expanded rapidly. The top twenty processors, which were major factors in an average of more than five divisions of the industry at the beginning of the study period, had nearly doubled their areas of influence at the end.

Meanwhile, in a process that the economists call "vertical integration," the big companies were expanding upward into retailing and downward into agricultural production. At the same time national supermarket chains were expanding into manufacturing operations. About a third of the total sales volume of the 200 largest food manufacturers came from retail stores that they operated.

The "vertical integration" of the food manufacturers into agriculture has now given them control of 22 percent of all farm production, according to the Economic Research Service of the Department of Agriculture. And those figures do not include the big, highly concentrated broiler-chicken industry.

The national commission's concern, of course, was over effects on competition, which—short of government control—is the only protection that consumers have for the value and quality of the food they buy. Most disturbing to investigators was the conglomerate trend, for the market power of a big company in any one phase of business tends to multiply the effects of its dominance in others. In summing up, they cited the testimony of a leading authority, Professor Corwin Edwards of the University of Oregon, before a Senate Antitrust and Monopoly Subcommittee:

"When one large conglomerate enterprise competes with another, the two are likely to encounter each other in a considerable number of markets. The multiplicity of contacts may blunt the edge of their competition. A prospect of advantage from vigorous competition in one market may be weighed against the danger of retaliatory forays by the competitor in other markets. Each conglomerate competitor may adopt a live-and-let-live policy designed to stabilize the whole structure of the competitive relationship."

Edwards, in fact, had more damning things to say in his testimony about the nature of the conglomerates, including this:

"Each may informally recognize the other's primacy of interest in markets important to the other, in the expectation that its own important interests will be similarly respected. Like national states, the great conglomerates may come to have recognized spheres of influence and may hesitate to fight local wars vigorously because the prospect of local gain is not worth the risk of general warfare."

Their effect on smaller companies is even greater, as other authorities have proved. Without the necessity of any threat or even a veiled signal, smaller rivals know how badly they can be hurt if they compete too vigorously. John M. Blair, in his recent book, *Economic Concentration, Structure, Behavior and Public Policy*, put it this way:

"To most of the small producers these leading companies of U. S. industry must loom as veritable giants. This is all the more true if the large company derives monopoly profits from some other industry in which it is also engaged. To any one of the hundreds of small firms in such industries, making a competitive move which might invite retaliation by a giant competitor could well appear to be an invitation to disaster."

Thus the very existence of the giants constitutes restraint of trade. It is obvious that, as Mann, the F.T.C. official, said, the big powers in the food industry do not need to resort to overt plots, skulduggery or any readily recognizable violations of antitrust law. And yet they do. In fact, the F.T.C.'s problems with food manufacturers on that score were shown in the study by the Commission on Food Marketing to have been far out of proportion to the size of the industry. More than 25 percent of the agency's complaints for restraint of trade had been against big food manufacturers.

The charges run the full range of all the predatory practices that big companies can think up against their neighbors. They vary from price-fixing to discriminatory pricing that victimizes the smallest and weakest firms and from conspiracies to divide markets to reciprocal dealings and abuses of patents.

The worst offenders, naturally enough, have been among the industry groups where financial power is concentrated in the fewest hands, such as the milk and dairy industry, grain milling and bakery products. National Dairy (now Kraftco), for example, tried to take over the Baltimore, Washington and Richmond markets by offering its jams and preserves at half-price discounts—an all too obvious preface to jacking up its own prices once competitors were disposed of.

In most cases, big firms have tended to discriminate in favor of other large companies, not surprisingly in light of a long history of favoritism resulting from what investigators in the United Brands case called "a web of mutual interests and interrelationships." There were many such as these:

Pacific-Gamble-Robinson Company, a big wholesaler of fresh fruits and vegetables, charged some stores as much as 16 percent more than those stores' larger competitors.

Foremost Dairies gave rebates on milk to one big chain, thus victimizing its competitors.

Food Fair and Giant Foods were able to get promotional

and advertising allowances ranging from $100 to $5,750 from several processors, which did not allow comparable benefits to competitors.

And in one of the boldest power play combinations, all three major television networks solicited payments from suppliers to provide free advertising to big supermarket chains. Some of the suppliers' payments to individual stations to help promote sales of the supermarket chains ranged from $12,000 to $178,000 over a twenty-four-month period.

But Consolidated Foods at least was no respecter of size in a case of reciprocal dealing. It refused to buy supplies from any manufacturer that bought its garlic from a competitor of Consolidated's garlic-handling division.

The giants do not have to stoop to such practices. They have other, more powerful weapons to overcome competition and repel newcomers into their fields.

One of the simplest is what economists call "product differentiation," a practice that is abetted by discriminatory rate structures in the advertising media. Product differentiation, as the economists use the term, does not mean the creation of differences in products. It merely means making the same product seem different from others.

This "differentiation," F.T.C. economists say, is "the primary barrier to entry in food manufacturing." And it is one of the costliest so far as the consumer is concerned. In essence, it is a device through which the consumer himself pays to be barred from the benefits of competition— from better products and reduced costs.

The costs to consumers for the advertising itself are considerable. Over $4-billion a year is spent on food advertising, most of it to persuade shoppers to pay more for food than they need to. Those who stick to the heavily advertised products, of course, pay more than their share of that big promotion bill. If they chose carefully they could find products of equal quality among low-ad-budget lines costing substantially less. "Store brands," for example, cost an average of 15 percent less for products of comparable quality than those for which advertising has created, as the hucksters say, a "consumer franchise"—that is, a clientele of brainwashed customers.

Naturally, it is the biggest corporations that dominate television advertising and promotion. The reason is that the industry's preferential rate structure increases the already overwhelming advantage of the big corporation's vast resources. Because of their big budgets and the discriminatory rates, they can buy more advertising for each dollar spent. As a result they can saturate the airwaves, which are barred by cost to their smaller competitors, however good their products might be.

A look at a series of mergers cited in the F.T.C.'s study shows the effects of "product differentiation" and the advantage that advertising gives to giant corporations. Procter & Gamble, for example, tripled the advertising budget of Duncan Hines cake mixes, from $1.2-million to $3.5-million the year after acquiring the company, and within three years Procter & Gamble was spending $8-million a year to advertise the mixes of its new division. Sales scooted upward, from 12.3 percent of volume in the cake-mix field to 28.2 percent, and in terms of market share the Duncan Hines products climbed from Number 3 to Number 1 without change in anything except the advertising budget. The only difference was "'differentiation."

When Coca-Cola bought Minute Maid, it raised the advertising budget from $2.8-million to $6.7-million, and soon more patrons than ever were reaching like automatons for Minute Maid orange juice rather than for equally good but less costly brands in the same freezer case.

Similarly, Heinz raised the television budget for Starkist tuna the year after acquisition from $300,000 to $1.2-million, and there have been other increases since. Soon millions of people were acting as if they believed the ridiculous little fish that swims across the TV tube to advise stupid Charlie—who is trying his best, naturally, to get himself caught and put into a can—that only the best-tasting tuna can be Starkist. Chicken of the Sea, of course, makes a similar claim. And shoppers corraled into the companies' "consumer franchise" are led to behave as if less expensive cans did not contain the same cold discs of the same species of fish.

Among others, Consolidated Food raised the budget for Sara Lee cakes from a little over $78,000 to $2.5-million within a few years after acquisition. The response from the public was automatic. Sales increased tenfold.

Partly because of such reactions to advertising, mergers of one company often drive competitors into mergers. General Foods, for example, entered a field where two companies were already dominant when it acquired S.O.S. soap pads. S.O.S. had 51 percent of the market and Brillo had 47.6 percent. There was not a great deal to be gained from Brillo by increasing the ad budget for S.O.S.; Brillo was sure to respond. General Foods did it anyway, influenced perhaps by the realization that, because of its heavy advertising of other products, it could get a 23 percent discount for S.O.S. promotions. It flooded the airwaves.

The extravagant waste was quickly rewarded. Soon S.O.S. had 56 percent of the market and Brillo had dropped to 42 percent. But that was not the end of the battle. Brillo, mismatched in the fight with General Foods, was forced to find some "deep pockets" of cash. The company merged with Purex, another big food-industry conglomerate.

For the two companies, the fight only increased selling costs, which consumers would have to pay. For anyone who might come along with a better cleaning product, the ante had been raised to an impossible height.

The public will never know how many good products and product improvements they have been denied because of the high "barriers to entry" created by the "differentiation" of products that are distinguishable only by their packages. If an informed public ever came to realize how much it pays to be barred from the benefits of true competition, it might follow the example of some television viewers who make it a matter of honor never to buy the products of an offensive advertiser.

If anyone is inclined to hope that the incidence of giantism in the food industry might somehow have abated since the National Commission on Food Marketing completed its definite but ignored study, he can be easily disabused of the notion by an occasional glance at the merger columns of financial newspapers. A weekly that calls itself—and is—"the newspaper of agribusiness" provides clues enough. Issue after issue carries items like this, which appeared in the edition of February 26, 1973:

"ARMOUR MAKES TWO MORE ACQUISITIONS IN POULTRY AREA."

What they all add up to can be found in the Census Bureau's survey of business. The report that brings the story up to 1970 (such statistics always lag behind the facts) shows food processing among the most concentrated of the monopolistic industries. Among forty-three industry groups in food manufacturing, twenty-six meet or exceed the generally accepted standard of an oligopoly, that is, an industry group where monopolistic pricing is possible. Many others are close to that level—where four firms account for 35 percent or more of the volume—and soon may exceed it.

They range downward from the cereals, where the top

four firms have 90 percent of the volume, and include such basic commodities as the cheeses, condensed and evaporated milk, canned and cured seafoods, canned specialties, rice, flour, sugar, chocolate and cocoa products, flavorings, coffee, cooking oils and pickles, sauces and salad dressings.

Meanwhile, the trend toward increasing concentration of financial power in the food industry has continued. In the number of mergers reported by the F.T.C. that same year for twenty-two basic manufacturing and mining categories, food was among the top three, while it led all in value of assets of the companies that were swallowed up by others. The assets of food companies that were taken over totaled nearly one-fifth of the assets of merged companies in all categories.

But raw statistics give only a glimmer of the effect of increasing industry concentration on the consumers and their money. They do not reveal that the same big corporation is often among the top four in several food-industry groups or that it, in turn, is likely to be controlled by a company that is one of the oligopolists in several other manufacturing industries.

In fact, the Census Bureau and the F.T.C. are both required by law to conceal the names of the companies involved in their concentration statistics, and if any figure threatens to become revealing it has to be suppressed. That happens when one company has grown so large that to reveal a figure for the industry is tantamount to revealing that company's business.

The statistics can disguise the power of the oligopolists to practice monopolistic pricing in other ways, too, and thus conceal the impact on consumers. For one, the products of the top four concerns in an industry group may not be competitive. In canned seafood, for example, one may concentrate on tuna and another on salmon. In other canned goods, one may stand out in pineapple—as Dole has for years—another in tomatoes, which were the original basis of Hunt Foods' rise to power and fortune. And obviously figures on fresh fruits and vegetables—though these are not included in the listing of processors—would give no hint that Tenneco, with over 70 percent of the business, has nearly total control of the date market.

More important, actual competition depends on how many rivals there are at the point where products are sold. National figures conceal the lack of competition in local markets, for competition counts only at the cash register where the shopper's purchases are rung up. Dairies, for example, tend to have regional markets, and in an area where one appears to have sales sewed up, another is likely to avoid conflict, with the tacit understanding that the same consideration will be shown in its own spheres of dominant influence.

But nowhere do the figures more completely conceal the real state of competition than in the meat industry. The meat packers, on the basis of national figures, no longer appear to be a concentrated industry, for the top four had only 23 percent of the national market in 1970. Yet a closer examination by two government economists, Gerald Engleman and Arnold Aspelin, for the Agriculture Department provided some revealing insights on that figure.

"The meat-packing industry tends to be highly oligopolistic at the state level—much more so than nationally," they said in a research paper completed in 1973. "Four ranking firms account for 65 percent or more of the slaughter for different species at the state level in most cases."

The significance is that meat marketing tends to be regional rather than national, and, in the regions where the big companies operate, power is still intensely concentrated.

For example, Engleman and Aspelin showed, in the important North Central region, the top four firms had over 75 percent of South Dakota and Wisconsin's cattle slaughter, and over 65 percent in Indiana, Missouri, Minnesota and Kansas. In hog slaughter, the concentration was still greater. In seven states in the region, the top four firms represented over 75 percent of the market and in one, Illinois, the top four had over 71 percent.

For sheep and lambs the concentration was yet higher. In the top producing states, the top four companies' control approached 100 percent. In the marketing of sheep and lambs, even on a national basis, the concentration was high. The top four firms had 53 percent of the national market.

And yet, despite the regional concentration in meats, the Justice Department in 1971 decided to alter the old consent decree that had helped hold the packers in check since 1920. The idea was to unleash their power on the theory that they might increase competition against the big corporations that had gained control of over half of the other food industries. Great power was needed to combat great power. And the packers had plenty of power in reserve.

Three of the present top four of those affected by the original decree—Armour, Wilson and Cudahy—had become parts of giant conglomerates, and the other, Swift, had become a conglomerate itself, controlling thirty-one subsidiaries. Two of the conglomerates had other food-industry interests in apparent violation of the consent decree, but judicial opinions had cleared them of the legal problem if not of suspicion. All were on *Fortune* magazine's exclusive list of the top 500 corporations in the country.

General Host, which acquired Cudahy, had extensive interests in frozen foods, bakery goods, candy and coffee shops, and it operated at both wholesale and retail levels.

A chain of convenience stores that sold food as well as household items gave General Host a big part of its business. When the two companies merged in 1971 the deal gave them total annual sales of more than a half billion dollars and lifted them to 459th place on the *Fortune* list.

When Greyhound took over Armour & Co. in 1970, it was already in the food business through its restaurant services and industrial catering. That merger gave the growing conglomerate a mighty boost, to 29th place on the *Fortune* list, with $2.7-billion in annual sales.

That same year Ling-Temco-Vought, which had taken over the meat-packing business of Wilson & Co. and its $1.4-billion-a-year volume, was 15th on the *Fortune* list. The merger gave the aerospace, steel, electronics and meat-packing conglomerate over $4-billion in annual sales.

Swift & Co., the biggest of the meat packers, was high on the list, too. With its thirty-one subsidiaries and $3-billion a year in sales, it stood at Number 23.

It seemed obvious to many critics that the clash of giants that might result from the Justice Department's concessions to the meat packers would bring results quite different from the aim of restraining the power of the most monopolistic. If both sides rolled out all their weapons—and "product differentiation" in particular—it seemed likely that they would only take business away from struggling smaller companies.

What the department apparently sought, however, was to provide a counterforce to phenomenal increases of financial power like those of Consolidated Foods and Hunt Foods & Industries.

Consolidated Foods is a relatively young company, incorporated in 1941 as a Chicago-based wholesale house named the South Street Company. But it was not long before it had spread into all phases of food production and distribution and its methods of operation and expansion attracted the attention of federal investigators. In rapid succession it took over five other wholesale houses and began looking into other fields.

It moved into the processing end of the food business in 1948 by acquiring Rosenberg Bros. & Co., a firm that was already a major factor in dried fruits, nuts and rice in California. The rapidly growing conglomerate had hardly had time to assimilate Rosenberg Bros. when it began acquiring, in quick succession, three other big processors: Union Sugar Company of California, U. S. Products Corporation, Ltd., and Gentry, Inc. Union Sugar gave the young giant its first foothold in agricultural production. Besides its refineries, the sugar company had 11,000 acres of land in California.

The year 1955 saw Consolidated with annual sales of $225-million on assets of $78-million, but its growth had hardly begun. Between 1955 and 1965, it picked up nine other food processors, including such names as Columbia Canning, Philips Packing, Michigan Fruit Canners, Charles E. Hires and Chicken Delight.

At the same time it was plunging into retailing, to complete the food chain from field to supermarket. First it took over Piggly-Wiggly Midwest Company, then Fine Supermarket and Quality Food Stores, acquisitions that gave it a chain of 100 supermarkets bracketing four Midwestern states, Illinois, Iowa, Minnesota and Wisconsin. It also acquired Eagle Food Centers, with seven supermarkets in Chicago, and Lawson Milk Company, a move that put Consolidated Foods into both processing and retailing of milk. Lawson had about 220 dairy stores in Ohio.

By 1965 Consolidated Foods had taken over forty-one companies, mainly in the processing, wholesaling and retailing of food. But it had already begun, also, a process of more diverse conglomeration, finding new fields to conquer outside of the food business. The first was May's

Drugstores, Inc., a relatively small operation with only eight stores.

Today the company has moved into many other industries, ranging from ladies' gloves to vacuum cleaners. And though its major strength and source of income remains in the food business, the wide diversification makes it a more formidable competitor everywhere it goes. By 1970, it was 147th on the list of major American companies in terms of net income, which was far above average in relation to its assets. Its sales had passed $1.5-billion a year, its assets $726-million and its profits $54.6-million.

Aside from the rapid pace at which Consolidated Foods was wiping out prospective competitors, its methods attracted the attention of F.T.C. investigators.

By 1965 Consolidated Foods' processing plants could sell to its own wholesale warehouses as well as to competitive wholesalers. Consolidated Foods could sell also to its own retail stores as well as to competitive supermarket chains. It developed and promoted, meanwhile, its Monarch brand of processed foods, which it sold to wholesalers in areas where the company had no wholesale branches of its own, giving the wholesaler "its own private label in an exclusive territory."

The company's wholesaling division was promoting at the same time "voluntary" chains of independent retailers in an arrangement by which the "voluntary" members had to agree to buy all their nonperishable staples from Consolidated Foods. In Chicago alone, Consolidated chained 875 "independents" to its wholesaling division.

"What are the effects of Consolidated's acquisitions on competition in the markets in which the company operates?" the F.T.C. wanted to know. "Does the fact that the company is integrated materially affect the structure of the markets in which it operates?" The agency built a strong argument for an affirmative answer to both questions.

Would the fact that Consolidated had its own supermarket chains affect its pricing and policies in relation to the captive "independents"? Although the F.T.C. did not deal specifically with the question, the structure of the company gave it the power to discriminate in pricing.

What concerned the F.T.C. most was that, since Consolidated was buying some of its raw materials from other manufacturers, which in turn were customers or potential customers, there were "opportunities for reciprocal buying and selling arrangements wherein Consolidated will channel its purchases to those suppliers which in turn buy from it."

Such an arrangement simply freezes out competition, and, said the F.T.C., it wasn't playing the game fairly. The F.T.C. said this in a case brought against Consolidated that finally reached the Supreme Court.

The case involved the company's Gentry division, which was a major producer of dehydrated onion and garlic products, with only one principal competitor. The competitive company, Basic Vegetable Products, Inc., did not blanket the range of manufacturing, wholesaling and retailing as Consolidated did, and for that reason it lacked the leverage of purchasing power of its own to force others to buy. Consolidated and Basic Vegetables together dominated 90 percent of the market for dehydrated onions and garlic, with the rest of the business going to small scattered firms.

The F.T.C. did not need to prove that Consolidated actually practiced reciprocal dealing, although the proof was clear. All it needed to show was that the potential was there. The agency charged a violation of antitrust law "since the acquisition of Gentry by Consolidated has conferred upon the latter the power to foreclose competition from a substantial share of the market for dehydrated onion and garlic, thereby jeopardizing the competitive opportunities of its small, relatively undiversified competitors and tending to lend further rigidity to an already heavily concentrated industry and to discourage the entry of new competitors."

The Supreme Court agreed unanimously, saying that "reciprocity . . . results in an irrelevant and alien factor intruding into the choice among competing products, creating at the least a priority on the business."

At the same time, while Consolidated's interests in a broad range of manufacturing and processing gave it an unfair advantage and helped it overpower weaker competitors, the same interests made it necessary to try to get along amicably with its big retail rivals. It was necessary to restrain any inclination toward vigor of competition, as the company found to its dismay in Chicago. There Consolidated had seven of its Eagle Food Center supermarkets with a share of the market that would have gone unnoticed by the area's dominant giant, the National Tea Company, if Consolidated had not tried to carve out a bigger portion with some spirited price competition.

When Consolidated's supermarkets kicked off a "miracle prices" campaign with two-page ads in Chicago papers announcing "price levels smashed on over 5,000 items," the threat to profits stung National Tea into action. National Tea's president is said to have warned Consolidated representatives that "tomorrow there will be fewer of your lines on our shelves." And National Tea stores reportedly were told by their headquarters to drop Sara Lee bakery products, made by one of Consolidated's subsidiaries.

National Tea, which operated 237 stores in the Chicago area, was also the nation's fourth largest food chain. Such market power could not be ignored lightly, even by a conglomerate giant such as Consolidated.

The Eagle Food Centers quietly ended their price-cutting campaign and a short time later Consolidated announced that it was selling its Chicago stores. Soon thereafter the company signed a consent order agreeing to dispose of three food chains in response to a complaint by the F.T.C. that "substantial competition, both actual and potential, has been eliminated between Consolidated and other large chain grocery store companies which are actual or potential purchasers of food products processed by Consolidated."

However, it appears that Consolidated, like many other such companies, is irrepressible. A few years later its honorary chairman tried to buy control of A&P, the biggest name in the retail business. He failed because the Hartford Foundation, the food chain's major stockholder, refused to part with its shares.

The vigor of the F.T.C.'s actions on Consolidated Foods cases would be reassuring if it were the rule rather than the exception. In fact, however, whatever the agency might prefer, its operations are constrained by a severely limited budget. Only a fraction of the violations brought to its attention are ever investigated and still fewer are prosecuted.

Yet the public benefits of work in "certain industries" could amount to as much as $100-million a year, five times the F.T.C.'s budget, according to an estimate by H. Michael Mann, director of the agency's Bureau of Economics.

The F.T.C., regarded as an "independent" agency, is insulated to some degree from Presidential and congressional pressures. But the President holds an ax over agency heads through his appointment powers and his control of staffing and budgets. Despite the public-benefit potential of vigorous F.T.C. action, the Nixon Administration has reduced rather than increased its ability to act by keeping a tight restraint on its budget. The power of such an influence can make a mockery of any theoretical insulation from politics.

It is notable that the principal action taken by the Government to restrain the growing power of many companies, such as Hunt Foods & Industries, has been to unleash the meat packers in the hope that they will become a new competitive force in food lines dominated by the conglomerates—a hope with a dubious foundation, as noted earlier.

Hunt was a small regional company until 1943, when a new management took over, and then things began to change fast. By 1958 its annual report was able to say that Hunt "reaches from the tinplate out of which the company manufactures cans for its own products, to the millions of bookmatches printed on company presses every month carrying the Hunt sales message. It reaches from the farmers' fields to the Hunt trucks that deliver the packaged product to the grocer's door.

"The company developed its own machinery for canmaking with the result that it is now one of the major independent suppliers of this type of equipment in the country. Bottles were needed for Hunt catsup; today the company supplies millions of bottles a year to companies in the food, beverage, drug and cosmetic industries. Wood matches continue to be an important part of the match industry; to supply the white pine needed, Hunt is in the lumber business, with timber tracts and sawmills."

But Hunt was not really the initiator and innovator that its glowing claims would have people believe. It did not forge ahead into new fields by the vigor of its competitive and engineering genius. Rarely did it create a new product to enter into competition; instead, it bought up competitors and suppliers in fields that it sought to conquer. Like the legendary landowner who said, "I don't want all the land in the world—I just want the land that adjoins mine," Hunt followed an endless course, with the pace of acquisitions accelerating in geometric progression.

To make its glass containers it bought United Can & Glass Company, Glass Containers, Inc., and Nevada Silica Sands, Inc., and its acquisition of the big Ohio Match Company gave it a captive advertising medium. The company itself estimated at one time that one-fourth of the matchbooks in the United States carried its advertising message. Each acquisition, of course, gave it new strength to go after bigger game.

One of the big quarries in the food industry was the Wesson Oil & Snowdrift Company, which was itself the result of a merger of three companies, the old Southern Cotton Oil, the Southern Shell Fish Company and Blue Plate Foods, Inc. By the time Hunt started to stalk Wesson, that company had ten subsidiaries and two highly coveted brands—Wesson Oil, which was the biggest selling vegetable oil, and Snowdrift, a leading solid shortening. In acquiring the company, Hunt also obtained six major vegetable oil refineries, two food-processing plants and two seafood canneries.

Hunt's methods of pursuing acquisitions were also interesting. In many instances it put an agent in the coveted company's camp before moving in for the kill. It did that by buying up enough of the other company's stock to win representation on its board of directors.

Before acquiring McCall Corporation, one of Hunt's principal advertising media, Hunt bought up over 28 percent of McCall's stock; before taking over Canada Dry, Hunt already had a quarter interest in the company; and when Hunt started to negotiate for Knox Glass, it was negotiating from the inside, with 35 percent of the company's stock already in Hunt's expanding investment portfolio.

By 1965 Hunt had $415-million in assets, and its sales were growing at a pace four times as fast as the food industry in general, according to its own estimate.

Hunt's "product differentiation," meanwhile, kept pace with its mergers. In the last year for which such figures are available, the company was spending 3 percent of its sales for advertising, with much of that focused on its tomato products. With each new merger, spending on "differentiation" increased.

The effect on small firms when food giants meet in an advertising war was illustrated in the case of Wesson Oil and Crisco. Hunt's Wesson Oil had about one-third of the vegetable oil market when Procter & Gamble introduced a new liquid Crisco as a competitor, backing it with costly promotions of its own.

As a result, although Hunt lost none of Wesson Oil's share of the vegetable oil market, liquid Crisco took 20 percent of national sales. It was the smaller companies that lost ground, and it was the consumer—who must eventually pay for the extravagant advertising—who lost the benefits of real competition.

An industry group is considered "concentrated," that is, capable of monopolistic pricing, when four firms share 35 percent of the business. Here two companies, Hunt and Procter & Gamble, were dividing nearly half of the vegetable oil market.

Today Hunt Foods is more powerful than ever. It represents the biggest part of assets totaling about $800-million owned by Norton Simon, Inc. Ironically, the highly acquisitive Hunt was itself taken over by Norton Simon in 1968. The giant corporation has sales of more than $1-billion a year and profits of about $42-million. More significantly, its profit rate is 12.3 percent of assets, and rising.

X
The Puffed Profit Breakfast

The consumer's future can be read not in tea leaves but in corn flakes and crispies of all kinds. For the future in other food groups has arrived in cereals, where the top four companies take in 90 percent of the money.

After watching those four increase their market share from 68 percent to 90 percent over the last twenty years, the Federal Trade Commission has finally stepped in to file a complaint. And even though the agency has belatedly acted, many more years are likely to pass before there is any relief for the consumer from the industry's malpractices. Investigators who did the spadework on the case fear that it will drag on and on, through litigation and appeals.

The complaint purports to tell the story of how the industry consciously—almost as if with malice aforethought—hoodwinks the consumer, how it gyps parents on pricing and cheats both children and adults of proper nutrition. The charges range from fake "product differentiation" abetted by misleading advertising to follow-the-leader pricing.

Aside from excess profits, the industry is said to have taken hundreds of millions of dollars of the public's substance to pay for publicizing its misleading claims. It has wasted hundreds of millions more on proliferation of package sizes and brand names. And these have wasted retail-store investment by using up more and more of the stores' costly shelf space. The stores don't seem to mind, however, because ready-to-eat cereals are a highly profitable commodity for them, too.

The ready-to-eat cereals had become a $650-million-a-year business by 1970. The industry's physical volume had doubled in the past twenty years and its gross income had quadrupled.

A good part of that income goes to support the industry's waste. Each package costs more than the grain that goes into it, and there is good evidence that the companies spend more to package, promote and sell than they invest in their finished products.

The huckstering cost is perhaps the industry's biggest individual outlay. The total, higher than the advertising-to-sales ratio of any other industry except cosmetics, was $81-million a year in 1970, or 13 percent of sales volume. A good estimate is that this sum, added to other waste and excess profits, accounts for at least thirty-three cents out of every dollar a consumer spends on cereals.

Much of the promotional outlay is poured out by Kellogg, which is far in front of its industry, with 45 percent of all sales. It has more than $300-million a year in cereal sales and spends $36-million a year on advertising to help keep its edge over the rest of the industry. That is a ratio of about 12 percent of sales, close to the industry average. But that is not nearly so high as its profit rate, which was over 20 percent of assets in 1972.

The company closest to Kellogg in cereal sales is General Mills, which has 21 percent of the market and a cereal volume of more than $141-million a year. Of that $141-million, General Mills spends $19-million, or 14 percent of sales, for advertising. Its profit rate was only slightly lower—12.4 per cent in 1972. Right behind General Mills is General Foods, which has 16 percent of the cereal business, or more than $92-million a year in sales. It spends $9-million a year—about 10 percent of dollar volume—to promote its cereals. The company had a bad year in 1972. Its profit rate was 8.4 percent. But it was bounding back strongly in early 1973.

The last of the big four in cereals is the Quaker Oats Company, which makes a lot of noise but no waves in the placid business. To promote its sales of $56-million a year in ready-to-eat cereals, Quaker spends $9-million a year on advertising. That is an advertising-to-sales ratio of over 16 percent. It is no wonder, considering such high outlays, that it can get 9 percent of industry volume for its packages of air with an advertising message so patently meaningless as its claim of grains "shot from guns." Its profit rate was as inflated as its grains, at 13.4 percent in 1972.

Those big four in cereals were the only ones charged by the F.T.C. with violations, but there were two others cited as co-conspirators. Nabisco and Ralston-Purina, which share the leavings of the leaders, follow the same practices as the others, the complaint said. Nabisco had about the same advertising-to-sales ratio as Kellogg's, but Ralston-Purina was really pouring out the money. It spent $4-million a year in support of $20-million in cereal sales—an advertising ratio of 20 percent.

Cereals are a live-and-let-live business, and the nature of the companies involved in it provide a clue to the reason why their rivalry is confined to advertising claims and why there is no real competition in pricing and values. Kellogg is a big corporation, standing more than halfway up on the *Fortune* 500 list, at 191st in national sales ranking. But it is far easier to live amicably with others like General Mills and General Foods than to fight them for their portions of the business. For General Mills is a still bigger giant with vast resources with which to fight back. The company, 116th on the *Fortune* list, has $1-billion a year in sales, and the conglomerate corporation draws its income from a wide diversity of products, ranging from jewelry and flour to clothing and chemicals.

Even larger is General Foods, which is Number 45 among the *Fortune* 500, and its diversity is still greater than that of General Mills. Its sales total more than $2-billion a year in products ranging across each of the consumers' menus, from breakfast through dinner. Quaker is the smallest of the big four, but that only means it is the lesser among giants. It is 195th on the *Fortune* list. And even the two companies that bring up the rear in cereals, Nabisco and Ralston-Purina, are giants in other fields. Ralston-Purina, which is big in many areas of agribusiness, is among the leaders in all industry, with sales of over $1.5-billion a year placing it 71st among the *Fortune* 500. Nabisco is 140th with sales of more than $868-million a year. Ralston-Purina's profit rate was 12 percent of assets in 1972, and Nabisco's was 16 percent.

In such a society of giants, Kellogg cannot afford to come to grips with the others on the field of real competition, in pricing and values. General Mills and General Foods could withstand a struggle of almost any duration, supporting their costs on the cereal front with profits from their other businesses, and they could mount punishing counterattacks. The fact is, however, that each is content to see another pour its money into advertising promotions, and each is willing to follow a competitor up the price ladder.

So extreme are the industry's practices, as documented in the F.T.C. complaint, that they seem like a caricature of the malpractices that are possible in a monopolistic industry. However, what they do to the nation's consumers, especially the children, is far from funny.

The big four of the industry have introduced 150 brands of cereals since 1950 in uncounted numbers of package sizes. The results and the accompanying practices come through the F.T.C. legalese used at various points in the complaint:

"In introducing and promoting these new brands, respondents have employed intensive advertising directed particularly at children."

"Respondents have used advertising to promote trademarks that conceal the true nature of the product."

"Respondents produce basically similar cereals and then emphasize and exaggerate trivial variations such as color and shape. Respondents employ trademarks to conceal such basic similarities and to differentiate cereal brands."

The companies, in fact, were said to be conning the public in ways that could lead to a jail term if one individual tried them against another and for much smaller stakes. Their "product differentiation" advertising made misleading promises that the cereals would do all manner of good for anybody who eats them.

They would let him lose weight even if he doesn't stick to a diet and watch his calories, and they would keep him from gaining even if he takes in more calories than he needs.

Substantially worse were the claims of nutritive value, directed mainly at children. To believe them would be to believe that eating one of the cereals could turn an athlete into a champion while failure to eat that cereal could lead to failure for the athlete.

"In truth and in fact," the cereal makers lie on all counts, the complaint said. First of all, none of the cereals have any significant value in weight control, and, second, eating or not eating them is unlikely to have any effect whatever on whether an athlete or anybody else performs well or poorly at anything.

Nevertheless, the agency charged, the companies' "unfair methods of competition" tend to "mislead consumers, particularly children . . . thereby facilitating artificial differentiation and brand proliferation."

"These unfair methods," the agency went on, "have contributed to and enhanced respondents' ability to obtain and maintain monopoly prices and to exclude competitors from the manufacture and sale of RTE [ready-to-eat] cereals."

But this was only part of the cereal makers' strategy. They physically pushed competitors off the grocery shelves by the proliferation of their own brands and packages. And to make sure that the tactic worked, they put Kellogg in charge of managing the grocers' shelves and allocating space—with the acquiescence of the grocery stores.

"Through such services," the F.T.C. said, they "restrict the shelf positions and the number of facings for Nabisco and Ralston . . . and remove the cereals of small regional producers." All of them benefit from the scheme, the agency said, because it "protects and perpetuates their respective market shares through the removal or controlled exposure of other breakfast food products."

What put those companies in a position to control and manipulate the market, as the complaint showed, was a long list of mergers by which they absorbed or liquidated pesky competitors.

And what permitted them to benefit most was the final facet of the overall scheme, the game of follow-the-leader pricing. In general, the complaint said, they "refrained from challenging each other's decisions to increase prices . . . [and] followed the price increases of each other."

That it was a scheme there seemed no doubt. The F.T.C. complaint said that the companies "individually and collectively" maintained their "artificially inflated prices."

For other businessmen, all this is extremely important and, if trends in other industries continue to point in the same direction, is prophetic of a future of gradually disappearing opportunity. "Entry," the complaint said, "has been blockaded."

Aside from being abused by falsehood and misled into poorer nutritive habits, it means the public has been denied one of the principal benefits of true competition, in which rivals vie to produce better products and to give buyers a true choice among real diversity. "Product innovation has been supplanted by product imitation," the F.T.C. complaint said.

In addition, the F.T.C. charged: American consumers "have been forced to pay substantially higher prices . . . than they would have had to pay in a competitively structured market."

All this has happened, the investigators said in summing up, because the companies "individually and collectively have obtained, shared and exercised and now share and exercise monopoly power in and have monopolized the production and sale" of breakfast cereals.

The complaint never mentioned another scheme on the part of the cereal makers. It is one in which they seek to tighten their grip and keep a dominant place in breakfast diets as children grow into adults.

The companies have long worked together through an organization called Cereal Institute, Inc. Recently they have attempted to bring the schools into their strategy. The cereal makers have produced through the institute a variety of "teaching aids" containing propaganda that smacks of the old falsehoods in their advertising.

One of the latest is called a multimedia kit, titled "Project A.M./Today's Foods & Breakfast," which fits into an array of teaching materials designed as propaganda for children from pre-school to high school. This one, designed for intermediate grades, contains filmstrips, a teacher's guide and even worksheets for students. Devised to appeal to an overworked teacher's need for occasional relief from pressures and tedium, the new kit joined such others as "Breakfast and the Bright Life" and "Alexander's Breakfast Secret."

It should come as no surprise that according to the "teaching aids," Alexander's "secret" was cereal and that cereals were needed for a "bright life."

Americans, of course, should have a right to expect that their children will not be subjected to such propaganda in their schools, just as they are considered to have a basic right under law to be treated fairly, without misrepresentation or abuse of monopoly power. After a review of such abuses and trends toward abuses in the food-processing industry, one clear fact also emerges: The unfair methods simply would not work without collusion or acquiescence of the supermarket chains.

XI
Super Prices in the Supermarket

All the power that is concentrated in the food industry confronts the American shopper at the supermarket door. Among the stages through which food passes before dropping into the shopper's basket, the retail industry is the most powerful and closely knit in its web of mutual interests. It is even strong enough to protect consumers from the depredations of processors, such as the profiteering of the big four cereal manufacturers.

But it is not the business of the supermarket to protect consumers. It profits best, in fact, when it protects least. For after the processor has added on all its advertising and promotion bills and, particularly in the highly concentrated food groups, its inflated profits and the toll of creeping inefficiencies, the retailer steps in to take his markup. And that markup is inflated by the excessive costs that precede it.

The retailer's markup has gradually risen over the years since the early days of the supermarkets from about 12.5 percent to well over 20 percent. Obviously, 20 percent of a shelf full of cereals billed to the store for $300 is more than 20 percent of the $200 or so that the shelf load would have cost if all the inflators were taken out. The supermarket's purchasing agent might, and often does, try to obtain for his stores a consideration that his smaller competitors cannot get in the form of an under-the-table rebate or "promotion" allowance to fatten profits, but he has no interest in cutting the cereal industry's general pricing structure. Quite the contrary.

Overpricing by the processor, in fact, has augmented another form of supermarket profits. It puts an umbrella over the store's own profiteering in its private-label merchandise. While the supermarket normally enjoys a markup of nearly 22 percent for the highly advertised brands, it can undersell them by a few cents on each item and still enjoy a gross margin of nearly 25 percent on its store-brand groceries. Why should the retailer meddle with a good thing?

The store chains, in fact, far from showing any inclination to protect the consumer, have a long and lurid history of victimizing shoppers, and they are adding to that record every day with new and ingenious devices.

They run through the whole litany of restraint-of-trade laws, from price wars waged by a chain seeking to monopolize local markets to collusion to avoid profit-cutting competition on prices. They also include practices within the stores ranging from the devious but legal to outrageous deception.

Like the processing industry, the retail chains have gained their power by the merger route. In fact, had it not been for mergers, the growth of their market power would have been so slow as to pose no monopoly threat, or at least to push the threat far into the future. Local and regional chains, which still often do quite well in the shadow of the giants, could have held the growth of the big national chains within reasonable bounds. But the growth of smaller local and regional chains has tended, instead, to feed the merger appetites of the supermarket giants. For the small chains usually parallel the life spans of their founders and, particularly when they do well, fall sooner or later into the hands of a national retail company.

Until recently the price wars had been mainly a phenomenon of the earlier days of the merger trend. In a price war, there may have been some consumers who benefited but it was never a sign of free competition. The murderous struggles have usually been started by dominant companies that cut prices below cost over a wide range of goods, knowing that their companies could offset local losses by gouging customers in other areas.

And even in the price-war zones, any benefits in the form of low-cost foods could only be temporary. They would not have been started, the National Commission on Food Marketing noted, had not the prospect of monopolistic pricing promised higher profits for the aggressor companies.

As the merger movement continued, the big chains acquired bigger and bigger shares of the national market. By 1963 the top four—A&P, Safeway, Kroger and National Tea—had 20 percent of all grocery store sales in the country. That was not high enough to classify them, by normally accepted standards, as a concentrated industry, but national figures in retailing as in many other phases of the food business can be misleading.

The consumer cannot shop the nation or even an entire region for his food. The competition that affects him is the competition that he finds where he lives, among the stores that he can reach conveniently in a few minutes' walk or drive.

Thus, at the time when the top four retail food chains

had gained 20 percent of the national sales, there were other figures that were far more revealing. In regions across the country—in what the census calls "Standard Metropolitan Statistical Areas"—the top four firms regionally had an average of more than 50 percent of all grocery sales. That, of course, means a high concentration of market power in the regions, but even so the figures are not adequately revealing. A Metropolitan Statistical Area can cover hundreds of square miles and many different suburbs or even separate towns.

Obviously, a shopper who faces price gouging at Gristede's or Bohack in Manhattan is unlikely to drive out of town in search of a better buy for chicken, steak or eggs. And since others besides the top four regionally are likely to be among the dominant supermarket chains within individual shopping areas of the region, a broader gauge can be more indicative of the actual degree of competition. Thus the Food Marketing Commission's figure of 75 percent of food sales on average for the top twenty firms in regions across the country is probably more revealing. But even that is not so revealing as a shopper's own experience, and most shoppers know that they are unlikely to find more than three or four shopping centers within convenient range. And although there are no statistics for truly local areas, consumers are aware that the concentration of market power where it counts, in their own neighborhoods, is likely to approach 100 percent for the top four supermarket chains.

Even for entire metropolitan areas, a 1967 tabulation by the F.T.C. (the most recent available) based on census figures shows the chains that are in the top four locally often approaching total dominance of their markets. Some high examples included 66 percent of all grocery sales for the four leading chains in Denver, 66.7 percent in Pittsfield,

Mass., 68.2 percent in Meriden, Conn., 70.3 percent in Washington, D.C., and 80.7 percent in Cedar Rapids, Iowa.

Yet the fact that the area of competition in selling is relatively restricted does not detract from the evidence of market power of the big national chains. As the big chains have expanded their territories, they have tended to take on the same characteristics as the conglomerate giants in food manufacturing. The wider the areas of those individual chains, the more often they meet in local markets. And the more frequent their points of contact, the greater the danger that spirited competition by one firm in one market area might invite costly retaliation by its powerful rivals in other areas. As a result, the tendency has been to avoid vigorous competition and adopt a live-and-let-live attitude on pricing.

Alignment of pricing policies among the companies in the local market areas has become the general rule, as a good deal of evidence indicates. Prices on individual items may vary slightly, but they tend to balance over the range of merchandise that represents the stores' main volume.

That does not require collusion. All it needs is a leader. And the price leader need not even be the supermarket chain with the biggest share in the region. In fact, regardless of the share it might have in the local market, the price leader tends to be the chain with the most national power, as a study by the University of Pennsylvania's Wharton School of Business has shown. In the Philadelphia retail markets, the study found, A&P tended to be the price leader, although American Stores had the biggest share of the local market. Interviews with executives of other stores showed that they fell into line with A&P's pricing.

"Interviewers were frequently cautioned that external considerations cannot be ignored," a report on the study said. "A&P's nationwide strength was repeatedly cited as a factor explaining its ability to serve as price leader."

Although competition pales to insignificance when the rivals are all representatives of national chains, it is weakened still further when one of the local stores available to a shopper happens to be an outlet of a small regional chain. Such companies tend to behave the way smaller companies always do when they know they can be stepped on at any moment by a giant. However vigorously they might be able to compete in the local market, if they did not fear severe economic retribution, they bow to the reality of power.

Where they do not, the national chains have many methods to deal with them. One is zone pricing, a device explained at a hearing in an antitrust case [U. S. v. New York Great Atlantic & Pacific Tea Co., 1946] by a former employee of A&P, who said:

"Well, just in brief, I can tell you what the zone system means, how it is operated. [A] unit would be five or six zones, like the Rose Zone, the Pearl Zone, the Green Zone, the Gray Zone, the Violet Zone—each of those representing a particular territory. Some of the prices were the same in those zones, but if there was a particular zone where the volume of the A&P was low [and] competition was keen, they would reduce certain items in that particular zone so that it would not affect the general price range over the entire system.

"That works both ways. They would advance prices in certain zones where they felt competition was weak, and they hadn't much competition. That is the way they adjusted the prices up and down in those various zones—that was the purpose of the zones—to take care of a particular neighborhood."

A&P is not the only chain to use zone pricing to chastise

obstinate competition, as other litigation has demonstrated. It has been used by many others, most notably by Safeway, which is now almost equal with A&P in national volume, and by National Tea. The results underscore the effect of the power of such chains in local markets. Where their share of the market is biggest, their profit margins are generally highest, the National Commission on Food Marketing found.

Zoning as well as other anticompetitive practices have also been used by the big chains to freeze competition out of a favored market area as well as to discipline competitors who already had a place there. It should come as no surprise, for example, that prices are higher in the national capital than in most other parts of the country and that they tend to react quickly and often excessively to any increase in the wholesale cost of merchandise while they lag in response to a decline in costs.

For Washington is the special preserve of the nation's second largest retail chain and that company, Safeway, has a bigger share of the market there than in any other comparable metropolitan area. It has the biggest portion of the 70 percent of all groceries sold there by the four leading chains. Others seeking to move in and share the big profits in the capital have found prospective sites for stores bought up on some occasions and on others they have faced the threat of an overwhelming competitor planning to open a new supermarket on a site adjacent to one they had chosen. And those that have braved the dangers and moved into the market have often found their neighborhoods saturated with fliers advertising "murderous" prices at nearby stores.

The big supermarket chains have expanded their power most ominously in recent years through a process that economists call "backward integration." From dominance of retail sales they have moved strongly into food manufacturing.

The movement has given the big chains a growing list of "private label" merchandise, which consumer leaders have welcomed as increased competition against the big processors. The consumer experts also know that the "store brand" is usually as good or better than the highly advertised national brands, with labels that often identify much more clearly the grade and quality of the item. Private-label prices also average about 15 percent below the "branded" groceries. In case after case, consumers have gotten reports like that given this writer in an interview with a former executive of A&P, who said:

"For example, the same people who make Sealtest, they are the ones who manufactured our ice cream. And what most shoppers didn't realize was that they made it by our own specifications—and our specs were higher than Sealtest's. We were better in butterfat content, in everything."

But there are flaws in this seemingly good thing. For one, both the prices of national brands and those of the stores' private labels are higher than they should be and would be in a truly competitive market. The food marketing commission found that stores entered manufacturing in the first place in quest of a share in "the noncompetitive margins of oligopolistically structured supplying industries."

The stores clearly have no interest in shaking that friendly umbrella of national-brand prices over their own profits. They seem quite content to take advantage of the manufacturers' excessive promotional and packaging costs, which permit the stores to set their own prices at levels far enough below the national brands to bring in volume and yet high enough for a big margin of profit.

Here again there is no necessity for collusion, although such conspiracies have been proven. How widespread the collusion may be no one knows, but a typical case found by the F.T.C. was costing Seattle shoppers millions of dollars. In that case, Safeway was conspiring with Continental and other, smaller bakers to keep the general price of bread high enough so that it could sell its own bread at a discount and still earn a comfortable margin of profit.

Another problem is that whatever the retail chains gain in food processing the small regional manufacturers lose with no apparent dilution of the market power of the giants of food processing. And that problem points toward evolution of one of two states of commerce, both to be dreaded by consumers. In one, all the food business would be divided between the stores and the brands of a few big manufacturers. The other may seem farfetched, but it is one that the retail chains already have the power to create if they wished—and if the antitrust agencies should leave them to their own devices. They have the market power now to seize a monopoly on all food manufacturing. That power lies in their control over prices and shelf space.

Already many chains sell more milk under their own labels than they sell of the single independent brand they usually carry as a semblance of competition. And many chains also sell more bakery products from their own ovens than from those of all other companies combined.

The day is still far off, however, when a shopper can fill her whole list of processed foods from the store's own brands. The supermarkets have generally confined themselves to high-turnover commodities in which the manufacturers' concentration of power and their monopolistic pricing provide inflated profits.

XII
Ambush in the Aisles

Victimized in dozens of ways by the power of the processors and the big chains, the shopper is further assailed along the supermarket aisles by small stratagems, petty cheats and outright frauds and thievery. One by one they add little to the cost of food. Taken all together, however, they count heavily at the cash register.

Many of the stratagems are quite legal, perhaps even moral and ethical. There may be nothing wrong, for example, with the fact that in the normal store layout the departments and bins with high-profit goods are usually placed near entrances and in paths of heaviest traffic. It seems less than ethical, however, when the stores place regular-priced merchandise in big displays at ends of aisles. Because shoppers believe low-priced specials get those positions, their sales run 600 percent above normal.

And there may be nothing wrong with a manager's use of a knowledge of shopper psychology and habit that would surprise most consumers. As the shopper—still usually a housewife—pushes her cart along the aisles, her eyes move naturally along a path of shelves ranging from about eye

135

level to just below her waist. What manager with a normal amount of enlightened self-interest would not place his most profitable items along that path of normal eye travel? But the shopper, knowing this, can gain dividends by training herself to look up and down for the bargains.

That strategy, ethical though it may be in itself, lends itself to the old device known to merchandisers as bait-and-switch. The ten-pound bag of sugar, the "loss leader" advertised to bring shoppers in, may be far less easy to find in the store than it is on the advertising pages. Often it becomes part of a game of hide-and-seek: The clerk hides it down at ankle level, and the shopper must seek. But easily visible up at eye level and within fingertip reach will be the higher-profit two-pound and five-pound packages.

In another form of bait-and-switch, she may be told that a loss leader has already been sold out. She may even be offered a "rain check"—a device that many stores have used since several were caught a few years ago using the old conning trick. Few shoppers, however, will bother to ask for the low-priced special unless they see it on display, and still fewer will bother to ask for the rain check.

More often, the loss leader will be hidden in plain sight, like Poe's purloined letter. A store manager can reduce its visibility and manipulate volume of any item merely by narrowing the size of its display, that is, by reducing the number of facings that the item has at the front of a shelf. A brand of green peas, for example, in a display only two cans wide will have approximately half the sale of a display that is four rows wide. For most buyers, moving quickly down the aisles to fill a shopping list, a lower-priced brand can be completely lost, though in plain sight, if the display is narrow and placed among broad facings of competing brands.

Such practices, at least, are more defensible than behind-the-scenes ripoffs such as several that have been described to this writer in interviews with former supermarket executives and employees. One, a blatant fraud on cheese buyers, was detailed by a disillusioned former merchandiser who had left one of the big national supermarket chains to take a job in government.

"It was as simple as could be," he said. "I don't see how you could call it anything else but fraud. We'd get in the cheese in those big cartwheels, you know, and then we'd cut it up and wrap it.

"We'd cut it up into three parts. From the middle we'd take a long rectangle and divide it up, and that part we'd slice up and label 'mild' and sell for, say, forty-nine cents a pound. Then on each side there would be those half-moon sides left. We'd slice that up in wedges, and the wedges on one side we'd wrap and call 'sharp, three months old' and sell it for ten cents more. The wedges from the other side we called 'very sharp, six months old' and got another ten cents a pound for it.

"Then—and this was the best—the ends we'd carved off the 'mild' loaf and the other scraps, well, we'd dice those up into little squares, drop them into bags with a few toothpicks and call them 'party packs.' We got still another ten cents a pound for those."

Another former executive, once an official in the buying department of a different supermarket chain, told of other seamy sides of the business. They involved collusion between the stores on their advertising, behind-the-scenes payoffs by brokers to buyers and what he called "back-door" influences on store employees who supervised arrangements and displays of products.

In one instance he was offered $4,000 to introduce a new product into the company's stores. His reaction was revealing, although he says he did not accept the offer.

"No, I didn't report it," he said. "That would just have
tipped off the others that there was a chance to get a payoff for themselves."

There were other gratuities that he did accept because,
he said, he regarded them at the time as innocent and
harmless. He took a free trip to Florida on one occasion
and, on another, an expensive television set. The way he
got them was interesting, also.

Both were "prizes" offered by distributors of processed
foods. Those in competition for the prizes were the buying
agents for various food stores. The purchasing agent for
each store received "points" toward the prize according to
the volume of his purchase—the more he bought, the
more points toward the prize. The clear intent of the practice, he acknowledged, was to induce buying agents to
favor one product over another on a basis unrelated to in-
trinsic values or prices.

Among other frequent practices that he cited were several forms of collusion between purchasing agents and
brokers. In one instance, the buyer had a direct ownership
interest in a distributing company. In other instances the
buying agent installed relatives or friends in a distributing
company and channeled business to them. Such situations
created at least the circumstances where a kickback was
possible.

Through such relationships, he said, buying agent and
broker were often able to conspire in a special form of
profiteering in commodities. During periods when wholesale prices were low the stores' buying agent would advise his fellow conspirator to stock up on the commodity.
Later, when prices rose, he would place his order for the
supermarkets' needs and the two, buying agent and broker,
would split the difference.

Their risk was slight, for the law of nature has been
reversed in the food stores. It may not be true that when-

ever prices go up they will always come down; it is true that whatever is down will go up.

The former official cited an instance when such a profit was made in a frozen food deal. The broker advised the buying agent for a supermarket chain that the situation seemed ripe for a coup. Wholesale prices were low and the inevitable rise seemed not far off. Getting his signal from the buying agent, the broker stocked up and, once the prices rose, received his order from the agent. The difference ran into a sizable windfall for each of them.

The one-time chain-store executive had a curious way of rationalizing such behavior. "Well," he said, "the way we looked at it, nobody really got hurt. The store added on its regular markup, so it wasn't losing money. And the consumer wouldn't have gotten the benefit anyway, even if the stores had got the stuff at the low price. It didn't make any difference what the company might have paid. The retail price would have been marked up anyway because the wholesale price was rising."

In fact, retailing is a game in which the shopper can never win, as many other knowledgeable witnesses have been able to testify. The rules change as the score mounts. When wholesale prices drop, the store managers hold their price line as long as possible, reasoning that they must recoup what they paid at wholesale, before the decline, plus their normal markup. When wholesale prices rise the same store officials quickly mark up their retail prices to reflect the increase, rationalizing that they must allow for higher replacement costs.

It is a curious, twisted logic that has stood up over the years except in rare instances when it comes under the brief examination of an expert such as Weldon V. Barton, an economist on the Washington staff of the National Farmers Union. On April 12, 1972, he told the Price Commission:

"Consider, for example, what happened to the carcass value of pork during February–December, 1970, when the price of live hogs dropped from 27.4 cents a pound in February to 15.1 cents a pound in December. The figures indicate that, while the price to the farmer for the hog carcass dropped 45 percent over the ten months, the processors reduced their wholesale prices for pork by only 21 percent, and retail prices came down only 16 percent."

The economist added: "This is not an isolated instance. Statistics collected by the Economic Research Service of the Department of Agriculture show that, without exception since the statistical series was begun in 1949, retail food chains have lagged in cutting their beef prices in time of decreasing livestock prices, thus reaping windfall gains when prices to the farmer were falling."

On the other hand, he and other economists have noted, the retail stores are quick to respond to any increase in the wholesale prices, whatever lower-cost stocks they might have on hand.

Some of the costs of petty greed are quite small, but taken together with others they add up to a sizable toll on the shopper's budget. They include what the former purchasing official for a food chain called "back-door" tampering with the free play of competition.

"The brokers come in the back door, as we called it, and get to the sales people," he said. Sales supervisors are entertained at expensive dinners, tempted with gifts such as television sets and showered with services, such as the paneling of a recreation room, to mention one that the former executive cited.

"Just mention something you need done to your house," he said. "That's all you have to do."

What the brokers seek from the salespeople, of course, is help in pushing their products, cooperation with merchandise promotions, favored shelf space and the like. It is worth a good deal to a broker, for example, to have his product displayed at eye level rather than below waist level, and to have a few extra rows of his product on the shelf at the expense of a rival product.

Of such practices the former buying official said: "After all, it was all small potatoes. Nobody really got hurt." In defense of the brokers, who operate in a cutthroat business, he added: "If they wanted to stay in business they had to do it."

He remembered one instance, however, when a buyer had heavily overstocked on a new sandwich spread at a premium price and angered his colleagues. What seemed to bother them, he said, was that the buyer had acted so blatantly, not what he had done, for it was a "generally accepted practice."

Neither such "generally accepted practices" nor the stores corrupted by them could survive, of course, in a truly competitive market. A few good stores with efficient distribution systems, honest operations and tight cost controls could force a similar regimen on others in the same market area. But that clearly was not the sort of environment in which this former buying official worked, which was the region that included the national capital.

"You couldn't really say we fixed prices," he said, "but we didn't just trust to luck either. We would exchange price lists—under the table, of course. That told us what we needed to know, and generally we'd just try to stay in line, a little higher here, a little lower there.

"It wasn't anything overt that we did. It was what we didn't do. You might advertise an item a few times, but you didn't cut prices too much or push it too hard, because you knew if you pushed hard enough to hurt, the other store would hit back, and then everybody would suffer."

And then he added a fact of life in the retail business,

a tacit understanding on level of profits that economists have often cited and the F.T.C. at the time was quietly investigating:

"It was just good business to live and let live. Everybody knew what profit margin we all wanted to make, and that was really our best guideline."

Explaining how that guideline proved effective, he said: "Maybe we would find that profits were a little low one month. Then word would come down to slow down on the price specials and the price advertising. You would hope that the other stores would see what you were doing and hold off themselves. Usually they did."

The cheating that ranges from the petty to grand larceny, the deceptions big and small and the collusion made possible by growing concentration of power in the hands of a few all contribute to the fact that the margin between what a farmer is paid for food and what it costs the shopper has been steadily rising. The spread between the farm and the retail store increased 76 percent between 1949 and 1972. Meanwhile, for the first fifteen years of that period, farm prices actually declined, and they did not return to the 1947–49 average—except for some erratic movements during the Korean war years—until 1968. It is ironic that the recent sharp rise in farm prices coincided roughly with the period of massive invasion of agriculture by big corporations, although other factors, including government mismanagement of farm programs, must be given most of the blame for the phenomenon.

Studies by the Department of Agriculture have attempted to assign appropriate shares of the food dollar to each cost factor. The latest attempt, based on prices in 1971, showed that the farmer who produced the food got only forty cents out of each dollar that the consumer paid for it. Of the rest—the so-called "farm-to-retail spread"—46 percent went for retail labor, 12 percent for packaging, 8 percent for transportation, 6 percent for corporate profits, 4 percent for business taxes, 3 percent for a category including interest and repairs, 3 percent each for rent, depreciation and advertising, and 12 percent for "other" costs.

There was no effort to assess the costs of waste, internal cheating and price gouging. But there was plenty of room for those elements in the broad catch-all category of "other" costs and in the 6 percent cited for profits.

The profit figure was higher than retail spokesmen like to acknowledge but it was in line with a customary public-relations gimmick used to disguise the scope of profits in the supermarkets. They like to state profits as a percentage of sales in pronouncements for public consumption, but the practice is misleading in most businesses and especially misleading in a high-volume business such as food retailing. It distracts the public from the much higher profit statistic stated as return on investment, which is the only true reflection of profitability, because it shows the rate of income in relation to the cost of property and equipment needed to produce it.

The corporate profit from the consumer's dollar found in the Department of Agriculture study, however, conforms with an earlier finding by the National Commission on Food Marketing, which said:

"The return on investment for food chains consistently exceeded the level of return for all industry." And again: "Profits of retail chains were high relative to other industries." And they were highest of all in market areas where concentration of power was greatest, making monopolistic pricing possible.

More recent figures only confirm the commission's findings in an industry where the top two chains, A&P and

Safeway, each with more than $6-billion a year in sales, share more than 40 percent of the revenue from consumers taken by the eight biggest supermarket companies.

Safeway's profit rate was 15 percent of investment in 1972. Winn Dixie Stores and Lucky Stores had even higher rates, at 19.7 percent. But the average level for the whole industry was dragged down by losses of its poorly managed, inefficient giant, the Great Atlantic and Pacific Tea Company, which were aggravated by a brief price war that A&P started, apparently out of desperation. Safeway, which at one point in the year had pulled ahead of A&P in sales, continued to profit at a handsome rate on into 1973.

XIII
Supermarket Bunko

"Ladies, please don't blame the butcher," a union spokesman begged at a meeting of angry housewives in Washington following the nationwide meat boycott that they had led in April, 1973, in a protest against rising prices.

Well, why not?

Deceptions in meat departments contribute to the fact that their profit margins are wider than any other in a grocery store except for fresh produce, another area where malpractices are rife. And deceptions in meats are more detrimental to the American family than in any other commodity because meats represent the biggest part of the family budget.

The deception starts with the efforts of the stores to disguise the fact that wide profit margins exist in meats. The device used is relatively simple, as "Markets in Change," an unusually candid study by the Department of Agriculture, shows. The supermarkets simply juggle their figures, assigning more of the stores' overhead to the meat departments when that seems strategically advisable.

145

"The farm-retail spread for choice beef has been increasing much more rapidly than the consumer price index," the study found, noting a certain "rigidity" in retail prices even when supplies are large and farm and wholesale prices drop.

"In such cases," it said, "unchanged regular prices may put additional downward pressure on wholesale and live prices. However, the same rigidity very likely puts upward pressure on rising prices during opposite supply circumstances."

That may require a bit of interpretation. As the study makes clear, the "rigidity" of retail meat prices hurts both the farmer and the consumer. Because the stores hold the price line and merely widen their profit margins when wholesale prices decline, they keep demand from rising. It is a simple law of economics that declining prices tend to stimulate demand, but by their resistance to downward trends the supermarkets simply render that law inoperative. As a result of retail-price "rigidity" in the face of increased supplies, farm prices drop still further—and the stores' margins widen still more. At some point, farm prices hit a level where it is unprofitable for the farmer to produce and there is little incentive for him to breed more cattle and build up his herds. The result is a future restraint on supplies and another upswing in prices. On the upswing, the farmer may get some benefits, but not even on the downswing in farm prices does the consumer get the break that conditions would justify.

In periods of rising prices such as the sharp spiral of 1972 and 1973, the temptation toward deception in the meat department grows. Consumer resistance to the high costs of good grades and cuts further increases the temptation. For the potentially larcenous, the prospects of increased profits from short weights, from a little extra water or fat in the ham or hamburger, from mislabeling and other malpractices become almost irresistible.

Blatant examples of such practices were charged as a result of two investigations conducted during the sharp escalation of meat prices of 1973. One was made by 200 clergy and laymen organized as an "Interfaith Committee to Aid Farm Workers." The group sent a consumer task force throughout California to check on complaints against Safeway, the nation's second largest chain and one of the biggest sellers of meats. The malpractices that they said they found led to a series of lawsuits.

The investigative methods that the task force used were quite simple. Its members merely went shopping and took their purchases to the local meat-grading branch of the Department of Agriculture, where they were inspected by Charles Murphy, the branch supervisor.

They reported that the inspection official found twenty-three examples of mislabeling among their samples, in all of which cheap cuts were masquerading as more expensive cuts of beef. They included among other examples chuck steak labeled as T-bone.

Among other documentation kept by the investigators was a series of photographs of mislabeled meats. A typical photo showed a rib steak that was selling elsewhere at the time for $1.39 a pound. But the photographs purported to show that it was being sold at Safeway under the label of "club steak" for 49 cents more—$1.88 a pound.

A statement by the Reverend Wayne C. Hartmire, Jr., chairman of the interfaith committee, charged:

"The most blatant examples of this are:

"Safeway sells rib steaks as club steaks, charges club steak prices and thereby defrauds their customers by thirty to fifty cents per pound.

"Safeway sells clubs steaks under the label T-bone steak and overcharges customers by ten cents a pound.

"Safeway sells swiss steaks as round steaks and reaps an extra profit of ten cents per pound.

"Safeway sells beef liver as calf liver, thereby overcharging their customers by sixty to seventy cents per pound.

"The American housewife is not only defrauded by Safeway's practice. She is also surprised and frustrated when she serves meat to her family and friends that is less tender and of lower quality than she expected it to be."

The interfaith group filed a class-action suit asking $36-million in damages for consumers and an injunction to halt the alleged deceptions.

After another investigation, the same group also charged that they had found Safeway selling "lean ground beef" with as much fat content as ordinary "ground beef," which was priced at thirty cents a pound less. In that case, the group filed a $7.5-million punitive and damage suit in behalf of consumers who allegedly had been cheated in buying the product.

Safeway filed a $150-million countersuit against the group and the Farm Workers Union, charging libel and extortion, but at this writing none of the litigation has been resolved.

Allegations of such practices are not confined to Safeway, of course. In reporting the suit, the Los Angeles *Times* noted that:

"Similar suits have been filed recently against other market chains by the consumer protection division of the District Attorney's office for allegedly mislabeling ground lamb and ground pork as ground beef."

In still another case, the interfaith group also charged that Safeway had been up to an old trick, one exposed in 1967 and 1968 in a Washington investigation by the F.T.C. In a week in which Safeway was running ads in the newspapers to promote meat sales, a check on its stores showed that in some instances they were charging more for their meats than their ads indicated, the group charged. The one-week check followed a three-week survey by a consumer and clerical team of sixty-two stores in which they said they found 3,492 violations of federal trade laws. In all those stores, the team reported finding advertised items either unavailable or priced higher than advertised. The violations were said to involve not just a few scattered items but 27 percent of the 18,080 items promoted.

In the follow-up, the teams visited thirty-five of the stores and reported the conditions still prevailing. Overcharges were ranged from 1 percent to 38 percent.

When two Congressmen announced the findings of the interfaith group, Safeway protested in full-page advertisements in Washington newspapers. The company's chairman, Quentin Reynolds, charged that the investigations had been rigged and that the investigators were biased because they supported the United Farm Workers Union in its boycott of nonunion lettuce, which Safeway handled. The Reverend Mr. Hartmire said in a statement:

"It would be better for the consumer if Safeway advertised less and cut its prices more."

While Quentin Reynolds's pained denials were still echoing, an NBC investigative team was at work in New York and New Jersey, accompanied by Harold Sherman, the supervising inspector for the New York City Department of Consumer Affairs. In introducing the results on the *Today* show, Frank McGee said the team had "turned up evidence that meat buyers are getting flimflammed by misleading label practices." He said it had "visited sixteen supermarkets and found instances of such misleading practices at every one of them."

His introduction was followed by a film clip. Here is the reporter, Ken Alvord, talking as the camera scans a Shop Rite meat department:

"Butcher's Bunko is what we call the growing supermarket practice of selling the same cut of meat at one price under one name and again at a higher price under a fancier name. By the time we reached the Shop Rite supermarket in New Jersey's Bergen Mall, the pattern was clear. We'd uncovered it shopping from store to store. Here, as in other stores, the plain and pedestrian rib steak proved a fertile product for the creative labeler."

The camera focuses on Sherman, the inspector, and shows him examining two steaks.

"Right here," he says, "you have a His and Her Steak, marked $2.29 a pound. And here you have a rib steak, marked $1.29 a pound. If you take a good close look, you'll see that they're both exactly the same."

That was an overcharge of exactly $1.00 a pound for one of the less expensive beef cuts when it is priced fairly.

Then there was this exchange:

Sherman: "And now we have roast. Starting from this end, you have a rump round roast, for $1.89 a pound. Here you have something—I don't know what it is—it's called a 'Deli Roast.' "

Alvord: "Is that the same cut of meat?"

Sherman: "It's a—it's the other half of this cut."

Alvord: "Is there any reason why it should cost $2.09 a pound?"

Sherman: "$2.09? Well, because they don't call it a 'Rump Roast' that everybody knows. They call it a 'Deli Roast.' That makes it $2.09 a pound."

Next to the "Deli Roast," Sherman pointed out "charcoal steaks," which had been cut from the same part of beef "just as if you took a knife and sliced down the roast." The price was still higher.

To document the deception, Alvord and Sherman confronted the meat manager and, after he tried to dodge them, finally cornered him. Showing him the rib steak that was labeled "loin," Sherman demanded to know:

"Does it come from the beef loin?"

The almost pathetically flustered meat manager finally

surrendered to the badgering of the investigators and acknowledged:

"No, this is not a beef loin; this comes from the rib."

In a subsequent interview with Frank McGee, the inspector confirmed that mislabeling in supermarkets was a long-standing and widespread malpractice. But even more prevalent, he said, was the meat cutters' cheating on weights.

Although inspectors try to eliminate the deceptions, they are normally too overworked and the fraud too profitable for enforcement agents to suceed in prevention. About the only real protection a consumer has, he said, is to double-check the weights and approach fancifully named cuts of meat with caution, or, as McGee said:

"The fancier the name, the farther back you stand."

Deceptions in the meat department are more disturbing only because the stakes are higher there. But nowhere are the profit margins wider or the rake-offs more flagrant than in the departments where fresh produce is sold.

Prices can vary widely from town to town and even from store to store in the same town, for rarely are fresh fruits or vegetables offered as "specials" in the stores' promotions. And rarely is there real price competition. The stores enjoying the high profits from the department are unlikely to meddle with that green state of affairs. Overall, a study by *Chain Store Age* once showed, the average markup is 31 percent, but on individual items the stores have shown themselves able to set produce prices with little regard for producer costs.

A California grower, for example, told this writer of a deal that he made to sell his late-season peaches at what he thought was a reasonable price to the Los Angeles division of a retail chain. Concerned when the reorders were coming in slowly, he drove down from Fresno to Los

Angeles. The stores were not selling very many peaches, but those that they sold were bringing in a fancy profit. The stores had marked the price up to more than double what they were paying him.

The result of such overpricing shows up in the figures found by *Chain Store Age*. While produce accounted for 9.49 percent of store sales, it contributed 12.76 percent of supermarkets' profits.

Most large chains now have their own buying agents who set up their offices in the major growing and shipping areas, where they can buy for their stores in carload lots, often at good prices. But, as Jerome M. Stein, now an economist at the Department of Agriculture, found in a wide-ranging investigation for a master's thesis, they discover imaginative ways to avoid passing the savings on to shoppers.

Local wholesale markets, where smaller competitors must buy their produce, are weakened by the big chains' distant purchases. The volumes are low in the local markets and easily manipulated. The big chains simply reserve some of their buying for strategic use. Then when prices appear to be dropping to a competitive level for local rivals, the chain buyers step in and buy enough to drive the prices up again.

Stein also found widespread suspicion of under-the-table deals between buying officials of chain stores and the brokers they deal with. Such deals are difficult to prove, of course, but travels by this writer through major growing areas provided some evidence.

A San Joaquin farmer, for example, sometimes tries to sell his produce directly to the chain stores rather than through markets and brokers. Often he is told, as he was by the buyer for one large southern chain: "Sure we need your nectarines, be glad to buy them. But talk to our broker."

The broker's fee was 10 percent of the shipper's price. The grower-shipper could only guess how much of that fee found its way back into the buying official's pockets. But he did know one thing. The consumer was the ultimate victim.

Among chain stores, the style of operation in most markets is set by the biggest power. That power is now held increasingly by the fast-growing Safeway. And, if the past can be a guide to the future, the fact is not an encouraging omen for the consumer.

The protests of wounded probity advertised by Quentin Reynolds when Safeway was charged with mislabeling by the California interfaith group would have sounded more convincing were it not for Safeway's long record of charges of trade-law violations. A few years ago Gene Cervi, crusading editor of Cervi's Rocky Mountain *Journal,* put together what he called an "editorialized . . . incomplete history of violations" charged against Safeway. He listed them as the following:

In 1937 Safeway was part of a group charged by the F.T.C. with forming a company to collect illegal brokerage fees. When they agreed to dissolve the company, the case was dismissed.

In 1939, in a federal court in Denver, Safeway pleaded no contest and paid a $7,500 fine for fixing prices and restraining competition.

In 1941, Safeway faced a similar charge in Nevada. Again it pleaded no contest and paid a $7,500 fine.

Again in 1941 Safeway pleaded no contest when it was charged in California with fixing wholesale and retail food prices. This time it received a suspended fine.

In 1942, only a year later, Safeway again was charged with a price-fixing conspiracy. This time it was fined $5,000.

In 1943, Safeway was fined $30,000 when it declined to contest an indictment for conspiracy to restrain trade and monopolize a substantial part of commerce in food and food products.

In 1944, Safeway and the Grocery Distributors Association of Northern California defeated a price-fixing charge by the F.T.C., but two of the five commissioners thought they were guilty and voted for such a finding.

In 1954, Safeway was charged with misrepresenting the quality of its margarine. It settled without admitting its guilt.

In 1955, Safeway was fined $105,000, its president was fined $75,000 and a regional manager was fined $7,500 for a conspiracy to destroy competition through a price war.

In 1957, Safeway was given a $2,500 share of a $36,250 fine for a conspiracy with others to fix milk prices in Oregon.

In 1959, the F.T.C. ordered Safeway to stop falsely advertising its low-calorie bread.

In 1961, Safeway was found guilty in the conspiracy to fix bread prices in Seattle, Washington, by an F.T.C. examiner.

In 1963, Safeway was indicted in a conspiracy to suppress competition in trading stamps in California areas.

That was the end of Cervi's "incomplete history." But it was not the end of Safeway's record of alleged malpractices, as the F.T.C. found in investigations in 1967 and 1969 that led to a tightening of trade regulations. In a 1967–68 study of practices in Washington and San Francisco, Safeway was said to be one of the worst malefactors. In store after store it was found to be overpricing advertised specials and in a high percentage of cases the advertised specials were not available.

The worst victims were the poor of the ghetto areas, which had the highest percentage of cases of mispriced or unavailable "specials." In a recheck by the F.T.C. in 1969, investigators found a good deal of improvement, but the experience of the interfaith group in California points strongly to the suspicion that the chain is once again up to its old tricks.

Safeway was investigated again in 1972 and 1973 by the F.T.C. for its Washington operations. Investigators refused to discuss the case, but sources close to their inquiry said that this time findings were based on some entirely new grounds. The agents were said to believe that Safeway's share of the Washington market in itself constitutes restraint of trade.

They found that Safeway and Giant Foods—only two firms—had more than 60 percent of food sales in the national capital, a level well above the concentration of power that makes monopolistic pricing possible.

The investigators are likely to have found it particularly interesting when, in September, 1972, among similar instances, food prices declined in most other cities but rose 1.5 percent in Washington.

Nevertheless, higher officials at the agency decided against bringing a formal complaint against Safeway.

XIV
Where Are the Tastes of Yesteryear?

The scenes are as vivid as the events on the days they happened. Two boys about twelve or thirteen years old were sitting in the shade of a big live oak tree, eating their lunches. They had spent the morning chopping grass in a field. Occasionally they would exchange small morsels that had been packed for them.

At one point one of the boys handed the other a jar and a spoon. The jar contained garden peas floating cold in their own liquor. The spoon, loaded with peas, went from the jar to the boy, and he chewed slowly, savoring the taste. Though cold, the food tasted rich and sweet, with a flavor drawn from the good soil and the natural nutrients that produced it. It was a moment of simple pleasure, a fleeting vignette of cool shade and fresh air and a summer day, that always afterward could be evoked by the simple sight of a bowl of peas. The picture fades quickly for the key element is missing. The flavor of that spoonful of peas cannot be recaptured.

Another time, the same two boys were walking down a

country road, perhaps with fishing poles on their shoulders. This was a fall day, after the first frost, and the boys saw a persimmon tree beside the road bearing its ripened fruit. One of the boys climbed up and tossed fruit down to the other. Then the two walked on, munching its sweetness.

Today those experiences can be recaptured only in memory, not because of taste buds dulled by years but because of other changes. Vegetables have been bred for high production, with little regard to taste, and the flavor of garden-freshness has been burnt away by chemicals. And though persimmons in season were once available on fruit counters, they are no longer offered at the supermarket.

In such ways are consumers robbed today, in addition to the extra dollars taken from them at the checkout counter. Victimized monetarily, they are also cheated of taste, quality and variety in food, and often of quantity and purity as well.

Yet taste can contribute as much to the quality of life as sight and smell. And it is as important to the richness of memory as the beauty of a wild valley or the fragrance of flowers.

In today's supermarket chains, taste and variety have been sacrificed to a false efficiency. Buyers are dispatched to areas where high-volume fruits and vegetables are mass-produced, often picked green and shipped long distances, usually without regard to nearer, riper, tastier supplies that might be available. The flavor never matures or, if so, it fades before delivery.

The system leaves no latitude for the local store manager to make the morning trip such managers once took to local terminals or farmers' markets to pick out fresh fruits and vegetables in season, seeking to offer his customers the best in quality, variety and flavor. Fallout victims of the system are the local farmers, the local markets and, especially, the consumer.

The loss is easily verified by a trip to the supermarket. Looking for tomatoes? You'll find tomatoes that were bred for mass production, without regard to flavor, that were picked green, sprayed with an ethylene gas that turns them red but doesn't produce either the vitamins or the flavor of vine-ripened produce. In their cellophane-windowed cartons, they will be lined up on the counter, having been shipped across country, while nearby farmers may have vines heavy with tomatoes that are juicy and rich in vitamins.

Look for apples and you are likely to find only Red Delicious, whatever variety you might prefer. Persimmons have been forgotten. Rare too are blackberries, loganberries, raspberries and gooseberries. Like dozens of varieties of apples and pears, those fruits can no longer find a place on the produce counter, where each item must justify its space by high volume and the ease of acquisition by the store.

Even many of the finest species of squash have disappeared from most stores, and declining in availability are such old regulars as celery root, parsley, fresh turnip greens, mustard, kale, rape, rhubarb and fresh okra. And even fresh garden peas have faded from most counters.

It is not that no one would buy those items. The problem, experts say, is twofold. First, the low-volume produce does not produce as *much* profit as the others. And, second, the store officials know that in the current state of competition in the food industry they do not need to worry that their rivals will try to offer more. They can get uncomplaining customers to accept a basic, narrow offering that will maintain fast turnover and keep produce as the highest profit-per-dollar department in their stores.

And thus our children grow up unknowing of the wealth

of taste and variety that once enriched the quality of life and memory. They will never know the flavor-dripping richness of a home-cooked pie made with Northern Spy or Rhode Island Greening apples, the mellow spring taste of a Grimes Golden or the varied flavor in such apples as the Yellow Newton, the Pippin, the early Gravenstein, the Cortland or the Baldwin, and many may never know the mild, crumbling mellowness of the once ubiquitous Winesap.

Similarly, the Comice, the queen of all pears, has disappeared from most stores, as have the Kieffer, the Seckel and the winter Nelis. With these, too, something has disappeared unnecessarily from all our lives.

"I think, really, variety is the worst loss to the system," a top research economist at the Department of Agriculture told an interviewer, asking not to be identified. "And you know there is no real reason for it except arrogance. Every variety could pay its own way. They just don't feel it's necessary to bother." After a moment he added:

"As a matter of fact, you can't excuse the system on the grounds of efficiency. Often, they could even save money by buying good local fruits and vegetables when they are in season."

Aside from the loss of quality, flavor and variety, the consumer finds herself deceived in other ways when the bags are unpacked at home and the cans and packages opened. One of the worst hoaxes is in the so-called convenience foods. A busy working wife, tired after a day at the office, often finds something quite different under the foil of an oven-ready dinner from the sumptuous picture on the label. Nestling beside two or three ounces of dry chicken may be a skimpy spoonful of rubbery peas and another of mashed potatoes.

In one of the writer's most recent experiences with such products, he found under the crust of a "beef pot pie" a

tinful of gravy, two or three peas, a minute slice of carrot
and exactly two half-inch cubes of beef.

After many such experiences, Sidney Margolius, a consumer advocate doing research for a book, *The Great
American Food Hoax,* conducted a scientific study to see
exactly how much Americans were being cheated in their
packages and cans. He and his wife cooked up a long list
of convenience foods, then measured and weighed the
ingredients and estimated their true costs.

A package of Lipton's "Beef Stroganoff With Noodles"
was particularly deceptive. The package listed the cooked
serving weight—twenty-three ounces—after adding two
and a half cups of water. The actual weight of the ingredients was about six ounces. At a cost of 79 cents for the
package, he found he was paying at a rate of $2.61 a pound
for noodles worth 37 cents a pound. There were other
findings, such as these:

In a Swanson turkey dinner, then selling for 65 cents,
he found exactly two and a half ounces of turkey, two
ounces of peas, some stuffing and a bit of cranberry sauce
and gravy. The label pictured generous servings.

A cheaper dinner was a bigger gyp. It was a dinner of
beans with franks, priced at 39 cents. It contained one and
a half ounces of franks. For less than half the price he could
have opened a couple of cans and quickly served the same
dinner, without bothering to time it in an oven.

In several meat pies he found about one ounce of meat
and a few bits of vegetables and a lot of crust.

Again and again, convenience was a delusion. As Margolius pointed out, in a frozen omelet: "Look at the convenience. You save the work of breaking an egg."

Cereals, as might be expected, were the biggest deception. Besides a nutritional inferiority in a package of sugar-
coated flakes, he found that the sugar had added eighteen

cents to the cost of the package. Analyzing the sugar content, he found that consumers were paying for the frosting at a rate of ninety cents a pound, a somewhat high price to pay to avoid sprinkling a little sugar over a bowl of corn flakes.

Department of Agriculture officials in defense of food costs continuously return to the "convenience foods" and cite their "built-in maid service" for "America's busy housewives." What they fail to observe is that no maid could keep a job if she served such deceptive and pale, flat-tasting foods as consumers find in prepackaged meals. One wonders how the processors who perpetrate that kind of cozenry can keep their customers.

But deceptions in quality and quantity do not end when the shopper has passed the produce counters and the convenience-food sections. In subtle disguises of cans and packages, they follow the shopper throughout the store.

Backed by the power of the food industry, they have survived the attacks of consumer advocates in Congress and out. And they have weathered even the concerted campaign that led, in 1966, to the small gains contained in the Fair Packaging and Labeling Act. The act itself was the dying sputter of a fight that began with a roar in the early nineteen-sixties.

The deceptions then had reached scandalous proportions. Package sizes had proliferated in costly profusion, and their weights, stated in odd fractions, made it impossible for an average shopper to try to estimate the comparative costs and values. There were more than seventy sizes of cookies and crackers alone, most of them with odd-fraction weights.

Appearances provided little guidance. The giant-sized package of corn flakes, for example, might well be half empty. And with the weight stated in fractions of ounces the "large economy size" of anything might be more costly per ounce than a smaller package while the fraud escaped detection even by economy-minded shoppers.

Senator Philip Hart conducted extensive hearings that exposed the hocus-pocus confronting shoppers at every counter and, on the basis of his committee's findings, offered a bill containing a simple solution. His bill would have required standardized packaging, with weights in even denominations rather than fractions so that a consumer might have some chance to estimate how much she might be getting for her money.

But the Senator underestimated the power of the industry with which he had to contend. The processors wheeled their flacks and lobbyists into action, assaulting the eardrums of the public and its representatives in Congress with the specious argument that the truth squads were trying to regiment the poor grocers and food producers.

For five years the food industry managed to stave off any action, and when Congress finally passed the Fair Packaging and Labeling Act of 1966, it was written to a formula that was acceptable to the industry. There was good reason why the industry dropped its opposition before this final bill was approved, for it was almost toothless. It contained some tightening of labeling requirements, but in more important respects it merely gave the industry the privilege of adopting voluntary standards, which its members could then obey or ignore without peril.

The bill and the notoriety of the practices exposed while it was being debated did, in fact, produce some improvements. In some food groups, the number of package sizes was reduced slightly and the fractionalizing of weights was somewhat diminished, but the practice still persists.

The shopper was still confronted with the problem of comparing a 7¼-ounce box of cookies or crackers with a 9½-ounce size. In fact, there is evidence of a resurgence in the fractionalization game. Representative Benjamin Rosenthal, in hearings in 1969, three years after passage of the Fair Packaging Act, found long lists of products in which the abuse persisted. In some, even weights had been shifted to odd fractions.

Among Pillsbury products, for example, the housewife was faced with the confusion of a 5⅛-ounce package of scalloped potatoes, a 5¼-ounce package of mashed potatoes and a 7¼-ounce package of hash browns. The Pillsbury "family pack" of mashed potatoes was labeled 15¾ ounces. The same abuses persisted with Pillsbury's Fluffy White Frosting, which weighed 5¼ ounces, its hot roll mix, at 13¾ ounces, and with many others of its products.

It may be unfair to single out Pillsbury, for Betty Crocker, one of Pillsbury's few rivals in this highly concentrated industry, was marketing products showing the same confusion of weights and measures. It was still difficult to compare prices of Betty Crocker Fudge Brownie mix, at 22½ ounces, with the Duncan Hines Fudge Brownie mix, which weighed 15½ ounces.

Nor did the abuse stop among the mixes. It extended through product lines throughout the store, with varying fractions on jars of peanuts, cans of spaghetti, hash, stew, sardines, pineapples, pet foods and baby foods and so on.

One witness at Rosenthal's hearings, Edward Berlin, an attorney for the Consumer Federation of America, illustrated the deceptiveness of the fractionalized weights. The weights in one case—tuna from a processor that he did not identify—were in a series of three. The cans were labeled 6½ ounces, 9¼ ounces and 12½ ounces.

"I suggest that is a particularly outrageous example of

fractionalized packaging," Berlin said, "because the sizes, although they are not at all comparable, do suggest a comparative relationship."

With a shopping computer and the aid of a law partner, Berlin analyzed the prices of the three cans to arrive at the price per ounce. He found that the confusing fractionalization had enabled the store to get away with higher per-ounce prices for the two larger sizes than for the smallest size can of tuna.

The ineffectiveness of the Fair Packaging and Labeling Act was shown in a demonstration by Consumers Union. It compared results of a test conducted in 1962, four years before passage of the act, with a similar study two years after the law went into effect. In both instances five housewives with comparable educations were sent to the supermarket with a shopping list of everyday items.

They were instructed to pick the item in each category that offered the most for their money. In the earlier study, the housewives had been wrong 34 times out of 70, or slightly less than 50 percent of the time. In the second test, three years after passage of the act, the housewives were wrong 38 out of 70 times, or more than 50 percent.

And while some progress had been made, at least temporarily, on the problem of proliferation of packages, there was still a confusing array of sizes and weights. Edward Berlin of the Consumer Federation found six sizes of coffee between 2 and 10 ounces, twelve sizes of one manufacturer's candy between $5\frac{1}{4}$ and $8\frac{1}{2}$ ounces and twenty-two sizes of a single manufacturer's cereal below 24 ounces.

Government regulators had been lax, as might have been expected, in implementing the act. With thousands of items in the stores, the Department of Commerce had managed to obtain voluntary agreements from industry on package standardization in thirty categories.

A witness for the department testified that he could not

say whether it would be "one or twenty-one years" before all categories were brought into compliance, but he thought manufacturers had "responded magnificently." He brought amused smiles when he cited one example of the government-industry "cooperation" that is usually sought so eagerly by regulators in preference to enforcement.

The witness, Malcolm W. Jensen, acting deputy director, Institute of Applied Technology, National Bureau of Standards, recalled an instance involving kitchen cleansers, which all manufacturers but one had been producing in twenty-ounce sizes. The other had a twenty-two-ounce size. Triumphantly the official told of the manufacturer of that product "joyfully" coming into his office and announcing that he had found a way to fall into line with the others— by reducing by two ounces the amount of cleanser that buyers would henceforth get in his packages. That must have been a great consolation to consumers.

Another of the Commerce Department's triumphs had been a voluntary reduction in the number of package sizes for cookies and crackers—from seventy-three to fifty-six.

The proliferation of packages, of course, is not merely a source of confusion. It also imposes a heavy tax on consumers. As Colston E. Warne, who was president of Consumers Union, once described the problem, a profusion of package sizes "adds costs all down the line."

"The manufacturer who puts out his product in needlessly multiple sizes increases his labor and overhead costs as well as inventory costs of packing materials," he said. "The wholesaler and distributor costs are increased by heavier, slower-moving inventories. And the retail grocers' costs are pyramided by this meaningless product differentiation. And finally, of course, we consumers are befuddled and robbed of our ability to buy the best possible living our incomes might afford."

The fractions in many cases were a symptom of a new and insidious deception that had come to Rosenthal's attention. The Congressman called it "packaging to price." The practice was a method of short-weighting that fleeced customers in a fashion that is entirely legal by all laws in existence, including the Fair Packaging and Labeling Act.

Manufacturers adopting the practice have found that they can raise their prices secretly and indirectly by reducing the weights of the products in their packages. The customer gets no warning that she is getting a little less for her money, and there is no physical evidence in the form of a change in the size of the package, can or jar.

But a housewife accustomed to buying a 14-ounce package of Kellogg's Fruit Loops would have found one day, in the unlikely event that she checked the weight of her package, that she was suddenly getting only 11 ounces of the cereal for her money. Similarly, if she had bought Chef-Boy-Ardee Meatball Dinners one week she would have gotten 25⅔ ounces. On her next purchase she would have gotten only 23½ ounces for her money, again without detecting a difference, at least until she opened the can. Rosenthal and his staff found hundreds of products in which this same—quite legal—deception had been practiced.

When their deceptions are exposed by consumer advocates, food industry spokesman often seek to discredit the evidence by implying that the disclosures are exceptions singled out by zealots. There was clear evidence, however, that the findings of Edward Berlin and Congressman Rosenthal could not be so easily dismissed. They had lists of dozens of products that reflected the deceptive practices. And they were supported at the congressional hearings by spokesmen from the Department of Health, Education and Welfare, an agency that, like most others with a regulatory function in government, has never been noted for severity in its relations with industry.

One witness, Diane McKaig, who was director of H.E.W.'s Office of Consumer Services, provided examples that heaped new weight on the evidence. Noting that Rosenthal's committee had cited the confusion of trying to compare the price of a 15¾-ounce can of cheese ravioli with a 15-ounce can, she produced still another, a 15½-ounce can. There was no visible difference in size between the three.

In another example, she showed a 17-ounce can of kidney beans and a 16-ounce can of the same product, both made by the same manufacturer, with no visible difference in size. Both had been purchased in the same store, a few days apart. Ironically, the heavier can had been priced at two for 37 cents, while the lighter can, bought later, was priced at two for 39 cents.

Diane McKaig cited examples of even greater deception in the packaging of frankfurters and cheese. In one instance, she displayed two hot dog wrappers that had been mailed in by a Minnesota housewife. The first was taken from a 16-ounce package that had been purchased for 59 cents. The housewife's complaint was that when she returned to the store she found the package unchanged in appearance but, on close inspection, weighing only 12 ounces. A part of the deception was that the lighter package had been priced at 49 cents, implying a reduction to an unwary shopper. Actually the lower price represented an increase in the cost per ounce.

Miss McKaig's testimony on cheese showed further deception. She displayed three packages, all bought the night before she testified. One weighed 8 ounces, contained eight slices, and was priced at 39 cents. The second contained 16 slices, but it was not twice the weight. Actually it weighed only 12 ounces. It was priced at 59 cents. The third package, also 12 ounces and 16 slices, was priced at 65 cents. All three were the same brand, bought from the same counter at the same time.

"Now, contrary to what you would think at first glance," said Miss McKaig, "the smaller package is the better buy."

Was the varied pricing of the larger size an instance of inadvertent stamping? Certainly not, said Miss McKaig, because:

"There were lots of them at both prices."

During the hearings, Congressman Rosenthal and his staff pinpointed still another area of deception in packaging. He was concerned about the fact that a buyer, when shopping for most canned goods, could never tell exactly how much food she was getting, despite the net weight printed on the label. There was no way to know when buying a can of peas, for example, whether it was filled with peas or largely with liquid.

The problem was illustrated by a staff aide in a demonstration for the committee. The aide used portable scales, some cups and two Del Monte cans, both labeled Whole Kernel Golden Sweet Corn. One was vacuum packed, the other packed in liquid. The vacuum-pack can was labeled 12 ounces, the other 17 ounces. But when the aide drained the liquid in the larger can and weighed the remainder before the eyes of the committee, the scales showed only a half-ounce more corn in the 17-ounce size than there was in the smaller, 12-ounce can.

And yet the label on the larger can said it contained 2½ cups of corn, while the label of the other said only 2 cups—a half-cup increase claimed for only a half-ounce more corn.

The demonstration gave visual emphasis to the impossibility of determining from labels whether one can of fruits or vegetables is a better buy than another. And there was ample data for evidence behind the display.

For example, figures extracted from the Department of Agriculture showed that there is consistently more spinach in a 15-ounce can of the Town House brand than in a can of Del Monte spinach of the same size. Town House fruit cocktail consistently contained 4 to 5 percent more fruit than a Del Monte can of the same size, and 16-ounce cans of Hanover green beans contained 3 to 4 percent more beans than similar Del Monte cans. On the other hand, Del Monte cans of sliced beets contained 5 percent more beets than Libby's cans.

The lists go on and on. The point is that, without knowing how much of the weight in a can is vegetable or fruit and how much is liquid, it is impossible to tell which is the best buy, even if there were no other deceptions. The evidence obtained by the Rosenthal committee from the Agriculture Department is data of a sort that its researchers and analysts often accumulate. Those facts could help the shopper, but they are data that industry-oriented officials at the agency rarely disclose.

Even if uncertainty about the weight of real food in the cans were removed, another element necessary for comparison of values would still be missing. It is impossible under present practices to determine from most labels the quality of the product in the cans they cover. Del Monte, through its extensive brand promotion, has attempted to persuade consumers that its label alone is assurance of the highest quality. Inspectors in food purchasing divisions of the Department of Agriculture know that often isn't true. But the agency's officials regard such information as "trade secrets" and refuse to disclose the facts to the public that pays for collecting the truth.

Actually, "store brands" are often of higher quality than

any others, though they usually sell for less. The proof can be found on some of their labels. When cans of some vegetables are stamped Fancy they contain products that are as good, according to Agriculture Department standards, as can be found at any price. The big processors, however, prefer to compete through advertising claims rather than through quality designations that would allow direct price comparisons of comparable products.

Such honesty in labeling, however, would prevent the use of a practice that has proved profitable for one large canning company. The corporation, according to an expert at the Department of Agriculture, who refused to identify the name, puts its top label on a lower grade of peas for the Northeast, where a firm consistency is more popular. The rest of the country gets higher-grade, tenderer peas under the same label and for the same price.

The problem is not that the company gives the shoppers of the Northeast what they prefer under its top label; it is that those shoppers are not given the price benefit of their preference for a lower-cost product.

Standardized grades for many fruit and vegetable products have been established by the Department of Agriculture, but there is no requirement that the manufacturer use such an easy guide to quality on its labels. Abortive campaigns for such a requirement have been launched occasionally, but the food industry, with the aid of its friends in government, has successfully fought them off.

XV
Blood, Fat and Germs

Only at the meat counter, ironically, surrounded as it is with other deceptions, has grading as a concession toward fair play with the shopper won any headway, and there the practice applies only to beef.

In the beef tray, despite the confusion of misleading names that are often applied to the butcher's cuts, the shopper can be relatively sure that U. S. Choice beef in one store will be the equal of U. S. Choice in another—assuming that a guileful manager has done no mislabeling.

But this one concession to the customer is set like bait in a tangle of snares. For the unwary shopper, the traps range from uncertain quality through deceptions on ingredient to questions of wholesomeness.

For buyers of fresh pork and chicken there is no guide to quality. The chicken parts may be soaked in water, for which the shopper pays chicken-meat prices. And the pork-loin special that lures buyers to a store one week may be laced with twice as much fat as the lean pork they may remember from their previous shopping trips.

The absence of grading is particularly beneficial to the processors of branded pork products, most of whom have their own designations for top quality, trademarks such as Armour's "Star" or Swift's "Premium." Beneficial to the processor though the absence of grading may be, it can be costly to the shopper. For the top-quality designations of the processor can be highly elastic. In periods of limited supply, the standards can be lowered to encompass enough hams, shoulders or bacon to meet the demand for "top-quality" meat.

Another snare may lurk in hams, even if the label should accurately reflect the quality of the meat. The Department of Agriculture, acting in response to what it said was "consumer demand" for "juicier smoked meats," has permitted processors to pump water into hams up to a limit of 10 percent of the weight. The department, in fact, was responding to the industry's wishes. It has never been able to show that any consumer wanted to pay ham prices for water—or given any evidence to show that it sought seriously to determine the consumer's wishes.

The water in the ham and chicken is a bargain beside what the shopper may buy from the ground-beef tray. Chances have diminished that the ground meat will contain illegal extenders such as soy flour or dangerous substances such as sodium nitrites and sodium sulfite. Yet the nitrites and sulfites, which mask deterioration of the meat, still turn up in occasional tests. But what the shopper is more likely to get is a lot of loose fat added to red-meat scraps and colored during the grinding process with clots of beef blood. And all this is likely to be laced with high counts of bacteria.

Beef intended for grinding should be handled with special care, since the grinding process breaks down tissues and releases fluids that become a fertile culture for bacteria. The evidence, however, is that where most care is needed, least is given, as Consumers Union found in tests of ground meat from a broad sampling of offerings in three cities.

Investigators were sent out to collect samples in Philadelphia, New York and Los Angeles. Tests on the samples showed high bacteria counts, reflecting a history of careless handling of the meat itself and, in some cases, advanced stages of deterioration. Twenty percent of 126 samples from the Philadelphia area showed bacteria counts of 10 million per gram or more, a level indicating that putrefaction had begun. Over 60 percent had more than a million bacteria per gram—a level that can cause mild intestinal distress.

A more significant test was for coliform bacteria, the presence of which indicates fecal contamination. More than 70 percent of the samples exceeded what specialists set as a "reasonable" limit of 100 coliform bacteria per gram, and 52 percent had counts of more than 1,000 coliform bacteria per gram. In the Los Angeles samples, the tests showed insect fragments and rodent hairs, although those samples had somewhat lower bacteria counts.

The Consumers Union specialists concluded that the only safe way to obtain ground beef was to buy fresh cuts of meat and do the grinding at home.

The same was true if the buyer wanted to avoid adulteration of the ground meat with excess fat and blood clots. Many of the samples exceeded the legal limit of 30 percent fat, in itself an exceedingly high level, indicating a legalized deception. The deception grew worse if the buyers picked up ground chuck or ground round, for the prices were naturally higher and the expectation was to find a correspondingly better grade of meat. Samples of ground chuck ranged up to 34 percent fat content and ground round up to 27 percent fat.

The depth of the deception is illustrated by the fact

that fat contains no protein, the element for which meat is usually purchased. On average, when a patty of ordinary ground beef was cooked and compared with a patty of ground round, costing approximately fifty cents more a pound, both contained about the same amount of protein.

The cost of the protein, however, differed sharply. For the ordinary ground beef the highest cost of the protein content was $4.18 a pound. For the ground round, the protein cost ranged up to $6.78 a pound. At such levels, a good T-bone steak could be a better buy.

The deception was underscored when Consumers Union taste testers could find no appreciable difference in flavor between the lowest-priced and the highest-priced grades of ground beef.

The consumers who get water in their ham and blood clots and loose fat, laced with bacteria, in their hamburger receive still more for their money at the lunch meat and hot dog counter. There they get the 10 percent added water *plus* the 30 percent allowable fat content, plus a lot of other things unpleasant to mention.

Margolius found 127 types, brands and package sizes of luncheon meat in one store with prices ranging above two dollars a pound for lunch "meats" that were only half meat. Considering that half of them was water, fat and additives, the price of the meat ran to several dollars a pound.

The hot dog, one of the mainstays of the poor, can be one of the costliest buys in the store in terms of the grams of protein bought for a dollar.

The hot dog has a long history, and the longer it survives the less likely it is, considering its record, to give consumers their money's worth. First introduced into the United States at the Chicago World's Fair of 1893, it caught on quickly. Although there are no analyses available of the value of the early contents, it was apparently worth the few cents it cost, spicy and tasty. By the time of the World's Fair of 1939, it still offered reasonably good food value, with only 19 percent fat and a little over 19 percent protein. By World War II the hot dog had become one of the symbols of America, and it danced around the world alongside apple pie, home and mother in the visions of GI's. And when they returned it was still a reasonably good value, although already somewhat deteriorated. A survey in 1945 showed only 14 percent fat, but the protein level was also down, to 15 percent.

From there the hot dog continued downhill. Protein content trailed off, while prices and fat content soared. Aided by technological "progress," the industry has been able to use a new emulsifying process that gives the pulverized meat a stable consistency even when mixed with excess fat and water. By 1967, the average protein content was down to 11.8 percent, and the fat was up to 31.2 percent. In 1969, according to one report, the figures were 11 percent protein and 33 percent fat.

Now, as the adulteration of the hot dog threatened to erupt into a scandal, the Department of Agriculture, reluctantly and slowly, moved to set a standard of identity for what one writer called the "fatdog."

And where did it propose to set the limit for fat content? At 33 percent, of course. As one department official explained, the 33 percent line was chosen because it was the level prevailing in the industry. There was no mention of how consumers might feel except for some unsubstantiated industry claims that they really liked hot dogs with all that fat and water. Nutritionists were not consulted.

Consumers were soon heard from, however, and in a slight concession the department's regulatory officials drew the line at the still-high level of 30 percent fat, which was scheduled to go into effect October 23, 1969. Concerned about how that might affect the industry, Department of

Agriculture officials sent out a letter to regional directors telling them not to rush into enforcement but to give "cooperating management" plenty of time to make adjustments.

There was no mention at the time of all the other elements that consumers were getting for their money. A list of the normal contents sounds like the ingredients for a brew by Macbeth's witches.

Today your hot dog, the salvage pit of the meat industry, can legally contain parts of cattle, sheep, hogs and goats including such organs as the esophagus, diaphragm and heart with accompanying fat, bone, skin, sinew, nerve and blood vessels. It can also contain up to 15 percent chicken meat, normally the flesh of "spent" pullets—laying hens grown too old for profitable egg production and of little value elsewhere in the market. It can also contain as much as 2 percent corn syrup, $3\frac{1}{2}$ percent salt, spices and curing agents and $3\frac{1}{2}$ percent "extenders," including soybean and milk products and cereals.

Regulations do not yet permit lips, snouts and ears in the hot dog, but those may come. The industry began to demand the right to salvage them in hot dogs in 1973.

Into the mixture can go 10 percent added water, an addition that raises the total water content to more than 50 percent of the product, for meat itself is estimated by the Department of Agriculture to contain about 44 percent water.

Heart specialists have protested the allowance, unlabeled, of the high fat content of hot dogs because of the role of saturated fats in heart attacks, but little has been said about some other questionable ingredients. The "fat-dog" can also contain dyes of unproven safety as well as such potentially dangerous chemicals as nitrates, nitrites and nitrosamines.

The nitrates are considered harmless in themselves and

a potential danger only because they can be converted by bacteriological action in food or the stomach into nitrites, which are poisons that can be lethal in high concentrations. The nitrites are not merely a theoretical danger; several children have died from eating hot dogs containing concentrations far above the permissible limit of 200 parts per million. The nitrosamines, which can be created by interaction between nitrites and other chemicals in foods, are known carcinogens.

Ironically, chemicals are used in hot dogs primarily for cosmetic reasons, to help maintain a fresh appearance. Much smaller concentrations than are normally used would suffice for their one functional purpose, as a preservative. The hot dog can also contain, also for cosmetic reasons, such color fixers as sodium erythorbate, sodium ascorbate, ascorbic acid or citric acid, and to enhance taste appeal, the controversial compound, monosodium glutamate. The monosodium glutamate (MSG), which has been identified with the "Chinese restaurant syndrome," need not even be listed on the label.

There is also much more. Consumers Union, in a test in early 1972 similar to the one it conducted with hamburgers, found 40 percent of the samples examined to have bacteria counts above the level indicating the start of putrefaction—10 million per gram or more. One sample had far more—140 million per gram.

The tests also indicated that in buying hot dogs, you stand a good chance of purchasing a stomachache. Three-fourths of the samples had bacteria counts of more than one million per gram, a level that is likely to give a consumer some gastric distress. In 19 percent of samples tested for wholesomeness, Consumers Union specialists also found insect fragments and rodent hair.

Insect fragments may not be alarming in themselves, but they provide a clue to the level of sanitation in the meat plants where the hot dogs were processed. The rodent hairs were more sinister, for they were a sign of fecal contamination. Rodents eat their own hair.

In comparison with all that, one could hardly be offended by the Macbeth witches' "fillet of a fenny snake . . . eye of newt, and toe of frog, wool of bat, and tongue of dog, adder's fork and blind-worm's sting, lizard's leg and owlet's wing."

Aside from the foreign ingredients in this salvage pit of the meat industry, the hot dog proved to be an even poorer prospect than the hamburger for a family seeking a low-cost source of protein. The average cost per pound of protein in the samples, at early 1972 price levels, was $6.98 a pound for "all-meat" hot dogs and $7.98 for those labeled "all beef."

For lower quality, poorer values and diminished wholesomeness of foods found beyond the supermarket door, the consumer can justifiably blame the food industry. But it is not alone. The industry has partners among the friendly government regulators.

XVI
Golden Grain:
The Russian Wheat Deals

Regulators in government, friends and often close associates of officials in the industries they regulate, played a crucial role in the biggest raid ever made on the American economy. That was the series of secret deals in which canny Russian agents in 1972 outfoxed Yankee traders while buying up one-fourth of the United States wheat crop.

For the Russians, the deals constituted one of the world's greatest bargains. They bought largely on credit, with financing from the United States Government and with that same government footing part of the bill through subsidies, and they were able to repay either with cheap dollars that the deals helped to devalue or with gold that doubled in worth under the same influences.

For American consumers, the results were disastrous. The Russian deals left short supplies in the United States, and the devaluation of the dollar helped spur a run on farm commodities that left critical shortages. In addition, the deals overloaded the American transportation system to the point of delaying deliveries of vital feeds and of the fuel and fertilizers needed to produce the next year's food. And they put prices of America's meats and staples on a skyrocket.

It might be unfair to imply that such results were intended by anyone involved but, inadvertently or not, two secret visits by a Russian trading team to the United States in the summer of 1972 have cost American shoppers more than $3-billion a year, according to an unpublished study made for the staff of the House Agriculture Committee.

Certainly, government officials who should have been responsible were not meeting their obligation to get the information they needed to guard against damaging consequences. Meanwhile, information that they had was withheld from the farmers and consumers to whom the officials owed their greatest loyalty. Whether they were so chary with information in their contacts with big grain companies was a question.

In the aftermath, the officials involved have professed an ignorance that would disqualify most men for office, but they have done so to guard against more serious charges. Whether those professions of a lack of vital data were true became more and more dubious during congressional investigations. How much did they know and when did they know it? As to that, enough conflicts in testimony and failures of memory developed to equal a Senate Watergate hearing.

The whole story was like the plot of a mystery farce with a denouement that turned to disaster. Its principal actors included top officials of multibillion-dollar grain corporations versus the wily group of Russian traders. In the supporting cast were several shortsighted government officials with strong ties to the grain companies. And offstage through part of the drama was a mystery voice, that of a still unidentified "John Smith."

The two leading corporations in grain, one of the most highly concentrated of all industries, are Continental and Cargill, which make over half of the world's shipments. The top five—including Dreyfus, Bunge and Cook Industries—have 90 percent of the business. All but one, Cook, are closely held private corporations.

This means that those companies, controlling the most vital element in the nation's food supply, do not have to give an accounting to the public on their operations or even, to any important degree, to the Government. Secrecy, in fact, has been one of the key elements in the business, as it was in this drama.

Its plot actually began early in 1972 with a letter from Henry Kissinger, President Nixon's chief adviser and operator in foreign affairs, who was seeking ways to improve relations with the Soviet Union. The letter, asking for plans to increase agricultural trade, started a flurry of activity and conferences at the Department of Agriculture.

The response from Agriculture was an approach that led to a massive giveaway and a design to fatten the profits of the grain companies.

The leading figure in the discussions and planning was Clarence D. Palmby, who was the Assistant Secretary of Agriculture with responsibility for foreign trade, a man who had beaten a path between industry and government and was soon to make the return trip.

Among the topics of the internal discussions was a proposal to offer the Soviet Union a line of credit sufficient to aid massive grain purchases. Another subject was a planned trip to Moscow to discuss agricultural trade. Palmby was scheduled to lead a negotiating team, although Secretary of Agriculture Earl L. Butz would be the nominal head of the delegation.

While such internal discussions were under way, Palmby was also talking to the president of Continental Grain, the giant multinational corporation with offices in forty-four countries and more than $2.5-billion a year in revenues.

Michel Fribourg, the president of Continental, offered Palmby a job. Palmby has testified that he immediately told Fribourg he was not free to discuss the possibility so long as he held his current responsibilities.

Yet in late March, shortly before he was to leave for Moscow for the secret negotiations, Palmby made a trip to New York City, the headquarters of Continental Grain, and closed a deal on an expensive cooperative apartment. He gave Michel Fribourg as a reference.

On April 8 Palmby departed with the negotiating team for Moscow, still having told no one at the department of any plans to resign or of his contacts with Continental Grain.

Also on the trip besides Palmby and Butz was the general sales manager of the department's Export Marketing Service, Clifford G. Pulvermacher. Like Palmby, Pulvermacher was soon to leave government service. He would retire and take a job with the Bunge Corporation, another giant multinational grain company.

At the time of their departure for Moscow, Palmby was to testify later, he still had not made up his mind to go to work for Continental, even though he had bought an apartment in the company's headquarters city. He acknowledged that he had already decided to resign, but he said he had bought the apartment in New York with confidence that he could get a lucrative position with any one of several world-trade firms. He admitted that he never discussed a possibility of a position with anyone besides Continental.

Pulvermacher, in an affidavit to the Senate Permanent Subcommittee on Investigations, swore that he never discussed a position with Bunge until after the Moscow trip.

He said he had made his retirement plans known to his superiors much earlier.

An important issue that was soon to arise was how many clues the United States officials gathered, both in the trip to the Soviet Union and later, to the possibilities of massive sales of wheat and other grain. A related issue was the available data that was withheld from the public, and from farmers, who rely on government reports, and on the other hand how much information the grain companies were able to get from their friends in the Department of Agriculture.

During the talks in Moscow, Russian negotiators flatly rejected the credit terms that the American team offered—three years and the lowest legally possible interest rate, $6\frac{1}{8}$ per cent. Yet they were to return to the subject again and again, seeking more information on the terms offered.

There were several signs that the rejection in Moscow was not the Russians' final answer. Even before the Americans' departure on the trade mission, there were important clues. On February 9, 1972, the United States agricultural attaché in Moscow had reported that the Russian winter wheat crop had suffered severe damage.

The problem with the Russian crop was an inadequate snow cover and extremely cold temperatures that had resulted in severe winter kill. A good snow cover is important, not only to protect the wheat in the ground but also to provide moisture for spring-planted grain.

Again, on March 31, more than a week before the start of the trade mission, the agricultural attaché made a report on winter damage to the Russian crop. This time the news was worse. He reported that twenty-five million acres of winter wheat—an area nearly half as big as the entire United States wheat crop—had been killed by the severe Soviet winter. Furthermore, he reported, the low moisture

in the soil made conditions unfavorable for spring re-
planting.

While the American team was in the Soviet Union they
had a chance to confirm those conditions for themselves.
On a two-day tour through the Crimea, they found the
winter kill as severe and the soil as dry as reported.

In the past the members of the American mission might
have reasoned that the Russians would have an alternative
to buying abroad and certainly an alternative to buying
from the United States. As Agriculture Department officials have pointed out, the Soviet Union has had crop failures before and merely required its people to tighten
their belts.

But no one knowing the heavy reliance of Russians on
bread in their diet would suspect that they would accept
the deprivation indicated by a failure of the vast proportions threatened. Besides, the American mission knew that
the Russians had made a commitment to improve the diet
of their people and that, as part of that commitment, the
Soviet leaders had promised to increase the protein com-
ponent. To that end the Russians had begun developing
big livestock herds, which needed great quantities of grain.
The Russians normally use part of their wheat crop for
livestock feed, as do farmers in the United States.

In previous years, also, the Department of Agriculture
officials might have reasoned that the Russians could turn
elsewhere besides the United States for the grain they
needed to buy. But this time the experts knew that crop
failures in competitive nations had left the United States
with the only supplies large enough to provide the massive tonnages that the Russians would have to obtain
abroad.

All this the American officials were aware of—or at least
they should have known. Besides, the Russians were talking of large sums, discussing a $750-million line of credit

from the U. S. Government, with as much as $500-million of it available in any one year.

The Russian negotiators were playing a shrewd bluffing game when they sent the American team home with a flat "no" for an answer to the credit proposal. Yet some members of the United States delegation remained convinced that the Soviet Union would be importing American wheat, with or without credit terms. They knew the need and they were aware that the Russians had ample reserves of both currency and gold.

More enlightening information came soon after the officials returned to their posts in Washington. On April 24, the agricultural attaché in Moscow submitted a new report, this time advising of the possibility of a spring drought to follow the dry winter, a condition that was unfavorable even to the germination of spring-seeded crops. He told of unseasonably warm and dry weather in Moscow and gave indirect evidence of warm and dry conditions throughout major crop areas.

About two weeks later Soviet representatives paid a call on Clarence Palmby, then the Assistant Secretary of Agriculture. This time the extent of their interest was unmistakable—or should have been. They talked for an hour and a quarter, discussing credit terms, the possibility of a barter agreement and of buying grain directly from government-held stocks.

A government-to-government deal would have had at least three advantages. It would have given responsible officials a precise knowledge of what the Russians were receiving from U. S. stores; it would have saved over $300-million in subsidies that the Government was soon to pay to private grain companies, and it would have had a restraining influence on the price spiral that accompanied heavy buying from private stocks.

Palmby flatly turned down the direct-purchase proposal.

Whatever deal should be made, he said, purchases would have to be channeled through the private grain companies. In less than a month he was to join the company that made nearly half of the 1972 wheat sales to the Soviet Union and that gained proportionate shares of the subsidies and profits involved.

All this knowledge could have been enormously valuable to Continental or to the other grain companies. It could have been equally valuable to farmers if the Department of Agriculture had given them accurate information in the reports on which they base their decisions. Palmby carried that knowledge with him when he left office June 8, before the Russian grain deal was consummated, but after a big agreement had become one of the surest bets in history.

Palmby joined Continental as a vice president at a salary of $60,000 a year plus liberal bonuses. He has sworn that he passed none of his inside information on to his new employer. Certainly before he left neither he nor anyone else in the department let farmers know that they might be wise to expect better prices for their grain or advised them not to sell too cheaply. A May "Wheat Situation" report only cautioned farmers of the possibility—already an unlikelihood at that point—of a big "carryover" of surplus grain stocks after harvest and all possible sales.

Information continued to flow into the department, although it did not flow out of the department's offices so easily. On June 16, the agricultural attaché in Moscow, reporting on travels in the Ukraine and Moldavia, said he had found the spring grain crops poor to only fair. Ten days later he raised his estimate of the winter kill. He said about one-third—27 million acres—of the winter grain had been killed by the severe weather.

On July 5, in response to an urgent request, the attaché submitted an estimate that the Soviet grain crop would fall twenty million tons below production goals. The report was stamped "classified" and never released. Officials said later they had been skeptical because, despite all the indications of crop failure they had been receiving, the attaché's production estimate seemed low. It turned out to be higher than actual yields. When the department's top grain expert in Washington later gave a still lower estimate, the officials also stamped that "classified" and withheld that report from farmers and the general public.

The urgent request for new advice from the attaché in Moscow resulted from another piece of new information. On June 27, 1972, the department was notified that two teams of Russian grain experts were on their way to Washington. One was a group of negotiators that included the Soviet Minister of Foreign Trade, the other a group of specialists in grain buying. This too was information that was withheld from all except the grain companies, which did not need to be told.

On its arrival, the trading team set up a command post in Washington's Madison Hotel and began making telephone calls while the other group began negotiations with agriculture officials. One call went to Continental, another to Cargill.

At the time, Continental's president, Michel Fribourg, was on vacation in Spain after a business trip to Paris with two aides. One was Bernard Steinweg, his brother-in-law and senior vice president in charge of grain dealings, and the other was Gregoire Ziv, a Russian-born customer relations man. Cargill's vice president for grain sales and chief trader, W. B. Saunders, was away from his Minneapolis office. He was located in Chicago.

Steinweg and Ziv, who were still at work in Paris, immediately boarded a plane for the United States. They arrived in Washington on the evening of June 30, 1972, and immediately began talks with the Russian traders. They were asked for offers on four million tons of wheat and three million tons of corn, and next morning the Russians added a half-million tons to their request for a wheat offer.

For this, the biggest grain deal in history, Steinweg wanted help. He put through an urgent call to Europe asking Fribourg to interrupt his vacation and rush home. He then agreed to meet with the Russians again on Monday afternoon in New York.

The next day Saunders of Cargill arrived from Chicago. The visitors approached him in different fashion. The Russians used a classic strategy. They talked all day about corn, although what they wanted most was wheat. And although they knew they had a critical need, they temporized in their talks. At the end of the day, Saturday, July 1, the Russians closed the talks with a nonchalant dismissal of Saunders, the chief trader of one of the two biggest grain companies of the capitalist world and a controller of supplies that they vitally needed. What they said was, in effect: "Don't call us. We'll call you."

On Sunday, July 2, Continental's Gregoire Ziv arrived at the Madison Hotel and picked up members of the Russian trading team to take them on a sightseeing tour of the national capital. His next stop was at the Virginia home of Clarence Palmby, who by this time had left his Agriculture Department post.

Continental was as cool as the Russians, if Palmby's report can be credited. He said later that no business was discussed that day. He entertained the Russian traders at dinner in his home and went along on the sightseeing tour, he said, merely to help out his "old friend," Gregoire Ziv.

The next day, Monday, July 3, the Russian team moved to a plush suite in the New York Hilton Hotel, where they resumed talks with the Continental executives. Palmby also traveled to New York to sit in. He went as an observer only, he testified later in response to suggestions of a conflict of interest that might be involved in a trade role for a man who had dealt the Government's hand in initiating negotiations.

On through Independence Day the talks continued, and finally, on July 5, with handshakes and glasses of vodka, the traders toasted the biggest grain deal in history. With nothing more formal than a handclasp, the Russian traders had bought four million tons of wheat—nearly 150 million bushels—and 4.5 million tons of corn. They were still talking about another half-million tons of wheat, and before all the talking had ended Continental's total wheat sales to the Russians reached 5.5 million tons.

So far as the Continental executives knew, theirs might be the only deals that the Russians would make, and they were sworn to secrecy. They did not really need to be told the deal was to be kept secret, for secrecy was as vital to them as to the Russians. They did not have the grain they had sold. They still had to go into the domestic market and buy it. If word of their deal leaked out the grain they needed would become very expensive.

Still, Continental's traders showed far less uneasiness than anyone might have expected, considering that they were selling nearly a half-billion dollars' worth of grain that could, in response to no more than a rumor, cost them far more than their asking price. The reason for their strange confidence apparently lay in a meeting that took place in Washington on Monday morning, July 3, while the Russian traders were waiting to resume talks with Continental.

Negotiations were under way in the capital between the other Russian team—the government representatives—and officials of the Department of Agriculture. The United States side of the talks was led by Carroll G. Brunthaver, who had succeeded Palmby as Assistant Secretary of Agriculture. Like Palmby, Brunthaver had a background in the grain business, having served as an executive of a firm that was affiliated with Cook Industries.

In response to an urgent request, Brunthaver broke away from his other duties for a meeting with Bernard Steinweg, the senior vice president of Continental Grain. Steinweg was accompanied to Brunthaver's office by two other vice presidents of the company, James R. Good and Samuel H. Sabin.

As to what specifically happened in the meeting, there has been conflicting testimony, and a strange vagueness of memory developed on the part of Brunthaver, who kept no logs either of the session or of subsequent phone calls.

On some points, however, there is no disagreement. Steinweg asked for assurance that the Agriculture Department would continue to subsidize exports of wheat. Under long-standing policy, the department had been paying the difference between the world price of wheat—then $1.63 to $1.65 a bushel—and higher prices that exporters might have to pay to acquire the grain they contracted to ship. At the time they were paying over $1.70 a bushel to buy wheat for export and the subsidy rate to enable them to sell abroad for less was 11 cents a bushel. The domestic price would spurt within seven weeks to more than $2 a bushel, and the Government would be obligated to pay 47 cents of it.

Brunthaver did not provide Steinweg with an immediate answer but later, in a telephone call, gave him the assurance that he sought. It was a can't-lose guarantee. Continental could then, alone, sell nearly one-eighth of the American wheat crop with little fear of losing money when it went into the market to buy. The subsidy, in fact, gave a guaranteed profit.

From that point on, the stories diverged. In later testimony both Secretary Earl Butz and Assistant Secretary Brunthaver swore that at the time of the deals neither had any idea how much wheat the grain companies were selling to the Russians. Butz, in fact, told a House subcommittee at a hearing on September 14, two months after Brunthaver's meeting with Steinweg and the two other grain company executives:

"We have been scrupulously careful not to converse with the private trade and they with us. . . . They have been scrupulously careful with us and with each other not to converse with us about this."

At the hearing, on the same day, there was this exchange between Brunthaver and Graham Purcell, then a Democratic Representative from Texas:

Purcell: You don't know how much Continental sold?

Brunthaver: No I do not.

Purcell: You don't have any idea which company sold how much of the grain?

Brunthaver: That is correct.

A quite different account came from Steinweg, Good and Sabin, the Continental Grain vice presidents, who described their meeting with Brunthaver to the Senate Permanent Subcommittee on Investigations in sworn testimony and affidavits on July 20, 1973. Steinweg testified:

"So it was that I met Mr. Brunthaver on July 3 [1972]. I told him we had been contacted by the Russians, told him the specific amounts of wheat they wished to purchase from us. . . . On July 6, I spoke with Mr. Brunthaver by telephone and told him that we had consummated the sale for four million tons of milling wheat and were still negotiating the durum wheat sale."

That testimony was supported in the affidavits of Good and Sabin, the other Continental executives who attended the July 3, 1972, meeting with Brunthaver.

In response to questioning, Steinweg asserted: "We did not ask the department to keep it secret." There is little doubt, however, that he felt confident the department would keep quiet about the company's information.

Steinweg was followed to the witness chair by Brunthaver, who swore: "I do not recall receiving any such information and have reason to doubt that it was ever communicated to me."

Five days after the Continental officials' visit with Brunthaver, on July 8, the United States and the Soviet Union jointly announced, with great fanfare, a $750-million credit arrangement. In a news briefing, Secretary Butz talked mainly about corn and told reporters that the Russians "have plenty of wheat for now." That was after all the reports the department had received of wheat distress in the Soviet Union and only two days, according to the Steinweg testimony, after Brunthaver had received confirmation of the biggest wheat deal in history.

In subsequent days, the Russian traders closed big wheat contracts with five other grain companies. Officials of three of them—Cargill, Bunge and Dreyfus—gave the Senate investigations subcommittee affidavits saying they, too, had asked for assurance on continued subsidies and had told Brunthaver and an aide of discussions on "large" wheat deals.

No knowledgeable observers could see how Brunthaver or anyone else in the Department of Agriculture could have given assurance of subsidies to the grain companies without demanding some knowledge of how much wheat was going out of the country and how much they were guaranteeing to subsidize.

By August 4 the Russian team had finished their secret deals, after a trip home during which they apparently found the crop news worse than ever. At that point they had quietly cornered more than eleven million tons of American wheat—one-fourth of the United States crop.

In an August "Wheat Situation" report, the Department of Agriculture told farmers: "There are indications that Soviet wheat purchases could easily exceed 65 million bushels." That was less than half what Continental alone had sold early in July, when, according to Steinweg's testimony, the department, through Brunthaver, was so informed.

In theory, at least, the Soviet traders could have bought up the entire U. S. grain supply and left the American consumer holding the bag. As it was, the impact on the consumer has been serious enough. Yet the Agriculture Department officials who were responsible for orderly management of grain exports were doing nothing to assess the volume of the outflow or the possible consequences. They were doing little besides standing on the sidelines and cheering while they promised to continue to pour out tax dollars to subsidize what turned out to be a gigantic raid on the American economy.

Also while all this was going on, American farmers were harvesting their wheat and selling much of it off at what turned out to be bargain prices. While the Russians were buying up wheat, Secretary Butz was going around the country talking about corn sales. He and other officials at the department seemed more concerned about guarding the big grain corporations' secrets than meeting their responsibilties to protect the interests of farmers and consumers.

As late as August 8, when it was clear that the Russians had been buying on a massive scale, the department was still withholding from farmers information that could be important as an aid in making decisions that would be vital to their economic interests. The department stamped "classified" a reassessment of Russian needs by its top expert, an economist named Fletcher Pope. Pope estimated that the Russian crop had fallen ten million tons shorter than previously supposed.

About halfway through this period a mystery element entered the plot. It was brought in by a strange voice that began calling from London to talk with the editor of a trade publication in Kansas City. The caller identified himself as John Smith and said he was a reporter for the *Financial Times* of London. He never explained why he was calling.

As it turned out, however, he was passing along extremely accurate news on the Russians' trading. It was information that he could hardly have gotten anywhere else except from the Russians themselves.

"John Smith" made his first call to Morton I. Sosland, editor of *Milling & Baking News,* on July 15, offering a "scoop." At that point, he said, the Russians had bought five million tons of wheat. Actually, when the Russians returned to Moscow six days later they had bought seven and a half million tons, much of it after Smith's first call. But even the five million tons that the mysterious caller reported seemed too massive for the Kansas City editor to believe.

On July 31, the day the Russian trading team returned to New York from Moscow, "Smith" called Sosland again to report that fact. Meanwhile, Sosland was checking on his caller's reports.

By August 2, the editor had verified enough information to publish a story in his trade paper, which is considered the "bible" of the grain business. He wrote that the Russians had bought seven million tons of United States wheat and were planning to buy more. Actually, the Russians had already cornered most of their eleven million tons, but the figure that Sosland reported was sufficiently large to throw the grain markets into turmoil.

On the day when Sosland published his report, wheat jumped 8 cents a bushel, and in the next four days it spurted from $1.80 a bushel to $2.05. It would keep climbing, eventually in early 1973 passing the historic record of $5.00 a bushel.

Sosland, naturally curious about his mysterious caller, had begun checking. The *Financial Times* of London told him there was no reporter named John Smith on its staff, but it too had been getting mysterious calls with the same sort of information that Sosland had been receiving. The *Financial Times*'s caller had identified himself as an East German named Veovosky. By August 7, when Smith called again, Sosland was prepared to confront him with the results of his checking. Smith blithely admitted the imposture and then told Sosland that he was really operating in a "secret information office."

There was one more call from Smith, on August 10. That time, once more accurately, he reported that the Chinese were about to buy American grain.

Sosland did some further checking. He recalled that his John Smith would often address the editor as Mr. Morton Sosland, using both the given and the surname, not just Mr. Sosland. Checking with linguists, Sosland was told that such a characteristic was peculiar to Russian speech patterns.

That fact led John Fialka, a Washington *Star* reporter, to wonder in an installment of a four-part series on the grain deal:

"Could the Russians, as a final finesse of our marketing system, have financed part of their purchase by speculating in wheat futures in U. S. commodity markets?"

Certainly that would have been easy enough for the Russian traders to do, operating through some third party such as the Swiss-owned Garnac Grain Company. The logic of the theory is almost inescapable, for the Russians were the only ones who knew enough about the scope of the deals they had made to gauge their effect on the commodity markets.

When Fialka asked Brunthaver about that, he was told

that the department had been checking and could not confirm his theory. But then again it could not be ruled out. At least one broker had queried the department about the legality of representing the Soviet Union in buying and selling of grain futures. He had been told there was no legal barrier.

Sosland, however, scoffed at the idea. What the Russians could have made in the futures market would not have made a dent in the bill for their grain purchase—a total of $1-billion. Besides, he said, it would have been a drop in the bucket beside what they had gained in their raid on the American economy.

Consider these elements, he said: First, the Russians cornered eleven million tons, one-fourth of the U. S. wheat crop, at what turned out to be bargain-basement prices. Half of that they bought with their line of credit rather than paying cash. Shortly afterward the dollar was devalued. Meanwhile gold, which the Russians have in large supply, was climbing and within a year reached a peak about twice as high as its dollar value when the Russians were making their deals.

Those developments meant that the Soviet Union could pay off its debt for bargain-priced grain, incurred when the dollar was worth a good deal more, either with dollars that could be acquired cheaply or with half the amount of gold they would have had to use to pay for the grain when they were buying it.

The effect on the American economy, however, was far more serious than the relative profitability of the deal itself or the fact that the Russian traders outfoxed both the grain companies and the United States officials.

The first effect was felt by farmers. Those who sold out to the grain dealers early, before the impact of the Soviet buying became evident, found themselves double losers. First, they lost the possible benefits of a rising market, and next they found themselves losers again when the Government computed subsidies that were due them.

Farmers' wheat subsidies at the time were based on an artificial concept of "parity," a price level considered fair to growers in relation to the cost of the things they have to buy. What they were getting as a subsidy was the difference between parity and the average market price over a five-month period. The five-month period used was July through November.

The higher the market rose during that period of spurting prices, after most farmers in the Southwest had already sold out, the lower their subsidy would be. The farmers' lost benefits, in terms of the subsidy, have been estimated at more than $55-million.

When they discovered how they had been taken, the farmers turned their anger on the officials in the grain offices at the Department of Agriculture, who have a duty to keep farmers informed of market conditions. Those officials, in self-defense, pretended a nearly impossible degree of ignorance.

Brunthaver, Assistant Secretary of Agriculture, and the other grain-export officials had the authority to require from the grain companies the information they needed to protect farmers and the public interest. If they did not have that information, congressional investigators began asking, why didn't they demand it? It never became clear just how much they did know, but it was obvious that they had not been using what information they certainly must have had to meet their own responsibilities effectively.

As summer dwindled toward fall and farmers' subsidies continued to decline, the subsidies for the grain companies soared. Whenever market prices moved higher, so did the subsidies needed to permit the grain dealers to make a profit at the $1.65 for which they had sold wheat that many were still having to buy. By August 5 the export subsidy was up to 21 cents a bushel. Four days later it had jumped 10 cents, to 31 cents a bushel, and two weeks afterward it was up to 38 cents.

Public clamor grew to an uproar as the subsidies to the grain dealers mounted into hundreds of millions of dollars. Finally, the outcry was heard at the White House, and the Department of Agriculture officials began to sense discontent in the Office of Management and Budget over their generosity. They realized that something had to be done.

Much of the public clamor focused on regulations, established by the department's officials, that gave wide latitude for profiteering to the grain companies. All any company had to do to record a claim for a subsidy was to tell the department that a sale had been made. They did not need to provide proof or even to name the date when it was made.

Whatever the actual date of the sale, or the date of purchases by exporters to cover their sales commitments, the subsidy that the grain company would get would be the payment that was in effect on the date of the filing of the claim. Since prices—and therefore the subsidies—were rising, it was to the advantage of the grain companies to hold back their filing of claims in expectation of later windfalls.

The extent of their profiteering became evident in one big week between August 25 and September 1. The developing crisis had brought the department's managers to the point of panic by August 24, when a series of phone calls were made that became one of the most controversial episodes of the whole mismanaged business.

To Assistant Secretary Brunthaver and other Agriculture Department officials it had become obvious that they had let the drain on United States supplies go beyond the point of wisdom and that the costs had gotten out of hand. They realized that they would soon have to back away from their promise to continue following a rising grain market with continually increasing subsidies. Brunthaver ordered calls made to the six biggest grain companies.

Charles W. Pence, director of the grain division of the Export Marketing Service, began making the calls on the morning of August 24. He testified later that he told officials of the companies—Continental, Cargill, Bunge, Cook, Dreyfus and Garnac—two things. He said he informed them that as of the close of business the previous day they could no longer count on the Government, through subsidies, to keep the world price of wheat down at $1.65 a bushel and that there would be a meeting on a change in policy next day in Brunthaver's office. The six big companies were invited to send top executives.

The next day, August 25, the day of the meeting in Brunthaver's office, the Department of Agriculture announced that for one week the grain companies would be allowed to continue to file for subsidies on the old basis, on sales made by the end of the day of August 24 or earlier. That was an extra day beyond the cutoff that Pence said he had passed out in his telephone calls. There was one other important change. For that one big week, the subsidy would be 47 cents a bushel, up from the 38 cents that was in effect the previous week.

There were widespread suspicions that Pence might have passed out much more information in those telephone calls than he acknowledged. If he told the grain companies that the cutoff date would be the end of the day of his phone calls, there was still time for them to get busy and close some more sales. If he told them that for the next week the plan was to increase the subsidies, they would have had all the more incentive to try to pick up more of the windfalls. All the officials involved, however, have denied that he could have given such information. The decision to add an extra day and to raise the subsidy rate was only made after he had called his friends at the grain companies, they said.

Brunthaver, however, denied at one point any knowledge of Pence's phone calls, although they were made on his orders. When confronted by Representative Melcher at a hearing with evidence of the calls he finally acknowledged that he had ordered them. What he had not known, he said, was that Pence was the man making the calls. His first denial could have been merely a lapse of memory, but it seemed curious to many that Brunthaver, when questioned, would not have somehow connected the calls that Pence had made with the calls that he had ordered.

Whatever may be the case, the next week was to provide windfalls enough for the big grain companies. It was also to show how they had been riding the market upward, holding back their filings for subsidies on earlier sales until they could get the biggest possible handout from the Treasury.

In that one week they collected nearly half of the more than $300-million that the Department of Agriculture paid in support of the grain deal, subsidies that in reality were a gift to the Russians. They were receiving, for $1.65 a bushel, wheat that was costing exporters over $2.10, with U. S. taxpayers making up the difference. The extent of the administrators' mismanagement became clear later when the General Accounting Office, in an investigation, found that the department's officials had known all the time that subsidies were unnecessary to make it possible to sell grain to the Soviet Union.

They had been advised in urgent messages from other major grain-producing nations that the United States was the only country with enough supplies to meet the Russians' needs. There was no reason, therefore, why this country should not have got a fair market price for its shipments and no reason to pour out taxpayers' money to provide bargain rates on American wheat for the Soviet Union.

The subsidies were necessary, however, if the administrators were to give their friends the grain dealers an ironclad assurance of a profit rather than letting them take their chances in the marketplace, as other businessmen must do.

The $128-million in subsidies paid out in that one big week included such staggering sums to individual companies as the $41.5-million that went to Continental and $39.4-million for Dreyfus, a French-owned company. Garnac, the Swiss-owned company, and Bunge, owned by an Argentinian conglomerate, seemed pikers in comparison, with their receipts from the United States Treasury of $16-million and $10.6-million during that week.

Of more than $13-million booked for subsidies by Cargill that week, over $600,000 represented unfounded claims, most of them filed in an attempt to collect a payment on wheat for which it had waived subsidies to a third party, the Office of the Inspector General found in an investigation. In the same type of effort, Continental's claims totaled $789,600 more than the company was entitled to, the investigators reported. Excessive claims by Dreyfus totaled $623,854.

But all those figures seemed like pittances in comparison with other costs of the Russian wheat deal to the American economy.

The Soviet traders were not finished with their tough bargaining when they bought the last of their eleven million tons of wheat, on August 2. The next stage was to negotiate on how the grain would be shipped, and that was not settled until late November. The agreement finally reached then seemed to be one that could have been settled in August. It provided that one-third of the grain would be carried in Russian ships, one-third in American and one-third in vessels of other countries. The arrangement was a compromise designed to satisfy American shipping interests.

It is unlikely that there was pernicious intent behind the delay, but it did show a failure to perceive the urgency of an early start in moving the massive amounts of grain involved, and the results were disastrous. The mountains of grain sold to the Russians were thrown suddenly on an American transportation system that was ill equipped to handle them. The settlement came as corn harvests were under way and had to be moved and just before the Mississippi River, a major grain artery, became locked in its winter freeze. All the Russian grain, in addition to normal harvests, was thrown at once onto the railroads.

Suddenly, as the managers might have foreseen and the railroads themselves had warned, all ports became clogged with rail cars waiting to discharge their cargoes. And because the rail cars needed were sitting in idle paralysis at ports and terminals, back-country warehouses could not move the grain that they had already bought. With business at a standstill, their operators had to borrow ever more money, and the strain on bank credit raised interest rates.

Meanwhile, because those country warehouses were full, farmers who were reading about record prices at terminals found themselves unable to move their crops at any price. What was worse, they soon found, the rail tie-up was hampering delivery of feeds for livestock and fuels and fertilizers for the next year's crops.

Normally, part of the wheat crop is used as feed for livestock. But in 1972, because of the record wheat prices, no one could afford to feed wheat to cattle and hogs. The result was a new pressure on corn and other feed grains, and those too began escalating. Farmers who might have expanded their cattle- and hog-feeding operations held back, unwilling to take the risk of pouring costly grain into troughs in the uncertain hope of a future profit on meat.

All those and other problems, including an unusually severe winter, caused one of the worst peacetime periods of inflation the United States had ever known. All grocery prices soared, but meat prices shot skyward. The inflation soon led to the second devaluation of the dollar in a little over a year, and devaluation, in turn, fueled further inflation.

The Russian wheat deal, of course, was not responsible for all of the inflation, but a report by an economist, prepared for the staff of the House Agriculture Committee, indicated that higher food prices directly attributable to the deal and the way it was handled amounted to about $3-billion a year.

That, obviously, is a high price to pay for the risk of empty warehouses and dependence on the vicissitudes of weather for the next year's food. As luck would have it, the worst floods in history struck the Mississippi valley just before planting time. And until late spring no one knew whether there was a chance for crops big enough to replenish the nation's depleted supplies.

The crunch came in the summer of 1973. Suddenly, with food prices still soaring, administrators at the Department of Agriculture made the discovery that this country had sold more grain than it had available. Only a belated move to embargo soybean shipments prevented a food crisis of historic proportions.

Among all those problems, there seemed little besides the weather that could not be ascribed to the cozy relationship between Department of Agriculture officials and their friends in the grain industry.

Just as such disastrous results were becoming evident, a member of the Russian Embassy in Washington approached a staff member of the House Agriculture Committee, urging him to help quiet criticism and suggesting that efforts toward moderation would prove worthwhile to him in the future.

"This deal," the Soviet diplomat insisted, "has been good for both our countries."

XVII
Of Milk and Money

While the grain companies, like other powerful segments of the food industry, have their friends and former associates in positions to protect their interests at the Department of Agriculture, all of them have men in key places elsewhere in government. They operate in Congress and inside the White House as well, backed up by bottomless funds with which to buy favors and enhance their influence, much of it passed under tables.

Men borrowed from the grain companies often represent the President and, ostensibly, the public interest in foreign trade negotiations. Others have their men more strategically placed. Procter & Gamble, a conglomerate with vast interests in food, lent Richard Nixon its chief lobbyist, Bryce Harlow, to help run interference in Congress. The company received in return an administrative assistant of Presidents Kennedy and Johnson to aid its Washington lobbying office.

But not even the International Telephone and Telegraph Corporation, which managed to get its message to the President through such high offices as the Attorney General and the Vice President, could compare with the pervasive influence of a dairy lobby that represents one of the broadest reaches of power in the food industry. Its purchases of political decisions and influence have been documented through court cases as well as through exposures resulting from scandals of the 1972 Presidential campaign, that dirtiest of all episodes ever studied by the Fair Campaign Practices Committee.

This dairy lobby, representing milk-farm cooperatives, is the outgrowth of a long fight begun in the days of the Depression when milk producers were totally at the mercy of the processing companies that bought their output. Congress then passed laws to try to provide farmers a counterbalancing weight by allowing them to form cooperatives and by exempting them from provisions of antitrust laws. Now the balance has tipped to the other side. Giant co-ops control vast proportions of food supplies.

There are several like Sunkist, which includes big corporations among its members and which has a near-monopoly on California's citrus crops. But none have been so successful in their grasp and use of power as the milk co-ops, which technically are owned by their farmer-members but operate in autocratic fashion. They have become giant combines like Associated Milk Producers, Inc., which controls the sale of milk to processors in broad sections of twenty Midwestern states. AMPI, as it is usually called, also has close working relationships with other giant combines, such as Mid-America Dairymen, Inc., and Dairymen, Inc.

All the big milk co-ops, accounting for 75 percent of the nation's milk production, are also joined under the umbrella of the National Milk Producers Federation, which helps apply their political pressures in Washington.

And now the individual dairymen are once more at the mercy of a powerful industry, for the co-ops have become big business. The co-op managements control the dairy farmers' affairs in a more dictatorial manner even than the giant conglomerates. They flood markets when small groups of producers attempt to retain their independence and ride roughshod over internal opposition. The co-ops even levy assessments on the incomes of farmer members to build political war chests for support of favored candidates and policies.

Nor have they been stingy or partisan in their favors. Their aid has gone to both political parties and even to opposing candidates for the same office. With more than $2-million on which to operate for the 1972 campaign, the dairy co-ops spread their favors far and wide, but the biggest flow was traced through a number of dummy committees to the campaign of Richard M. Nixon.

The money was not wasted. It bought the co-ops a decision that has increased their incomes by more than $500-million a year, paid directly or indirectly by consumers, according to their own estimates.

The episode began when Secretary of Agriculture Clifford M. Hardin, on March 12, 1971, under pressure from consumers and others, denied demands by the milk co-ops for an increase in price supports. Those price supports apply only to milk that is used in processing of cheese and other manufactured products, but they form a base from which higher-grade, bottled milk can rise. In 1973 the support price exceeded five dollars a hundredweight of milk.

Hardin gave what sounded like a plausible reason for his action. He said that an increase in price supports would lead to overproduction and that in turn would actually reduce prices paid to farmers while increasing government costs of buying surplus milk.

"They [the milk producers] know from past experience that they do not benefit when dairy production substantially exceeds demand and excessive surpluses pile up in government warehouses," Hardin said. "We must avoid this."

But the milk lobby was not buying that argument. They were already in the market for another decision and they had already made substantial investments. They turned first to Congress and then to the White House with promises of still bigger outlays for the campaign to come.

The friends of the dairy co-ops in Congress, previous recipients of money raised by levies on farmers, now moved in behind a bill that would require Hardin to reverse his decision and raise price supports. Associated Milk Producers, Inc., even wrote the legislation that was to be introduced.

There were many powerful members of Congress in the group. They included the Speaker of the House, Carl Albert, and the chairman of the House Agriculture Committee, W. R. Poage. The dairymen had spent $2,000 on a testimonial dinner for Albert but much more for Poage during the 1970 campaign. The aid to Poage included $5,000 in campaign contributions and $11,500 for a testimonial dinner. Neither man had any opposition in that campaign.

Among other contributions from the dairy co-ops, there had been $10,625 for Senator Hubert H. Humphrey and $7,132 for Senator Edmund Muskie, both of them prospects to run against Nixon for the Presidency. Senator Harold Hughes, another Presidential possibility, had received $5,000 and Senator Gale McGee $2,000. These men were all members of the Democratic majority in Congress, but Representative Page Belcher of Oklahoma, a Republican, also got $5,000.

All those prominent Congressmen could now be called on to return past favors, and they responded. They backed the legislation. By that time the milk lobby had also got to the White House. On March 23, 1971, sixteen leaders including officials of AMPI, Dairymen, Inc., and Mid-America Dairymen, Inc., spent an hour with the President —more time than he often allowed to heads of state.

The next day, March 24, five committees of the President's party received the first installment on nearly a half-million dollars that would be spent by the milk lobby to support the Nixon campaign.

When Hardin, on March 25, less than two weeks after his negative decision, reversed himself and gave the dairy lobby the milk-price increase it had been demanding, there were many observers who thought he had merely crumbled under congressional pressures. He lamely cited new evidence of rising production costs and made no reference to his previous argument against the action.

The new evidence available to him, however, was word of the political gifts rather than a sudden rise in production costs.

The first installment was $25,000, but the additional money was not long in coming. On April 5 there was $45,000 more, split among nine committees.

Other similar contributions followed in regular procession, but as they went along the co-op officials became steadily more sophisticated in disguising the route of their contributions. The money was split and parceled out in small but regular portions to a variety of seemingly unaffiliated committees.

There were names like Americans Dedicated to Greater Public Awareness, Americans United for Better Federal Administration, Citizens for More Effective Community Involvement, Americans United for Sensible Agricultural Policy, Association for Fair Press Reporting and Americans United for Objective Reporting.

The committees were not merely a means for disguising the contributions. They were also a device to dodge the strictures of the Corrupt Practices Act of 1925, which made it illegal to contribute more than $5,000 to any one recipient.

The lobby was less circumspect, however, in some of its contributions to the Nixon campaign. One big gift of $50,000 was traced by the General Accounting Office to the Lehigh Valley Cooperative Farmers although the contribution was never reported. The money, in hundred-dollar bills, was turned over to a secret fund that was later used to buy the silence of conspirators in the Watergate political espionage scandal. It was among $422,500 in milk-lobby gifts that have thus far been identified as going into the Nixon campaign.

The direct link between the political contributions and the milk-price decision has been acknowledged in letters by an official of AMPI, who explained merely that this was a recognition of reality—the way things get done in Washington. It was also among peripheral findings of investigators looking into the Watergate scandal.

The thoroughly documented accounts of this dark succession of favorable economic decisions—there were subsequent additional increases in milk-price supports preceded by political gifts—have both a prologue and a sequel. For Nixon was not the first President to grant favors to the milk lobby nor were the Congressmen of 1971 the first to demand them.

A previously undisclosed instance of a similar episode recounted to this writer by one of the officials involved also traced pressures from the office of a powerful Congressman through the White House and back to the Department of Agriculture. The account has since been confirmed confidentially by one of the highest aides to then Secretary Orville L. Freeman.

The time was 1967 and then, also, the milk co-ops wanted an increase in price supports, but they were meeting resistance at the Agriculture Department. However, a representative of the co-ops, David Parr, was a good friend and supporter of Wilbur Mills, one of the most influential members of Congress as chairman of the House Ways and Means Committee. Parr was also one of the $1,000 contributors to the President's Club.

Parr, along with Harold Nelson, who was to become general manager of AMPI, visited Mills and told him about their problem. At about that same time President Johnson was also trying to work his famous persuasion on Mills.

Johnson was concerned about inflation and he thought a tax surcharge was needed to slow it down. Mills, as head of the tax-writing Ways and Means Committee, was the man most able to get the job done for him. Mills told the President a budget cut was needed. Mills also informed Johnson about problems of his friends, the officials of the milk co-ops.

The White House, in turn, passed that information on to the Department of Agriculture. Mills, meanwhile, sent the two milk spokesmen to the department, where they saw George Mehren, then an assistant secretary of agriculture, and his deputy, Rodney Leonard. A series of discussions followed, sometimes in the Department of Agriculture and sometimes in Mills's office, under the watchful eye of the Congressman.

Leonard was the top man for the department's staff studies that were required to justify any change in milk-price supports, and he continued to maintain throughout the discussions that no increase could be justified. He held to that position even when he was called in and pressed by Secretary Freeman.

Leonard was troubled, sources close to the discussions say, because he was apparently making an inevitable decision more difficult for Freeman, who indicated that pressure for an increase in the support price was coming from the White House. Leonard stuck to his guns. Eventually he was overruled and Freeman approved the increase, despite Leonard's figures showing none was justified.

Ironically, the same George Mehren, the assistant secretary on the Government side of those discussions, was eventually to become the top official at AMPI, one of the biggest forces on the dairy industry's side.

The sequel to the political dealings of the campaigns of 1970 and 1972 came early in 1973, when the Senate Agriculture Committee was considering a new farm bill. Nearly all the members of the Senate committee had been recipients of contributions from the co-ops.

It was thus in an atmosphere of friendliness nurtured by past favors on each side that the National Milk Producers Federation sought some changes in farm law. They wrote several amendments and presented them for the Senators' consideration. Many of the changes were highly technical, but their effect was to increase the co-ops' control over milk supplies.

The Senators on the committee adopted most of the proposals almost verbatim, without an opposing vote, although many of them acknowledged later that they had not understood the provisions.

Not so agreeable, however, were the National Farmers Organization, which tries to represent farmers in the sale of milk, and the Justice Department. Both had filed suits against the co-ops on antitrust grounds.

Assistant Attorney General Thomas E. Kauper protested that Justice had been denied an opportunity to testify on the effects of the changes.

One provision of the bill would permit farmers in areas of scarcity to maintain high prices by paying farmers in surplus areas to withhold shipments. The overall effect, Kauper said, would be to increase the monopolistic power of the co-ops and raise consumer prices. Had the amendments succeeded, they would have provided a generous return on past milk-lobby favors to the senators.

After public exposure and wide protests, however, the co-ops' maneuver failed to gain their objective in the final form of the agriculture bill that emerged from Congress.

XVIII
The Laboratory Invasion

While agribusiness has been making good deals for itself by placing its friends and associates in high places and winning favors with its political gifts, it has also seized one of the world's best bargains by buying and burrowing its way into the Government's agricultural research establishment. That entity consists of the Federal Government's Agricultural Research Service, administrators in Washington, the land-grant universities that they deal with, and associated experiment stations.

The land-grant university system, the principal segment of the agricultural research establishment, was originally established to promote the well-being of consumers as well as farmers and other rural people. Today it appears to have been torn away from its roots by the enticements of big conglomerates, agribusiness corporations and the retail chains.

Agribusiness executives dominate advisory committees that set research goals for the agricultural colleges of the system, and agribusiness corporations bid for the attention

214

of its researchers and professors with handsome consulting fees and appointments to boards of directors.

Meanwhile, the corporations rivet the attention of the researchers on projects that serve agribusiness interests, and from the seeds of relatively small grants they reap the profits of publicly financed research.

While the nation's small towns and rural villages wither, tax-paid agricultural researchers work on systems that will help agribusiness sweep away the remaining rural families and turn the countryside into vast factories in the fields. While ecologists worry about the environment, the researchers at the land-grant universities focus on ever more deadly pesticides. They breed vegetables for survival in mechanical harvesters rather than for taste and food value. And they develop hormones to promote livestock profits with no recorded advance research into attributes that might be harmful to health, as the notorious cancer-causing DES turned out to be.

If all that seems difficult to accept, one need only ask the men who have been through the system. Many have testified before congressional committees to the distortions of priorities. And one of the most knowledgeable men produced by the system, a former administrator at one of the top land-grant universities who is now a research official at the Department of Agriculture, said in an interview:

"Well, that's all true. But I don't think it's the result of some vast conspiracy. I think it's just that agricultural research and researchers lack a sense of direction. Agribusiness steps into the vacuum and pushes. I think, also, that there is simply a common point of view between agribusiness and the men turned out by the land-grant system."

Farm groups and consumer leaders had long been aware that the agricultural colleges and the research stations had been diverted from their primary goals. Men like Oren Lee Staley, president of the National Farmers Organization, and Tony Dechant, president of the National Farmers Union, had publicly charged that the institutions were more concerned with development of factory-style production for agribusiness than with the plight of rural people or the consumers' welfare.

But it remained for James Hightower and a task force of eleven researchers to document the full extent of the distortions. In their year-long effort for the Agribusiness Accountability Project, a Washington-based public-interest research group, they found exorbitant social costs, a way of life under attack and the purity as well as the quality of food threatened. Hightower wrote of their findings in a book-length report, "Hard Tomatoes, Hard Times."

The problems, as they frequently do, start in the Department of Agriculture in Washington. They begin with the way the research budget is drawn, for that action sets the priorities.

The final recommendations on the research budget are made by officials of the department, the states and the land-grant institutions, but those administrators are advised on an official basis by a group called the National Agricultural Research Advisory Committee.

In 1971, the investigating team found, the committee was dominated by representatives of agribusiness, including the Del Monte Corporation, the Crown Zellerbach Corporation and Peavey Company Flour Mills. In addition, there were representatives from Agway, a diversified co-op that sells many farmers most of their needs; the Nutrition Foundation, which does research—often of a promotional nature—sponsored by food-processing companies, and the American Farm Bureau Federation, which purports to be a farm organization but which, investigations have shown, is a conglomerate that sells to farmers and others rather than serving them. It generally espouses big-business causes, often in opposition to the interests of farmers.

Another strong Washington influence on research at the agricultural institutions is the National Association of Universities and Land Grant Colleges. The organization is an inbred group that endorses the agribusiness approach.

The association's point of view comes naturally. In 1970 its budget was $394,349. Of that, $277,335 came from membership dues. Most of the other money needed— $93,500—came from grants by the Ford Motor Company Fund, Olin Corporation Charitable Fund, U. S. Steel Foundation, Sears Roebuck Foundation, Burlington Industries Foundation, International Business Machines Corporation and the W. K. Kellogg Foundation.

When the agricultural research budget goes to congressional committees for hearings, the chief voices heard are those of Department of Agriculture officials and the National Association of State Universities and Land Grant Colleges. "Public" witness lists are crowded by representatives of corporations that have already applied their influence to the drafting of the research budgets.

But those corporations do their most influential work on the campuses. Their officials are prominent on the membership lists of advisory committees that determine research priorities for the individual agricultural colleges, and, through their ties with divisions of the colleges, they propose specific projects that will be undertaken. They cement those ties with money.

A small investment goes a long way, for the basic funding of the research, including the payment of salaries, is taken care of by tax money. All agribusiness normally needs to get projects started is a little seed money—and that is tax-deductible.

The public-interest task force found the research at

three representative universities—the University of Florida, North Carolina State and Purdue—was promoted by such agribusiness giants as American Cyanamid, Chemagro, Chevron, Dow Chemical, Eli Lilly, Geigy, FMC-Niagara, IMC Corporation, Shell, Stauffer, Union Carbide and the Upjohn Company.

The individual grants were not large but they bought a lot of value, for the projects were usually closely related to the company's specific needs, and they were often designed for testing the company's proprietary products. Chemagro, for example, with a grant of only $500, was able to have university researchers test an experimental pesticide called Chemagro 7375.

Tests of such proprietary products at universities gives them a credibility that they would not otherwise have. The Texas A & M University, for example, helped Union Carbide develop Temik, an insecticide that was later described by an expert as one of the most lethal poisons ever developed for general use in the United States. And, although an A & M entomologist protested his university's role in developing a poison that was not safe for use even in a university laboratory, the pesticide was later cited before the Senate agricultural appropriations subcommittee as one of the praiseworthy products of university research.

The corporations often become heirs to the benefits of university research even without the necessity of a grant. Such was the case in the research that gave the nation—and Eli Lilly, the drug company—diethylstilbestrol and its inherent threat of cancer.

The product, known as DES, a growth-promoting hormone for livestock, was produced with tax funds by Iowa State University but it was still licensed to the university's old friend, Eli Lilly, without competitive bidding. It was a publicly funded product that netted the drug company tens of millions of dollars before the Food and Drug Administration, after long soul-searching, finally forced it off the market because of its cancer-causing potential.

The agricultural research establishment decided in 1966 to review its activities and priorities. As might be expected, it was an in-house job, led by Agriculture Department and land-grant college administrators. There were technical panels to aid them, but, of sixteen outsiders on the five panels, twelve came from agribusiness. Predictably, there was no revolution in research functions or priorities.

In January, 1973, a long article in *Science* magazine described the national scientific community's contempt for the sort of research conducted by the agricultural establishment. The reasons were similar to the case that had been documented by Hightower's task force.

In the face of great needs for protection of the consumer and for aid to struggling family farms and the rural poor, the task force found many researchers at the universities working on projects that were merely absurd.

Cornell University, for example, worked seriously on a project to determine how hard to squeeze a grapefruit to check firmness and texture. Cornell also—with a grant from Superior Pet Products, Inc.—conducted studies on methods of cleaning dogs' teeth.

Meanwhile, the Agricultural Research Service was working on more direct benefits for agribusiness. The agency, a division of the Department of Agriculture through which hundreds of millions of dollars of tax funds are channeled, had one project aimed at developing a computerized checkout system for supermarkets. Another project was perfecting a method of removing tomatoes' natural wax and thus making canning easier for food-processing companies. Other researchers were developing a mechanical unloading device for poultry processors.

As if this were not enough, the Agricultural Research

Service was also paying money directly to corporations to help them improve their processes. The agency handed out grants including $149,850 to General Mills for work on the treatment of industrial and municipal waste waters; $200,000 to B. F. Goodrich for studies of starch-reinforced rubber and $89,000 to Ralston-Purina for "limited commercial-scale preparation of cottonseed protein isolates." Other recipients of A.R.S. grants included such agribusiness interests as Cargill, the giant grain corporation, and the National Canners Association.

In the 1972 budget for agricultural research there was money for studies on "Levels of Living," a category that might be expected to produce some help for people rather than industry. But by the time it filtered down to the campus, the money was being spent on such projects as a study of "consumer acceptability of permanent-press shirts," at Texas A & M, and "location and distribution of methylene croslind in formaldehyde-treated cellulose," at Cornell.

Similarly, projects purporting to be designed for the consumer often turned out to be "mere gadgetry." Michigan State, for example, was spending 20 percent of its vegetable-breeding effort on developing a seedless cucumber.

"One suspects," Hightower said, "that the effort is made simply because the seeds are there."

Michigan State was also trying to develop a green cauliflower by crossing broccoli with the old-fashioned white variety. Hightower commented:

"It is not likely that the consumer particularly wanted a green cauliflower; it is likely, however, that consumers would choose that such food products be researched and developed privately, not with his tax dollars."

Hightower and his team counted up 232 new varieties of fruits and nuts that had been developed by government-supported research over the last thirty years, including

37 varieties of peaches, 35 different kinds of strawberries and 29 varieties of blueberries, but found no evidence that taste had been improved or even seriously considered.

Others have noted that none of the blueberries that now reach the grocer's counter, large and blue though they might be, equal the tart-sweet juiciness of the berries that they once pulled from wild bushes growing in thickets along country lanes.

At a Senate hearing on the agribusiness-college report, Alice Shabecoff, executive director of the National Consumers League, which has been a supporter of consumer causes since 1899, illustrated the point. She displayed a container of big, red strawberries bred by agricultural research and grown on a corporate farm. She also displayed a pint of smaller strawberries of a kind that every farm-grown adult can remember, produced with old-fashioned organic fertilizers on a nearby family farm.

The big berries were mouthfilling, pulpy—and nearly tasteless. The smaller berries, which had been less expensive, were full of juice and flavor.

"Who has decided for consumers that we want a fruit all year long if, as its cost, there is no season when it tastes good?" the witness asked.

The task force had found several projects that had produced tomatoes hard enough to withstand the rough tossing and tumbling of machines that move through fields, pluck up the plants, shake off the fruit and spit out the vines. But no thought had been given to taste or vitamin content, as a researcher from the University of Florida, which had produced one of the hard tomatoes, later acknowledged.

Interviewed on *Caution,* a television program produced in Washington, about the fading of taste in tomatoes, he argued that there had been no reason to believe that the University of Florida's hybrid product would lack the quality of the original varieties and so no thought had been given to the problem.

A few university researchers, however, have begun to sense the outrage of consumers. Some are reported even trying to breed taste back into commercially grown tomatoes. It could take years.

"The consumer is not just studied and sold by land-grant research; he is also fooled," Highwater reported. "These public laboratories have researched and developed food cosmetics in an effort to confirm the consumer's preconceptions about food appearances, thus causing the consumer to think that the food is good."

For example, Iowa State found that vacuum-packed bacon has more consumer appeal because its color stays brighter, and the South Carolina agricultural experiment station found that green tomatoes could be reddened under a fluorescent light treatment. Other research found a plant compound named Xanthophyl that could give chicken skins "a pleasant yellow tinge," while spray-on coatings could enhance the appearance of apples, peaches and tomatoes.

The report continued: "Sold, studied and fooled by his tax-supported researchers there finally is evidence that the consumer actually is harmed by food engineering at the land-grant colleges."

The report of the Agribusiness Accountability project also cited chemical ripening agents such as a compound called Ethrel, and ethylene gas. Both were said to produce tomatoes of lower quality and vitamin content than those that were naturally produced.

Consumers, the investigative team found, may have still more serious questions to ask about some of the research for processors and some of the chemicals used. At Ohio State, for example, a method was developed for the "chemical peeling of tomatoes, with wetting agents and caustic soda." And Mississippi State found an easy way to skin the catfish that are now grown in large commercial ponds for human consumption. The researchers simply used a bath of hot lye, followed by a rinse, which in turn was followed by a dip in a solution of acetic acid.

Knowledgeable Americans might more easily swallow the tax-paid aid to agribusiness if there were evidence of equal concern for consumers and their health and safety.

XIX
Let Them Eat Cancer

While agricultural researchers have concocted chemicals, enzymes and hormones to speed growth of products and alter appearance and taste, government agencies responsible for safeguards have shown a strange laxity.

The reluctance of the Food and Drug Administration to defy agribusiness lobbyists and protect the public from the cancer-causing hormone DES is only the latest of many unheroic demonstrations.

Food dyes have stayed on the market long after they were proved harmful. Drugs have remained on shelves for decades without any effort to demand that their producers substantiate claims of efficacy or safety. Cyclamates were a known hazard while soft-drink producers continued to fill the grocers' shelves with them.

The F.D.A.'s crackdown on DES was long and painfully slow in coming. When the substance was finally prohibited the protests from drug companies, meat packers and feed-lot operators were less clamorous than expected. The reason was simple. The chemists had a substitute on their shelves that would do the same things as DES. It would also promote growth. And it, too, could cause cancer.

The F.D.A. had acted in painfully slow stages. First it only banned an oral form of DES, but it continued to allow pellets to be implanted in the ears of livestock. Meanwhile, Syntex Laboratories was standing ready, and it was already advertising:

"You can't sell oral DES, but you can sure sell Synovex."

The main reason why Synovex had attracted little attention earlier was that it was more expensive and had not been widely used. With DES gone, Synovex could come into its own and its manufacturer could trust that it would be a long time before a sluggish F.D.A. could stir itself into action. Yet Dr. Mortimer Lipsett of the National Institutes of Health was disclosing no sudden discovery when he told a reporter:

"Whatever dangers you want to attribute to DES you can attribute to Synovex."

Synovex, like DES, contains an estrogen, and, as an internal memorandum by a top F.D.A. aide noted, "all estrogens that have been adequately tested have been shown to be carcinogens in animals." Progesterone, which Synovex also contains, is considered to be another carcinogen, since the body converts it to estrogen.

Synovex, in fact, was only one of sixteen known or suspected cancer-causing agents still being sold for livestock consumption when DES was banned. One was a substance called melengestrol acetate, or MGA, made by the Upjohn Company, which has been fed to heifers since 1968. Another was estradiol monopalmitate, an estrogen, which was being injected into chickens to work as a growth promoter the way DES did in cattle.

Among the known cancer-causing products still in use were two that were used for turkeys—dimetridazole and ipronidazole. Others suspected included compounds of nitrofuran and sulfa, though they are used to promote growth and prevent disease of hogs and chickens.

The F.D.A. approaches its job of protecting the public with a strange order of priorities. Its administrators do not require a chemical firm to prove that its product is safe before it can be marketed, and many of the drugs used in livestock have continued as potential threats to human health, despite the lack of appropriate testing methods to determine the amount of residue they might leave in meat. For some products such a test may never be developed because of the difficulty of distinguishing their residues from the animals' natural hormones. Yet they have continued to be sold although they could be causing imbalances that could lead to cancer.

Many of the drugs and hormones used for livestock have been said to be possible contributing agents to the 60 to 80 percent of cancer that at least one expert believes to be "environmental in origin."

The internal memorandum, a report on the problem written by Dr. K. K. Johnson, research director of the F.D.A.'s Bureau of Veterinary Medicine, concluded with this comment:

"Unless F.D.A. resolves this drug residue problem, we will soon be in direct confrontation with Congress and the consumers, defending an untenable position. For F.D.A. to ignore this problem would be disastrous."

The report was dated September 27, 1972, but by March 20, 1973, when a copy was obtained by Senator Abe Ribicoff, its urgent recommendations had produced no evidence of action by the F.D.A.

The lethargy seemed incomprehensible in light of several alarming situations highlighted in the report. In addition to substances suspected as carcinogens, a long list of others were being used in livestock despite indications that their presence in meat could cause toxic reactions.

Another problem underscored in the Johnson memorandum should have been relatively easy to resolve, yet it has continued to weaken efforts to develop and enforce safeguards. The difficulty is caused by a fragmentation of responsibility within the F.D.A. and between that agency and the Department of Agriculture.

It is the F.D.A.'s duty to set standards for use—to say how much residue of a drug can be allowed in food and, if none should be allowed, to say so. But it is the responsibility of the Agriculture Department to develop tests to detect the residues and to monitor slaughter to make sure that the tolerances are not exceeded in the tissues of meat that gets to market.

The F.D.A. often has information that would help the Agriculture Department in its monitoring, including data on where and how much of a chemical is used. But there seemed to be no regular system for transmission of help from the F.D.A. to researchers and inspection officials at the Agriculture Department.

Within the F.D.A., the report also showed, responsibility was split between the Bureau of Veterinary Medicine and the Bureau of Food. As a result, researchers in veterinary medicine could identify hazards, but they could not advise the Agriculture Department about which dangers were most serious and what actions ought to be taken. That was the responsibility of the Bureau of Food.

For lack of adequate methods of testing, inspectors were not even checking for residues of several of the carcinogenic and otherwise dangerous substances.

When Senator Ribicoff obtained the report, he angrily charged:

"Congress has given the highest priority to the search

for a cancer cure. At the same time that the Government has been searching for a cancer cure, however, government agencies have permitted introduction into the food supply of substances which may themselves cause cancer."

What seemed to anger him more than anything else was the continued use of MGA to promote growth in heifers without any monitoring to determine whether the carcinogenic compound was leaving dangerous residues in meats. The F.D.A. researchers had considered the substance so dangerous that they prescribed a tolerance of zero. Absolutely no residue should be allowed in meats.

The reason inspectors were not monitoring for MGA was simple. They had no way to determine whether any of the chemical was being left in the meat that was going to Americans' dinner tables.

The Government depends on the chemical companies themselves to develop testing procedures that are needed. But since they can go on selling their products while they try to find ways to assure safety, they have little incentive to put a high priority on the effort. Meanwhile, Americans can go right on buying and consuming cancer-producing agents.

One reason why MGA especially ignited Ribicoff's anger was that two years earlier the Senator had written the Secretary of Agriculture to express his concern about the chemical and inquire about safety tests. The Secretary had replied:

"The validation of the MGA procedure has been given a high priority so that the Department may initiate a monitoring program at an early date."

Ribicoff charged: "It is clear that government regulation of animal drugs is not protecting American consumers. Substances classified as suspect carcinogens are allowed to remain in the food supply until there is absolute proof that they do cause cancer. Even then, the Government moves slowly to remove them. Animal drugs, the safety of which are in serious doubt, are given the benefit of every doubt, and little is done to investigate the risk they present to consumers. By the time corrective action is taken, it may be too late for many Americans. In the past several decades, the incidence of cancer has grown alarmingly at the same time that the use of animal drugs which are suspect carcinogens has proliferated."

The F.D.A. responded with wounded dignity. Its officials thought it was unfair for Ribicoff to seize on an internal report, even one from someone as high as the director of research at the Bureau of Veterinary Medicine. They were, they said, really working on the problem.

Ribicoff might have feared that they were working on the problem with about the same degree of urgency as that of the Department of Agriculture's search for a monitoring program for MGA. Or perhaps with the same attention to detail that the F.D.A. inspectors had been giving to their responsibilities for protecting consumers against health hazards in food-processing plants.

The agency is required by law to assure sanitary conditions in plants that process food for shipment across state lines. How well it was doing that job was the subject of an inquiry made in late 1972 by the General Accounting Office, which is an investigative arm of Congress.

That investigation showed F.D.A. inspectors were often giving consumers very little protection, for the G.A.O. investigators found conditions of unspeakable filth in plants that were processing food for Americans to eat. In some instances, F.D.A. officials did not seem even to know which plants they were responsible for.

In their investigation, the G.A.O. agents checked up on ninety-seven plants in twenty-one states. Projecting their findings on the basis of that random sample, they said in a report:

"We estimate that 1,800, or 40 percent, of the food-manufacturing plants in 21 states were operating under insanitary conditions and that serious potential or actual food adulteration existed in 1,000 of the plants."

In 23 percent of the plants they found "conditions serious in terms of either having potential for causing product adulteration or having already caused product adulteration," and in an additional 16 percent of the plants they found unsanitary conditions that posed somewhat less serious "potential for product adulteration."

The summation tended to obscure the nauseating details of the filth that the investigators found.

Rat excrement, cockroaches "and other insect infestation," the report said, were found "in, on or around raw materials, finished products and processing equipment." Equipment and work areas were often dirty and pesticides were being used "in close proximity to food-processing areas."

Becoming more specific, the G.A.O. cited some examples. One was a candy factory that F.D.A. inspectors had declared to be in compliance with sanitation regulations. Instead, the G.A.O. investigators found raw materials adulterated with rat excrement and live insects in raw materials that were being processed. The raw materials were moldy and they were being processed with dirty equipment in an area that was infested with cockroaches.

In a bean cannery that the F.D.A. had classed as in compliance with sanitation standards, the investigators found rat-infested, moldy beans, many of them spilled on dirty floors and then scooped up and poured back into a line for canning. The surrounding area was infested by roaches and flies, including an "inoperative" can-washing machine through which open cans were passing.

Lurid pictures illustrated the report and gave striking proof of the conditions that friendly government regulators allow to exist in processing plants that produce food for Americans. Nauseating photographs showed rat-gnawed bags of flour littered with rat pellets, open cans of dough flecked with trash, beans spilled on a dirty floor in an area where they were being regularly scooped back into the canning line, and a pile of rotting potatoes that, the caption said, "had already been screened for final processing."

The report did not identify the culprit firms, but Representative Les Aspin later reported that their names included large and substantial concerns, such companies as Coca-Cola, Pepsi-Cola, Thomas J. Lipton, Inc., and American Bakeries.

The G.A.O. put the blame for the problem, in relatively mild terms, on the F.D.A. The filth and health hazards in the processing plants were caused, it said, by "lack of timely and aggressive enforcement actions" by the agency. All that was needed to correct the problem was "more timely and aggressive enforcement action by the F.D.A."

Such a consequence hardly seemed likely. Newspaper offices across the country continued to receive regular reports of people sickened by contaminated food. And it was more than a year later when the notorious case of food poisoning by tuna from a Starkist plant was exposed.

At least 232 people were sickened in the spring of 1973 by eating decomposed tuna canned by Starkist. And it was not as if this were a freak accident. F.D.A. inspectors had found thirteen unsanitary practices in the plant that was responsible, long before the rotting tuna was sold to the public, but the agency had taken no action beyond notifying the company. Officials said later they could see no case for legal action.

Yet the conditions found in that early inspection made the results almost inevitable. Fish were being thawed in untreated bay water, cans were not being cleaned, rain leaked through a roof onto cooked fish that was awaiting processing, and cockroaches were running around in a storage area.

The fish that sickened so many people were decomposed before they were canned, an investigation found. And this happened in a plant owned by a company that emphasizes quality in its advertising. The company said it was tightening its "quality control" procedures.

The F.D.A. inspectors work against heavy odds, for their ranks are undermanned in the face of an overwhelming task. But no obstacle should excuse the agency's failure to take strong enforcement actions against abuses when they are found or its failure to sound the alarm that short staffing in such a vital agency turns food shopping into a game of Russian roulette. The shopper can never tell which can might be loaded.

No such excuse is available to the meat-inspection service of the Department of Agriculture, which has a built-in conflict of interest. The same department that is responsible for promoting production and consumption of meats is also responsible for protecting the consumer. The two hats teeter awkwardly on the heads of its top officials, who are political appointees.

The problem was acknowledged by Clarence Palmby, the former official who was involved in the Russian grain deal, during a Senate investigation. The department is "producer-oriented," he said, and he thought "that is a weakness."

The inspection service itself would seem to be failsafe, since it must keep men on watch whenever any plant that ships meat or poultry in interstate commerce is in operation. In fact, however, the service is tainted from top to bottom by political considerations and industry influence. The facts about its problems have been verified in interviews with congressional and department staffs and from other sources, including a team of Nader's Raiders. A report of the Nader team, written by Harrison Wellford and later published under the title "Sowing the Wind," provides much documentation.

Nowhere has the taint of politics and industry influence been more evident than in the fight over the Wholesome Meat Act and the breakdown in enforcement that has followed, turning a victory by consumer advocates into a delusion.

It was late in the year 1967 when Aled P. Davies, the archetype of old-fashioned lobbyists, walked into the office of Representative John McCormack, then Speaker of the House. As friends and others describe him, Davies, a big Welshman, can be alternately cajoling and thundering, suave with a Congressman he wants to influence and terrifying to uncooperative bureaucrats. He storms into their offices, pounds his fist on their desks and demands, browbeats and threatens.

In the late stages of the fight over the Wholesome Meat Act there were two contending bills slated for consideration in the House. Davies and the American Meat Institute, which he represented, favored one bill and McCormack the other. And McCormack held the pivotal power.

As Davies later told the story to friends, he called his "people," the industry group, and said he might need help with McCormack. He was told to meet a visitor in McCormack's outer office at the Capitol.

A day or so later, Davies was waiting in McCormack's lobby when a stranger from Boston arrived. The descriptions given of the man have been vague, and he is said not even to have given Davies his name. But the two were ushered into the Speaker's office, where McCormack greeted the visitor from Boston like an old friend. After a few pleasantries, according to the accounts, this is what happened.

"John, my people like the Mondale bill," the Bostonian said.

McCormack responded with arguments used by the proponents of the opposing version of the meat act, whereupon his visitor cut in with words like these:

"John, I don't know anything about that. My people like the other bill."

And that was all the argument he offered. The bill that "his people" liked soon became law.

Oddly enough the bill that the American Meat Institute preferred was the stronger version of the alternative proposals. But in the explanation of why the meat industry came around to support a vigorous inspection law lies a long and convoluted sequence of events.

The conference in the Speaker's office was really the climax of a long fight to clean up execrable conditions that existed in meat and poultry plants that were under the jurisdiction of state rather than federal officials. The meat-plant horrors were well known to the Department of Agriculture, but its top officials wanted no part of a clean-up. They were all too aware of the patronage and entrenched power of state politicians that were involved.

It was a fight in which the institute that represented the big meat packers retreated from one prepared position to another, finally to wind up under public pressure in a reversal that placed them on the side of the clean-meat forces.

The Department of Agriculture had known since 1963 that the state-governed plants, which avoid federal regulation by shipping their products only within the states where they operate rather than across state lines, were often buying diseased animals and processing them amid filth, rats and cockroaches.

But the department's findings, the result of a national survey, had been kept secret. They would probably have never been disclosed had it not been for the persistence of the Nader-Wellford crew and an investigative reporter named Nick Kotz, then of the Minneapolis *Tribune* and more recently with the Washington *Post*.

As pressures and exposures grew, Davies and other meat lobbyists were forced from their first entrenchment. After trying to smother the consumer effort, preferring no bill at all, they supported a mild, toothless measure and helped push it through the House.

To his credit, it was Davies who was the first to recognize that the consumer movement to clean up state-controlled meat plants had grown irresistible, and he persuaded his employers that it was not in the best interest of the meat industry to appear to oppose wholesome conditions of production. He threw his considerable weight behind a strong bill sponsored by Senator Walter F. Mondale, and it was essentially that bill that finally became law after his visit, along with his mysterious companion, to Speaker McCormack's office.

Oddly, the last to yield to the forces of clean-up were the political appointees at the Department of Agriculture. Orville L. Freeman, then Secretary of Agriculture, continued to issue statements opposing strong measures even after the White House fell into line and he is said by associates to have been enraged when the White House finally ordered him to endorse the Mondale plan.

Pressures on Freeman were coming from the state commissioners of agriculture, who were jealous of their powers and the patronage that went with it and who, in turn, were under pressure from the plant operators within their states, who were generally owners of smaller firms usually unaffiliated with the meat institute. And one of the loudest voices among those opposing a clean-up was the man who was soon to become the Under Secretary of Agriculture in the Nixon Administration, Phil Campbell.

As passed, the Wholesome Meat Act was a stern law. It required the states to bring their inspection practices up to federal standards within two years. If they did not do that, the law required federal inspectors to take over. It allowed one exception, however. If the Secretary of Agriculture found that a state had failed to meet the law's requirements by only a narrow margin he could allow that state a one-year extension of time to bring its plants and procedures into conformance.

By the time the deadline rolled around, in 1969, there was a new Secretary of Agriculture, Clifford M. Hardin, who brought into office with him the very man who had been an outspoken opponent of the Wholesome Meat Act, Phil Campbell, as his Under Secretary.

It came as no surprise when Secretary Hardin played the kindly uncle to the powerful state commissioners and their operators of dirty plants. Although the law imposed strict conditions on extensions of the deadline, Hardin found reasons enough to allow additional time for most of the states. He found only three in conformance with federal standards, but allowed all but one of the others to continue to expose their citizens to health threats that result from lax inspection systems and unsanitary packing houses.

A year later, with no legal extension available, he again temporized, announcing only an "intention" to take over inspection of thirteen states and the territory of Puerto Rico.

In addition to the Agriculture Department's relaxed approach to carrying out the clear directions of the Wholesome Meat Act, it has taken great latitude in interpreting the intent of Congress as reflected in the law. Decisions on whether inspection of meat plants by the states is "equal to" federal inspection have been based largely on size of staffs and methods of organization rather than on whether state inspectors are forcing operators to keep their plants clean and making sure that they are selling only wholesome meats.

A still bigger problem, however, is that equality with federal standards does not mean excellence or anything close to it. Top-echelon Agriculture officials, swayed by the whims and pressures of industry, have eroded morale in the inspection staff and encouraged corruption, as Nader's Raiders found in their wide-ranging investigation.

Nader's investigations found a general failure of government officials to back up the inspection staff, a situation that allowed inspectors to be harassed by plant operators with impunity. In many cases, inspectors had been summarily transferred by their superiors because of complaints from operators that rigorous inspection practices were interfering with production.

Such working conditions at least encouraged the corruption that the investigation also found. There was bribery in forms ranging from the subtle to the blatant, from money to sex.

In some instances the bribery was disguised as extra overtime pay and in others it was supplies of free meat for the inspectors. There were also cases in which inspectors, as part owners of poultry houses, were given shares in lucrative contracts.

Among the cases cited was one in which superiors overruled the inspector on the scene and allowed a poultry plant to run its production line so fast that the inspector could not thoroughly check each fowl passing through. This was a violation of the department's own regulations, which quite logically gave the inspector the right to set production speeds at rates that permit him to give careful examination to each carcass.

The result of the violation was that fowl with diseased parts and others that had been incompletely plucked were being dropped into cooling water along with the clean chickens.

In such cases the cooling water becomes a culture for disease germs. Feathers left on the carcasses are not merely unsightly. They are potent bacteria carriers, and their contamination seeps through all the cooling water and soaks into all the chickens in the vats. There is no chance that any of the fowl will come out germ-free, for the eviscerated chickens are systematically left in the water long enough to soak up as much as 12 percent of added weight—an invisible, germ-laden and costly tariff for the consumer.

In this instance the speed-up backfired because large quantities of the plant's production were condemned by the inspector. Eventually, after long harassment, he was transferred by his superiors, who seemed to be more intent on satisfying the complaints of a plant manager than insuring sanitary conditions.

Inspectors themselves, in confidential accounts, told the investigators of bribery through handouts of free meat and extra overtime pay as well as sex. The seduction, it was explained, was quite subtle. "Trim girls," assigned to work with the inspectors and cut away bruises and other imperfections in the meat, also were reported to have duties to perform for their inspectors that often went beyond the end of their work days. Some were said to be on call to satisfy their inspectors' needs twenty-four hours a day.

The evidence is strong that political leaders of the department put a higher premium on good relations with the industry and its lobbyists than on their duty to protect the public. For if it wished, the service could easily enforce any findings of unwholesomeness.

It has the most powerful of all weapons. If a plant refuses to clean up unsanitary conditions, the agency can simply withdraw its inspectors, a step that would require a plant to suspend operations. It is a weapon that the service, however, systematically refuses to use on its friends in meat production.

From the outset of his administration, Secretary Hardin gave clear evidence of the extent of his own dedication to wholesome meats. The evidence came in a fast shuffle through which he tried to ease a pressure that had long been building within the poultry industry. He tried to help them sell cancer-infected chickens, according to the Nader report.

The problem was a virus that causes tumors on about 2 percent of all chickens, enough to prove costly since inspectors were condemning all the chickens on which such tumors appeared. The industry wanted the condemnation practice quietly changed to allow the plants merely to cut away an infected part.

One of those ubiquitous committees of advisers to the department, in this case a panel of twelve veterinarians, had always favored continued condemnation of the whole infected carcass by a majority of 8 to 4. Hardin quickly changed that. As one of his early actions, he ousted six of the eight members who opposed any change in the practice and named three new members, each of whom favored the industry position. Suddenly the balance was reversed. Now the committee favored relaxation of the cancerous-chicken standards, and it secretly gave the department a recommendation to that effect.

The ploy might have worked except that Assistant Secretary Richard Lyng saw political dangers in such a change and referred the issue to the Surgeon General, who killed the proposal after a review by another committee, this one including cancer specialists. The committee's reasoning was that, while the chicken-cancer virus had not been found infectious to humans, neither was there absolute proof of human immunity.

Both Hardin's own Office of the Inspector General and the General Accounting Office had found seriously unsanitary conditions in federally inspected meat plants even before Nader's Raiders made their investigation. One survey made as late as 1970 had found unsanitary conditions in thirty-six out of forty plants, with the old nauseous litany of rat infestation and contaminated products but no evidence of serious enforcement efforts.

After the Nader report and some other embarrassments, including the indictment of several inspectors, the department began some token reforms.

But another investigation by the Inspector General's office showed the extent of progress that was being made. Completed in 1972, it revealed that 43 percent of a broad sampling of meat plants were still threatening the public health with unsanitary processing conditions. It also exposed serious laxity among inspectors at ports of entry, which allowed possible dangers from imported meats.

Meanwhile, over in the inspection service's counterpart at the F.D.A., the agency that is charged with the duty of overseeing the processing of other foods, a strange decision was being made.

The F.D.A. in March, 1972, established standards of allowable filth. The guidelines established precisely how many rat pellets could be allowed per pint of wheat and the number of rodent hairs and insect fragments that could be allowed in other foods. The levels of allowable filth were higher than a moderately cautious processor would permit in the foods issuing from his plants.

But the standards reached the level that might be expected from regulators in both the F.D.A. and the Agriculture Department, at the height of the lowest common denominator.

XX
The Politics of Food

"In hindsight, my vision is twenty-twenty, without glasses," Secretary of Agriculture Earl L. Butz was heard to say with heavy sarcasm several times during the sharply spiraling food inflation of 1973.

The Secretary was protesting what he considered to be unfair criticism of policies formed, decisions made and actions taken by his department and others in the Administration in which he served. He resented hearing critics point out that the policies and actions had not only failed to arrest the rising costs but, in many instances, had aggravated problems with which they were intended to deal. Though his hindsight might have been 20-20, his foresight was considerably less than 20-40.

To many Americans it did not seem unreasonable to expect better vision from officials with an army of economists and researchers at their command. More than six hundred work in the Agriculture Department's Economic Research Service.

A series of predictions noted in the public press reflect

the quality of vision of the Secretary and his colleagues. On January 14, 1972, he was predicting the best of all possible resolutions of his responsibilities: improved income for farmers and a smaller price increase in the future than in the past for consumers. A month later, his department predicted a 4 percent increase in food costs for all of 1972, down from more than 5 percent the year before. In August, the Secretary predicted a drop in meat prices.

What followed the Secretary's prediction of January 14, 1972, is now history. In the next two years, the inexorable march of food inflation exacted a heavy toll from consumers. By August, 1973, they were paying $25-billion a year more to feed their families than they did in 1971. The prices of their food would rise by nearly one-fourth. And the cost of the meats they needed for protein would climb enormously. The prices of beef and pork as well as chicken would rise more than 50 percent.

All this was accompanied by repeated failures to assess the dimensions of developing problems, mismanagement and half-measures as crises approached and a singular weakness of will in the face of political stresses. For such negative achievements, the food and agriculture officials who were in charge between the end of 1971 and the end of 1973 established an unparalleled record.

In light of such performance, the criticism has been relatively mild.

It might have been stronger had the critics generally recognized that consumers were paying for a political decision made late in 1971.

At the time, farm prices were down and farmers were grumbling. The sounds were ominous with an election year coming, for the Midwestern farm vote had been the margin by which Richard M. Nixon was elected to the Presidency in 1968 over Hubert H. Humphrey. The decision was to raise farm prices, whatever the cost, and the

Administration began to act immediately. The nation has paid a bitter price for the farm votes gained in the strategy pursued in October, November and December of 1971 and January of 1972.

One part of the plan was to rid the Administration of a Secretary of Agriculture who had become anathema to farmers through no fault of his own, a former chancellor of the University of Nebraska named Clifford M. Hardin. Secretary Hardin was the political victim of two widely varying years of agricultural fortune and of a measure that he took to guard the nation against scarcity.

His problems stemmed from a corn blight that swept the major producing areas in 1970, cutting production and causing sharply increased prices both of the grain and the livestock that are fed with it. Fearing that the blight might persist in 1971 and aiming to assure adequate supplies of feed for cattle, hogs and chickens, Hardin released for production some of the land that had been kept idle under previous farm programs. Had he had not taken that precaution, Secretary Hardin could have been accused of gross negligence, a charge to which his successor would soon expose himself.

As it happened, the blight did not recur in 1971, and a good growing year produced a record crop that dropped the price of corn to 95 cents a bushel, down from the lofty price of $1.40 the year before. The result was a twofold worry for farmers. They were concerned not only over the price of corn but also over the old axiom that "cheap corn means cheap livestock." Secretary Hardin's unpopularity raised fears of a repetition in 1972 of Republican losses in farm states such as those suffered in congressional races of 1970. Hardin had to go.

The other part of the plan was to shore up farm prices by a two-pronged maneuver, and it was this plan that became the precursor of food troubles of 1972 and 1973. In

October, 1971, the Administration announced a program to increase subsidies on corn and other grains for livestock feed by $600-million in order to induce farmers to reduce their plantings. The next step, taken in December, was a government move to buy corn off the market and bolster prices quickly rather than awaiting the effects of crop reductions scheduled for 1972. It was a move that assured higher prices for meats as well as corn, for, in view of the expected high cost of feed, farmers would decide to breed fewer hogs.

Secretary Butz could not be blamed for the original decision to cut corn production, for it was made before he took office, although he neither protested the action nor warned about prospective repercussions. In fact, when it became known in January that farmers were planning to cut corn production only 4 percent, he offered further inducements leading to a total cutback of 8 percent. He also announced the decision to buy corn off the market in an effort to raise prices only one day after he assumed office.

The new program brought quick results. Butz, whose nomination had narrowly won approval in the Senate in December, 1971, was being hailed as a farm hero by March, 1972, when it was apparent that, aside from increases in prices, farm subsidies would rise from $3.3-billion in 1971 to more than $4-billion.

The subsidies were an expensive way to aid farmers. For every dollar in government payments that went to supplement the returns of the lower-income producers under the subsidy program, the Department of Agriculture had to give about ten dollars to farmers whose incomes were already above average.

But the goal was achieved. The farm vote returned safely to the Republican fold.

The risk being taken by the Administration to recover the farm vote escaped general notice, but there is no reason to believe that Secretary Butz and other policy-makers in government were unaware of the stakes in their gamble with the public interest. For it was already apparent that world conditions were undergoing rapid change. To men aware of those conditions it should have been clear that the limitations on production imposed for the crops of 1972 left this nation and others that depend on United States exports vulnerable to the effects of droughts and floods. Inflation was almost inevitable and famine was far from an impossibility.

Although a multivolume study completed as background for a report by a Presidentially appointed National Commission on Food and Fiber escaped general attention, no officials trying to deal intelligently with food and agricultural policy could have been unaware of its findings. One of the technical studies that went into the report, "Food and Fiber for the Future," submitted to President Lyndon B. Johnson in 1967, pointed out the limited nature of the world's land resources. Only 3.5 billion acres, slightly more than one-tenth of the world's land, was then arable, and most of that land was already under cultivation. About 2.5 billion more was potentially arable, in theory, provided technical solutions to problems such as desert conditions and the excessive water of the rain forests could be solved. But even then, after heavy costs, the added acreage would have only limited productive capacity.

The report was presented in the same year that two brothers, William and Paul Paddock, published *Famine 1975,* a book warning that world population was outstripping food production and predicting problems of critical proportions by the mid-nineteen-seventies.

Since then more than a half-billion people have been added to the world's population, and many other conditions have changed as well.

For a time it seemed that the so-called "Green Revolution," the development of higher-yielding grains for planting in poorly fed nations, might relieve some of the strain on resources. But the productive worth of such scientific advances was offset by the population growth and by increasing affluence both in the United States and abroad.

Only to agricultural economists like Secretary Butz and his colleagues is the immensity of the impact of rising affluence on food supplies easily apparent. Among the less knowledgeable, comments on the factor are likely to be skeptical. After all, one might say, how much more food can a wealthy man consume in comparison with his fellows of more moderate circumstances?

The answer is, a great deal. For as incomes rise, so does consumers' demand for meats. And the more meat one eats, the more land is required for his support. It takes far more grain to produce the protein in a pound of meat than it does to produce an equal amount of protein when the grain is consumed directly.

That factor is most strikingly evident in the United States, where consumption of beef has more than doubled in the last three decades, from 55 pounds a year per capita in 1940 to 117 pounds in 1972. At present rates of meat consumption, it takes nearly a ton of grain to support the average American, compared with about 400 pounds for the average person in most of the world's poorer countries. In a world that has less than an acre of cultivated land per person, it takes two acres per capita to support Americans in the style to which they have become accustomed, and their demand for meat is still increasing.

Meanwhile, meat consumption is rising with affluence in the more highly developed nations of Western Europe and Scandinavia as well as in the Soviet Union and Japan. And the more meat the increasing number of citizens in those countries eat, the greater the portion of the world's limited land resources that will be needed for their support.

It is unlikely that a great many of them can increase their meat consumption to the level now enjoyed by Americans and still leave enough grain to support the poor of other lands at even their present standards.

Realistic assessments of such conditions were available to the policy-makers of the United States when the ill-advised production cuts of 1972 were imposed, and it is evident from subsequent public statements of Secretary Butz that he was aware of the dimensions of the approaching world problems. It did not require 20-20 foresight for officials with the information that Secretary Butz had at his command to see that production was being cut to the point where natural disasters could create food crises in some parts of the world as well as sharply rising prices.

The principal buffer against such problems was the surpluses left over from the bumper crops of 1971. As Don Paarlberg, Butz's director of economics, pointed out in a speech in 1973, surpluses stored in United States warehouses have rescued the nation from problems nearly every time they have accumulated. Under present world conditions, many other economists believe, surpluses from the good years must be stored against the lean. Yet in 1973 Secretary Butz rejected proposals for a policy of continued government storage of grain reserves. He preferred to leave that function and the decisions involved, as well as the profits, to the private grain companies.

Luck was not with the policy-makers and the nation they exposed to the risks of food crisis and inflation in 1972. One after another, misfortunes in major producing countries unmasked the dimensions of their gamble. Drought struck the grain fields of South Africa and Australia. In the Soviet Union, drought coupled with a severe winter caused disastrous crop losses. Meanwhile, the cold Humboldt current mysteriously moved away from the Peruvian coast, as it does about once every seven years. The current is the habitat for the anchovies that Peru's fishing fleet supplies to the world as one of the two principal sources of protein for animal feeds. The other is the United States's soybeans.

Rising food prices were the inevitable response to production cuts at home and disaster abroad. The prices climbed steadily through July, when a new influence entered the scene and brought the greatest inflationary surge of all to the domestic market.

This was the entry of a Russian trading team, which secretly bought up one-fourth of the American wheat crop and large proportions of the corn crop and other livestock feeds. The Russians were acting understandably in behalf of a nation facing scarcities and consequent hardship as a result of its own crop failures. What was not quite fathomable was the behavior of United States officials in light of current world conditions and the clear needs both of American consumers and other nations of the world.

The responsible United States officials stood idly by, neither learning nor seeking to learn the scope of the Russians' buying until it became apparent, long after the last deal had been made, that more wheat had been sold than the nation could spare.

Secretary Butz hailed the deals with the Russians, which were aided by a credit arrangement with a federal agency and by bargain prices subsidized by the Government, as a historic benefit for the American economy.

And so it might have been but for the political decision of 1971 that left the nation with limited supplies to meet world and domestic demand.

Meanwhile, unmanaged conditions outside the food economy were making matters worse, among them failure to deal with the problem of serious deficits of the United States in the balance of international payments, a principal cause of which was soaring oil imports. In a nation increasingly dependent on foreign oil, the automobile industry continued to build cars with monstrous, gasoline-gobbling engines. While government officials failed to develop an energy policy to deal with excessive consumption or discover new sources of supply, billions of dollars in needed monetary reserves flowed out to pay for the oil imports.

As a direct result of increasing inflation in the United States, led by rising food prices, and extravagance in imports—primarily oil—came two devaluations of the dollar within a fourteen-month period.

Americans were led to believe that devaluation would primarily affect imports and exports, that it would have little impact on domestic prices. The falsity of that assurance was quickly exposed.

In the first week after the second devaluation the prices of food commodities surged. Pork bellies, from which bacon is cut, soared 8.5 percent and cattle and broiler chickens jumped 10 percent, while grains to feed such animals rose by comparable measures.

The reason was simple. Foreign buyers poured into the domestic markets to buy foods that were cheapened, in terms of their own more valuable currencies, although expensive to Americans using the degraded dollar.

Soon it became apparent that the nation's grain warehouses would be virtually empty by summer when reapers would begin to sweep across the wheat fields of Texas, up through the Midwestern plains and into fields of the North Central States. And then, by the time those harvests started, it was clear that soybeans had been oversold, and the pressures on the limited supplies drove prices as high as $12.90 a bushel.

This was a commodity that had sold at three dollars a bushel—a price considered glamorous to farmers at the time—as recently as early 1972. Only by imposing export controls and forcing sellers to break commitments to such longtime customers as Japan, which depends heavily on American soybeans, could United States officials hold back enough of the vital protein source to supply this country's livestock producers and prevent a runaway inflation that would have overshadowed even the soaring spiral of the preceding months.

While prices climbed and supplies tightened, the United States architects of food policy continued to react with half-measures. In January, 1973, Secretary Butz announced a decision to release more of the land that was being held out of production under the current farm program. But nineteen million acres were still kept idle.

Those nineteen million acres remained untouched through one of the worst springs in history, when rains soaked the corn belt and the wheat plains and floods covered millions of acres of the vast heartland through which the Mississippi River flows. Traders, knowing that a good crop was vital to world and domestic needs and that the heavy rains might delay plantings and cut production, bid up the prices of commodities on the futures markets. Yet United States officials took no action on those nineteen million idle acres.

It was not until late July, after all the crops had been planted and at a time when it was impossible to increase the acreages for 1973, that Secretary Butz announced an end of all crop restrictions and called for all-out production.

It was too late, of course, to relieve the current strains. The results of the relaxed restrictions could not be felt before 1974. With foreign traders buying heavily and nervous commodity markets watching each successive estimate of yields as 1973 crops matured, wheat soared past the historic mark of $4 a bushel and then on past $5, while corn climbed for a time above $3 a bushel, more than twice the $1.40 that had delighted farmers in early 1972. Yet even at such levels, foreign buyers dealing in contracts for future delivery bought up more than half the expected wheat production in July, the first month of the 1973–74 crop year.

The prices of grain are significant in themselves for they affect the costs of bread and pastries as well as cereals. But they are more important because of their impact on the prices of meat, which is the biggest item in the family budget. In general, when grain prices are high, farmers who would normally feed much of their production to livestock prefer to transfer the risks, work and worry of animal care to others and take their immediate profits from the harvest. The result is a decrease in livestock production and higher prices of meats for consumers.

But the story of meat production and prices of 1972 and 1973 cannot be explained so simply. Many complex factors entered the picture, among the most important of which were decisions made in Washington.

To understand the story of meat pricing in those two years one must first understand the market cycle of the animals involved, the commercial environment in which they are produced, processed and sold, and the effects of government policy.

Nearly two years elapse between the time when a beef cow is bred on a ranch in the West and when its calf becomes a fattened steer, ready to be turned into steaks and hamburgers on family tables in the East. In comparison, the time from breeding to table for pork is less than one year, while broiler chickens reach the dinner plate in only twelve weeks. It requires more grain to produce a pound of pork than a pound of chicken and still more to produce a pound of beef. The differences between the prices of the three meats normally reflect the time and the costs of production. Yet all three are interacting. When high prices of beef divert consumers to pork and chicken, their prices respond to increasing demand.

Supplies as well as the prices of each type of meat are affected by costs, market conditions and government policies in effect at the time of breeding or hatching and by similar factors throughout the market cycle.

Most broiler chickens today are grown in factory-like surroundings by farmers under contract to corporate processors. The corporations finance the buildings where the chickens are raised and supply the baby chicks that stand cooped in narrow pens with space enough only to dip their necks for feed. That feed is also supplied by the corporation. And when the chickens are grown they are taken away, processed and sold to retailers by the same corporation.

Because the corporations control the cycle from hatchery to retailers, they can more easily adjust production and influence markets and prices than can the processors of cattle and hogs, although corporate control and contract production of beef and pork has been increasing.

Some cattle and hogs are still fattened on farms where they are bred, but the usual cycle is a more segmented process. On the ranch or farm where they are born, the calves and pigs are raised until they are ready for fattening, when they are sold to operators of large feedlots. More and more often those feedlots are operated by big corporations, frequently by the packers who represent the next stage of production.

Because commercial feedlots represent sizable investments, their capacities are finite, and an operator is unlikely to expand in response to what may seem only a temporary increase in demand. Such restrictions on production are reflected in the prices paid by consumers.

From the feedlot the animals are shipped to packing-houses where the steers are slaughtered and quartered and the hogs are carved into hams, shoulders, loins and bellies, and sausage is ground from the scraps. From the packing-house, the meat goes to the retailers, where butchers carve the parts into family-size portions for sale to consumers.

In late 1971, when United States officials made their political decision to trade higher food costs for the farm vote, American consumers were already paying nearly a half-billion dollars a year in overcharges that were due to concentration of power in the meat-packing industry, according to an internal study by the F.T.C.

The study, made for its own guidance by the commission's staff, was obtained and disclosed by Senator George McGovern early in his drive for nomination as the Democratic Presidential candidate. Officials at the agency protested that the study was only tentative and the results could not be considered conclusive, but at about the same time H. Michael Mann, director of the F.T.C.'s Bureau of Economics, was citing its findings to illustrate public remarks on concentration of market power in various industries.

Whatever may have been the case, that half-billion dollars a year has been overshadowed by the consumer costs of government actions and inaction.

The steps taken in late 1971 and early 1972 to artificially raise prices of grain—because they affected breeding decisions at the time—would still be influencing the supplies and prices of cattle reaching the market in late 1973 and early 1974. The effect on hogs came sooner. By March, 1972, with grain prices rising, farmers had cut their swine production plans 9 percent below levels of the year before.

Before March of the next year those decisions forced consumer prices upward.

As grain prices persistently edged higher, the farmer continued to hold meat production in check and prices of beef, pork and chicken continued to climb.

Cattle on feed and available for feedlots were already limited in number when the severe winter and spring of 1972–73 spread serious problems through the major producing areas of the Midwest. Steers mired knee-deep in cold mud during the winter gained little weight no matter how much grain they consumed. Many, exhausted, lay down and died in the frigid muck, and many of the young cattle that might have replaced them in feedlots were killed in early spring blizzards. With supplies limited, beef prices could only climb higher and they in turn put added pressures on supplies and prices of pork, chickens, eggs, cheese and fish.

As the prices escalated, distressed consumers, not knowing where else to go, turned to Congress, and their representatives began calling for price rollbacks.

Secretary Butz had begun warning as early as March, 1972, that price controls would cause shortages and, in the long run, still higher prices. He was right, of course, and he had persuaded President Nixon that he was right. The President said so publicly in March, 1973.

The President's statement to that effect came just before he reversed himself and imposed ceilings on red meats and, shortly thereafter, on all foods.

The results of his caving in under the political pressures were disastrous. They were just as Secretary Butz had predicted and they followed the pattern President Nixon had said they would.

So long as the prices of livestock feeds remained uncontrolled—there were no ceilings at the farm level for any products—farmers could not afford to raise their animals for prices that packers, governed by the controls, could afford to pay. Newspapers and television programs were sprinkled with increasing numbers of stories of chicken producers destroying flocks that they could no longer afford to feed and of packing plants closing their doors.

By July 19, when the price freeze ended for all food except beef, the government-created shortages were approaching crisis proportions. And as a result of the brief siege of price ceilings, imposed as a response to political pressures, costs soared again, more than 25 percent in some areas in the first week of free marketing for eggs, pork and chicken.

Secretary Butz acknowledged to this writer in a television interview that the price freeze had been a political rather than an economic decision. With evident satisfaction he observed that, perhaps, it had taught consumers a lesson.

And yet, curiously, the Government continued to hold the ceiling on beef until September, while popular cuts gradually disappeared from many grocery counters.

In August, 1973, while the beef-price freeze and shortages continued, increasing the pressures on other meats, wholesale prices of farm products jumped 23 percent. By late September, when prices dipped somewhat below their highest levels, the relief for consumers was so great that they tended to forget their food was still costing them more than they would have been paying without government mismanagement of the food economy.

Throughout the period of soaring inflation, consumers grew more angry and frustrated, but they could find no culprit on whom to fix the blame. Few accused the farmers, whom they still pictured as the man on a small tractor pulling a plow rather than as the more typical owner of vast acreages or the corporations that hire the tractor drivers. More of the consumers accused a vaguely conceived element that they called the "middlemen" and many blamed the retail stores.

Though transportation can be included, the "middlemen" of the food industry are primarily the processors of food—the companies that manufacture and package the cereals, can or freeze the vegetables and slaughter, process and ship the meats. Spokesmen for these industries responded to the anger of the consumer with wounded probity, claiming a narrow rate of increase in the "farm-to-market spread." But that spread, the difference between what a farmer receives and the prices consumers pay, widened quite rapidly at times. In February, 1972, the "middlemen's" and retailers' share of food costs jumped 2.5 percent. And, despite price controls, the leading companies in the processing industries were able to pass through to the consumer their increased costs and tack a little more on for themselves. Their profit margins continued to widen.

The supermarkets had an outspoken defender in Clarence G. Adamy, president of the National Association of Food Chains. In testimony before a House Judiciary Subcommittee on Monopolies on July 11, 1973, he claimed that, in fact, he represented a distressed industry, with profits of less than 1 percent of sales.

But it was interesting to look at the facts behind Adamy's claims. Because of the high volume of supermarkets, a small percentage of sales can represent a big profit. Nevertheless, there had been a slight decline in average chain profits, but it was largely due to the operations of the industry's biggest member, the Great Atlantic and Pacific Tea Company. A&P had been poorly managed for years, failing to improve its stores and systems and doing little about creaky operations that eroded sales and profits.

When, for a brief period in early 1972, A&P found that it had fallen behind Safeway in sales, the company resorted to an old tactic, the price war. Its profits disappeared, and for the full year 1972 it showed a loss of $51-million. A&P's competition also dented the profit picture of some of its rivals.

But a price war is never a good omen for consumers. Normally it is merely a prelude to higher prices than ever. In the case of A&P, the losses were more than it could sustain for long and in 1973 the company began raising its prices and margins to recoup the losses.

Meanwhile, Safeway, A&P's biggest rival for prestige (although they meet each other in few market areas) was continuing to earn its profits at the high rate of 15 percent of investment. Kroger, the third largest chain, which was hard hit by A&P's war, earned at the rate of 5.2 percent of investment, but Jewel Companies, the fourth largest, had a highly satisfying rate of 12.5 percent, while the fifth largest, Lucky Stores, showed the towering earnings rate of 19.7 percent, about the same as that of Winn-Dixie, the eighth largest. Giant Foods, which shares the biggest part of the Washington market with Safeway, had a profit rate of nearly 17 percent.

Adamy's defensive protests have a hollow ring in the face of such profits and against a background of costly inefficiency and the pricing practices of his industry.

The simple fact behind all the arguments, however, and the principal cause of the food inflation that plagued consumers most severely during those two costly years, was that people were demanding more in relation to the supplies available. In short, there was scarcity, and at the bottom of the sharply rising cost of food was a commodity inflation, resulting from the scarcity. The commodity responsible was grain, which is the key element in the diets of most of the world's people, whether they are meat-eaters or not.

But the scarcity was man-made, manufactured by the very public officials who are responsible for assuring adequate supplies for consumers while promoting the well-being of the producers. And its origins were political.

In a democracy it is almost impossible to insulate men with such responsibilities from politics. Politicians must determine budgets and staff resources and help to establish priorities. But guidelines can be drawn for performance and ethical conduct. Standards of qualification also can be written for the appointment of officeholders whose jobs require knowledge and experience and whose actions and decisions govern the economic well-being of the nation and sometimes of the world.

And those men can be given better tools. Tighter laws against conflict of interest can be drafted. For even if expertise is required, it is not necessary to leave men with a background in the grain business to deal alone and unsupervised with the grain corporations. What's good for Continental and Cargill is not necessarily good for the country.

Other tools can help. Tax laws can be reformed to prevent the abuses of syndications that help some wealthy men escape paying their dues to the society that gave them the chance to prosper. New laws can be drawn to protect family farmers from the depredations of great corporate land-swallowers and the nation from their inefficiency. Others can be written to prevent discrimination in interest and advertising rates, to protect farmers and small business from unfair competition.

Legislation can also give greater protection to consumers. Grading systems can tell them the quality of the foods they buy and labels can give better information on ingredients and quantities. Advertisers might even be required to tell the truth.

But many of the laws needed to guard the interests of the nation are already in the code books. The water and reclamation abuses of the West were not for a lack of laws, and antitrust agencies quite possibly might be able to impose tighter curbs on the increasing concentration of corporate power with the laws they already have.

In the end, what is most needed is good men doing good jobs.

Principal Sources

Chapter I

This introductory chapter combines material from nearly all the sources to be identified later, besides drawing on the author's own travels and reporting, but it is fitting here to acknowledge special indebtedness to individuals and studies that have been unusually helpful. Among those are all the staff of the Agribusiness Accountability Project, a public-interest research organization based in Washington, which made available numerous studies as well as its extensive files. A special debt is owed to Jim Hightower, the project director, and A. V. Krebs, Jr., for their invaluable help.

The author is further indebted to the monumental work of the National Commission on Food Marketing, whose staff, directed by George E. Brandow, completed their report, "Food from Farm to Consumer," in 1966. It was released by the Government Printing Office. Two of the ten technical studies that went into the report were especially valuable. They are "The Structure of Food Manufacturing," prepared by the staff of the Federal Trade Commission, and "Organization and Competition in Food Retailing," which represents the work of the marketing commission's staff as well as contributions from several agencies: the F.T.C., the Bureau of the Census and the Bureau of Labor Statistics.

Also particularly helpful were Harrison Wellford's report, "Sowing the Wind: Pesticides, Meat and the Public Interest," and another Nader report, "Power and Land in California: The Ralph Nader Task Force Report on Land Use in the State of California," directed and edited by Robert C. Fellmeth. Both were issued in book form by Grossman Publishers, New York, in 1973, with the California study retitled "Politics of Land."

As in later chapters, the records of a series of hearings, "Farmworkers in Rural America, 1971–72," before the subcommittee on migratory labor of the Senate Committee on Labor and Public Welfare, was also valuable. The author is also grateful for the advice and help of Jerome M. Stein, an economist with the Department of Agriculture, and George Baker, an investigative reporter with the Fresno *Bee,* as well as other individuals too numerous to mention.

Chapter II

This chapter relies largely on travels and interviews in California as well as on the following sources, in order of primary use: Fellmeth, "Power and Land in California"; Peter Barnes, "Land Reform I: The Great American Land Grab," *New Republic* magazine, June 12, 1971; A. V. Krebs, Jr., "Agribusiness in California," *Commonweal,* October 9, 1970; Krebs, "A Profile of California Agribusiness," prepared for the Agribusiness Accountability Project, 1972; statistics from the California Department of Agriculture; various writings of George Baker in the Fresno *Bee;* "Administrative Complaint," filed by the National Coalition for Land Reform, California Coalition of Seasonal and Migrant Farm Workers v. Rogers C. B. Morton, individually and as Secretary of the Interior, and the U. S. Department of the Interior, 1972; hearings, "Farmworkers in Rural America, 1971–72."

Chapter III

This chapter was also based partly on personal travels and interviews. Other principal sources were prospectuses of tax-shelter syndicates and especially the prospectus titled "1971 Treecrop Company"; news articles from the Fresno *Bee* by George Baker and others; Charles Davenport, "Farm Losses Under the Tax Reform Act of 1969: Keepin' 'em Happy Down on the Farm," Boston College *Industrial and Commercial Law Review,* February, 1971.

Chapter IV

Aside from interviews, the following were primary sources: Fellmeth, "Power and Land in California"; hearings, "Farmworkers in Rural America, 1971–72."

Chapter V

The discussion of interlocking directorates here was based primarily on Krebs, "A Profile of California Agribusiness." Other sources: Barnes, "Land Reform II: The Vanishing Small Farmer," *New Republic,* June 12, 1971; hearings, "Farmworkers in Rural America, 1971–72."

Chapter VI

This chapter was based in part on personal interviews. Other sources included the following: Baker, "Agrimagnate Hollis Roberts: Tangled Ties to Nixon Pal," Fresno *Bee,* August 27, 1972; Robert Banks, "A Millionaire Marionette?" *California Business,* July 24, 1972.

Chapter VII

Material for this chapter was gathered in personal interviews as well as from a wide variety of news reports. Other sources: Annual reports of Tenneco, Inc.; files of the Agribusiness Accountability Project; hearings, "Farmworkers in Rural America, 1971–72"; Herbert Solow, "The Company Twice as Big as Rhode Island," *Fortune,* March, 1961; complaint, P. J. Divizich v. Bank of America National Trust and Savings Association *et al.,* United States District Court, Eastern District of California, filed July 3, 1971; Transcript of bankruptcy proceedings, "In the Matter of William W. Wiest," U. S. District Court, Eastern District of California, March 2, 1972.

Chapter VIII

Material for this chapter was obtained from interviews and the briefs of F.T.C. and United Brands attorneys and supporting papers, "In the Matter of United Brands Company, a Corporation," Docket No. 8835.

Chapter IX

Heavy reliance throughout this chapter was placed on the technical report, "The Structure of Food Manufacturing," prepared by the F.T.C. staff for the National Commission on Food Marketing, but the following were also important: H. Michael Mann, "Antitrust and the Consumer: The Policy and Its Constituency," an address by the director of the Bureau of Economics, F.T.C., before the Association of Massachusetts Consumers, Inc.; "On the Influence of Market Structure on the Performance of Food

Manufacturing Companies," a staff report to the F.T.C.,
1970, Government Printing Office; Arnold Aspelin and
Gerald Engleman, "National Oligopoly and Local Oligop-
sony in the Meat Packing Industry," research paper;
Kathryn Seddon, "Meat Packers' Consent Decree of 1920,"
research paper for the Agribusiness Accountability Project,
1971; "Current Trends in Merger Activity, 1970," Statistical Report No. 8, Bureau of Economics, F.T.C., March,
1971; "Annual Survey of Manufacturers, 1970," Bureau
of the Census, U. S. Department of Commerce, November,
1972.

Chapter X

The primary source here, aside from interviews, was the
F.T.C. complaint, "In the Matter of Kellogg Company, a
Corporation; General Mills, Inc., a Corporation; General
Foods Corporation, a Corporation; and The Quaker Oats
Company, a Corporation."

Chapter XI

As in Chapter IX, heavy emphasis was placed here on a
technical report to the National Commission on Food
Marketing, in this case its "Organization and Competition
in Food Retailing." Aside from interviews and annual reports, the other principal source was a 1967 tabulation by
the Bureau of the Census for the F.T.C., "Market Share
of Locally Largest 4, 8, and 20 Grocery Companies in 212
Standard Statistical Areas."

Chapter XII

This chapter obviously relies to a great extent on per-
sonal interviews as well as on the following: Beatrice Trum
Hunter, *Consumer Beware—Your Food and What's Been
Done to It,* Simon and Schuster, New York, 1971; Jerome

Stein, "Marketing Practices Influencing Equity in the Fruit and Vegetable Industry," master's thesis, University of Maryland, 1967; "Farm-Retail Spreads for Food Products," Economic Research Service, U. S. Department of Agriculture, Miscellaneous Publication No. 741; "Marketing & Transportation Situation," August, 1972, E.R.S., U.S.D.A.; "Agricultural Markets in Change," E.R.S., U.S.D.A., Agricultural Economic Report No. 95; "Organization and Competition in Food Retailing"; company annual reports.

Chapter XIII

The principal sources here were the following: "Agricultural Markets in Change"; "$7.5 Million Suit Accuses Chain of False Meat Labeling," Los Angeles *Times,* January 6, 1973; declaration of Frederick D. Eyster in Avelina Coriell, *et al.,* plaintiffs, v. Safeway Stores, Inc., *et al.,* defendants, Superior Court of the State of California for the County of Los Angeles; statement of the Reverend Wayne C. Hartmire, Jr., chairman of the Interfaith Committee to Aid Farmworkers, March 29, 1973; Krebs, "A Report on the Activities of Safeway Stores, Inc.," for the Agribusiness Accountability Project, December, 1971; "Food Chain Selling Practices in the District of Columbia and San Francisco," a staff report of the F.T.C., Government Printing Office, 1969; The "Today" Show, WNBC-TV and the National Broadcasting Company Television Network, April 3, 1973.

Chapter XIV

Besides interviews, the principal sources here were the following: Sidney Margolius, *The Great American Food Hoax,* Walker & Co., New York, 1971; hearings, "Packaging and Labeling Matters," before a subcommittee of the House Committee on Government Operations, June 3–5, 1969.

Chapter XV

The basis here was interviews as well as the following sources: Wellford, "Sowing the Wind"; Margolius, *The Great American Food Hoax;* "A Close Look at Hamburgers," *Consumer Reports,* August, 1971; "Frankfurters," *Consumer Reports,* February, 1972; Hunter, *Consumer Beware.*

Chapter XVI

Interviews and personal reporting by the author provided the principal basis for this chapter, but these sources were also used: hearings, "The Russian Grain Deal," subcommittee on livestock and grain, House Committee on Agriculture, September 14–19, 1972; hearings, "The Russian Grain Deal," Senate Permanent Subcommittee on Investigations, July 20–26, 1973; "Russian Wheat Sales and Weaknesses in Agriculture's Management of Wheat Export Subsidy Program," report by the Comptroller General of the United States, July 9, 1973; "Special Investigation of Wheat Export Program," Office of the Inspector General, U.S.D.A., internal report; John Fialka, "The Wheat Deal," series in The Washington *Star-News,* October 29–November 1, 1972; Martha M. Hamilton, "The Great American Grain Robbery and Other Stories," research report for the Agribusiness Accountability Project, 1972.

Chapter XVII

This chapter was based on a wide variety of news reports.

Chapter XVIII

In this chapter, the author is deeply indebted to a task force of the Agribusiness Accountability Project, which spent a year of research and investigation in preparation for the writing, by Jim Hightower, of "Hard Tomatoes, Hard Times," a report that was the subject of hearings before the subcommittee on migratory labor of the Senate Committee on Labor and Public Welfare and that was published in 1973 by Schenkman Publishing Company, Cambridge, Mass. Others whose work is reflected in the study include Susan DeMarco, Valerie Kantor, Toby Edelman, A. V. Krebs, Jr., Helen Lichtenstein, Susan Sechler and Kathryn Seddon. Other sources include the following: hearings, "Farmworkers in Rural America, 1971–72"; "Agriculture: Critics Find Basic Research Stunted and Wilting," *Science,* April 27, 1973.

Chapter XIX

The outstanding source in this chapter was Wellford, "Sowing the Wind." Others include: Daniel Zwerdling, "The Meat Risks," Washington *Post,* May 13, 1973; *Congressional Record,* March 20, 1973; "Dimensions of Insanitary Conditions in the Food Manufacturing Industry," report to Congress by the Comptroller General of the United States, based on inspections conducted May–August, 1971; "Tuna Fish," Associated Press, May 28, 1973; "Audit Report, Animal and Plant Health Inspection Service, Meat and Poultry Inspection Program," internal report by the Office of the Inspector General, U.S.D.A., 1972; "The High-Filth Diet, Compliments of F.D.A.," *Consumer Reports,* March, 1973.

Chapter XX

This chapter is based largely on personal interviews and travels as well as the outstanding article by Lester R. Brown, "Scarce Food: Here to Stay," Washington *Post,* July 15, 1973. Other sources include the following: "Requested Policy Papers," a technical report to the National Advisory Commission on Food and Fiber, Government Printing Office, 1967; Wellford, "Sowing the Wind"; Paul D. Scanlon, "FTC and Phase II: The 'McGovern Papers,' " *Antitrust Law & Economics Review,* spring, 1972; Clarence G. Adamy, testimony before the antitrust subcommittee of the House Committee on the Judiciary, July 11, 1973; Eleanor Johnson Tracy, "How A&P Got Creamed," *Fortune,* January, 1973.

Index